With grateful acknowledgement to Emily, Terri, and Tiger Creek Wildlife Refuge for allowing me the use of their beautiful photos and for all the great things they do for the big cats. Please check out and support their efforts at tigercreek.org

CATSKILL

by
Lisa Annette Powell
First part of the CATSKILL trilogy

TO ALL LOVER CATS
And to
MY SWIM

To George
Many Thanks!
Enjoy!

Lisa

FOR GRACE, AGILITY, CUNNING PATIENCE AND
INTELLIGENCE, NOTHING BEATS A CAT. AND HE
KNOWS IT.

Chapter 1

What a laugh! She thinks she can stuff me into her one-way, blinders-on-sorry-excuse-for-an-educational institution.

"We understand, Mr. Hawk, your school-age grandson is now residing with you." My Lakota grandfather sat non-committal, confronted by Cody's single, busybody social worker. "It's important that he is enrolled in the appropriate grade. Now, if you will give me some information, this will be simple and painless."

"Why is it the pale faces are always looking to the Indians for information these days? Perhaps you should take your own advice and attend some school somewhere. Maybe you would like to sign up for my meditation class. If you'll write your name here, this will be simple and painless."

I nearly laughed aloud at my grandfather's throwing the woman's words back at her. But that would have given away my eavesdropping position behind the single-curtain room partition.

Wearily, disdainfully and impatiently, Ms. Busybody tapped her legal pad, surveyed the sparse cabin, sans electric. I sensed her prejudicial scan of the one-room cabin.

A hand loomed rug separated one-fourth of the room for sleeping privacy. We used the fireplace for cooking, except for when it was too warm. In which case, we grilled out. No curtains, no refrigerator, no indoor facilities. Simply: a hand hewn wooden chest, a lantern, old scarred table with four equally embattled, semi-matching chairs, grandfather's leather recliner (the only concession to modernity), a dry sink with hand operated water pump and bucket waiting underneath. The inquirer had entered a different world.

I saw my grandfather through her eyes. Lean muscled, seemingly a 40-something man. No paunch, single black braid-no silver, impassive lined face, alert black eyes, at ease on his throne, clad in worn red flannel and frayed jeans. Yes, she was far from home.

As if addressing an Alzheimer's patient, she began her interrogation once more. "Now, Mr. Hawk," she gritted, condescendingly. One thing I could not accept was anyone talking down to my grandfather. Had all pale faces lost respect for elders?

I vacated my post and stood before her, defiantly. I am not slightly built and like all men I can appear more imposing when I want to.

"Well," she had to look up to address me- putting her at odds with her self-righteous attitude- a direct disadvantage. It was Custer-v-Crazy Horse.

"Pp...," she cleared her throat. My grandfather cast me a side-long look, a glint of laughter in his eyes. "Y...your name, please?"

I waited several seconds longer than politeness required, just to savor her unease. "CatSkill."

"First name or last?"

"What does it matter?" I could tell she wished to roll her eyes in exasperation, but my rebellious stance was keeping her nerves on jumping-jack stand-by. "Last." Grandfather was growing tired of these proceedings. Dinner time beckoned.

"First name?" She was diligently persistent in pulling teeth.

"Riordan," I acquiesced.

"H...how do you spell that?"

"Perhaps you should go back to your own school."

"Mr. CatSkill, your attitude is not helping. Maybe you would like to attend a juvenile delinquent boarding school?"

"Ah, you'd love to put an Indian in one of your boarding institutions, wouldn't you?" She ignored this.

"Last grade attended?" Grandfather's eyes lit up in anticipation of this answer. I shrugged. I did not admit that I was proud of the fact I'd not attended school, at least not the formal, American excuse for one.

"How about your date of birth?" Grandfather and I both smirked. "You don't know your date of birth? How is that possible? What hospital were you born in?"

"I was born on the road. Simple, no paperwork." She opened her laptop. I considered messing with the reception, but I felt my stomach protest. Rapidly, she punched a few keys.

"You're not in the system!" She murmured in disbelief.

"Thank the Great Spirit for that. You know, your so-called education system is for sheeple, people who only think and act as sheep."

"That attitude is not conducive to good citizenship and is improper in this day and age."

"Huh, I suppose the First Amendment is out of date, too?"

She closed her laptop, climbed back on her high horse and handed me a card. "Be at this address Monday, 10a.m. After you take an aptitude test we'll place you in the appropriate class structure. Miss this appointment," she warned, "and the wrath of the system will fall on your head. Good day."

"Ooh, I'm scared," I grinned at grandfather.

"What do you intend to do with this test?" Grandfather asked over cornbread and beans.

"I suppose high school senior will be the quickest, least painful," I mimicked the busybody while sopping up the last of my pinto beans with a suitable piece of Dutch oven-browned cornbread.

"Watch how you answer those questions or they'll declare you a genius and then where will we be?" His fingers summoned another bit of cornbread.

"I'm surprised she managed to get down our driveway." The drive lacked a formal base and the potholes led to hell or at the very least, a good mechanic's shop. "I'm also interested in how she knew about me." Grandfather gave a nonchalant grunt, confirming my suspicions. "Those busybodies, their noses direct and they must follow, eh grandfather?"

"She sure had a honker!" He barked and we both cracked up. "She thinks you're cocky."

"Among other things. I'm probably the only person she's ever met who is completely comfortable in his own skin and several others," I added. We shared a conspiratorial smile.

Moonless black night. My favorite time for a stealthy prowl and to reflect on my immediate path. Then I race. There is nothing like a great burst of speed. I enjoy the use of every muscle, every sense, especially those. . . My day vision is beyond any human's and my night vision. . . You'll see.

Chapter 2

As if a fly on the wall, I observed their observations.

"How old do you think he is?" The busybody/social worker/school counselor addressed Tom Gallagher, the test administrator.

"Now, just how would I know that? I thought that was another of your areas of expertise."

The busybody's nose sniffed and rose. "Your best guess, Mr. Gallagher."

Portly Mr. Gallagher, aficionado of all things involving numbers, adjusted his glasses, tilted his head to one side and then speculatively, to the other. He eyed the young man finishing an 8 page test.

"Could be anywhere from 17 to 25." He hunched his shoulders, accepted the pages from the tested with a smile and, "Thank you, Mr. CatSkill, an unusual name." The broad shouldered youth rested his eyes on the honest faced Mr. Gallagher, nodded, and without a glance at the busybody exited the room. I left my hearing closely tuned in.

"Will you look at the answer to question 27? Explain the Marshall Plan?"

Mr. Gallagher peered over the woman's shoulder and laughed, genuinely amused at my handwritten answer— Marshall Fields' plan for a department store. "You know, technically that response is not wrong."

"Mr. Gallagher," she remonstrated.

"Didn't you tell me he finished all the algebraic equations and probability problems without a calculator?"

"Yes," she grudgingly conceded.

"It seems our Mr. CatSkill is a very bright young man."

"Insouciant and ill-mannered is what he is."

"As Voltaire put it 'I may disagree with what you say but I will defend your right to say it'. It's heartening to find a young person who thinks outside the box." Whose brain hasn't been overly fried by this educational system of spit back institutionalized answers— he kept this to himself. "I'll be pleased to have him in my class."

"So where do we place him?" She asked.

Gallagher grinned, "Seeing as how we're not running a school for over-achievers and the brilliant minded, put him in the senior class. At least he'll acquire a diploma. Then he can entertain any college or future course of action he pleases."

"If he shows up for class. . ." she hedged.

"As long as he passes the exams, you mean, and somehow, I don't think that will be a problem," Mr. Gallagher added. He stifled a guffaw at the answer to question 36- explain a judiciary committee— a goofy group of tactless politicians, disguised as intellectuals, wreaking havoc. "God, I'd love to spend a day with this young man!"

Chapter 3

I'm not unaware of the stir of undercurrents as I enter a room. If I were conceited, I suppose I would enjoy the attention. But conceit has never been one of my failings.

This teacher, unlike Mr. Gallagher, has written me off with a short glance of disapproval. To him, I'm either a loser or a trouble maker and probably both. My old suffering jeans, t-shirt covered by worn, flannel shirt, moccasins (which I constructed myself) and especially, my long, loose hair, are all the proof he needs. He refuses to hold my eyes.

The intellectuals, very few in this group, know immediately I'm not a bully and therefore not a threat to them. Their relief is palpable.

Complete attention is garnered by the girls. The proverbial bad-boy is always desirable, his magnetism undeniable— a flame to most feminine moths. I can just see the plans forming in their limited cranial cavities. How are they going to draw my eye? I'm sure their mothers could tell them a thing or two and their fathers warn against.

Resentment flares in the wannabe men, especially those sitting next to the so-called prettiest girls. There are a few bullies who know right away I'm not an easy mark. Testosterone, however, will be tested.

A few of the jocks will unnecessarily intend to 'protect' their territory and I see calloused hands claiming feminine arms. Yes, challenges will be delivered— the girls will make sure of that.

I'll probably not be met man-to-man in the first match. No, it will be so-and-so and his buddies against the half-breed Indian— a veritable TV western of old played out on the high school grounds. Surreptitiously, of course. Mustn't be any teachers around to call off the festivities. There are no fair fights, certainly not according to the losers.

All of this flashes through my brain in an instant. No one reads scenarios better than I. Something else skips tantalizingly in my olfactory senses— a scent— I love a true scent and this one, unmolested by all the fad perfumes, deodorants, hair products, soaps, both male and female, is a true essence emanating from the back of the room. An empty seat beckons.

The only person who has not looked at and judged me has his/her head lying on the desk top. The body is the source of my admiring nose—sassafras, juniper, pine, honey and something else— ah, the body is a female. Finally, something worthy of my interest.

A backpack rests at her feet. Her clothes: jeans, flannel shirt, hiking boots, are old but cared for. No money here. Her hair, eminently touchable- long locks of sun-streaked gold, tumble about, hiding her face. I can feel my salivary glands doing overtime. I'm hungry. She's whetting my appetite.

She doesn't stir as I take the seat next to her. Heads swivel and return to the front as the instructor taps his desk. He rattles on about some piece of literary art. I half listen. My senses are locked on the girl beside me. Why is she napping so early in the day, in class, yet? I love a good bit of mystery.

There's a question hovering and a repetitive, "Miss Lance, would you care to grace us with an answer, please?"

The room has erupted in twitters from non-admiring twits. So, this one is considered fair game, by everyone, apparently.

"Miss Lance?"

My hand subtly rests on her knee under her hanging shirt tail. No one can see and I interject the jerk's question into her sleeping brain. At once, she moves, raises her head, blushes at being put on the spot, recognizes the question I've supplied telepathically and gracefully responds— correctly, to Mr. Crandall's dismay. My hand returns to my side.

The teacher rambles, endlessly it seems, for all my senses are solely intent on investigating my neighbor. She remains oblivious to me. Her attention is completely forward. I can feel her discomfort. She is physically and near mentally exhausted. Why? I wonder. I long to see her face, but my vision, though otherworldly, can't see around her tawny locks. It doesn't work like that.

Crandall issues an assignment. "Yes, Miss Lance. This will require the use of the internet unless you have the requisite antique copy of poetry lurking at home."

The girl looks down and then voices a respectful complaint. "You'll just have to use the library." He holds up a hand, staving off any further comments.

It's obvious that everyone in this room has internet access at home except her. It's not easy commandeering such access in a library, especially to fulfill homework assignments. Last time I checked, there was always a line to use the computer and a time limit once you had sat down.

A bell rang, signaling the end of class. I waited for the room to clear, knowing the melee I'd encounter outside if I hastened. Knowing I could not care less, because I would follow her scent.

"Do you think it is right to bully a student simply because your wife walks all over you and you've become disillusioned in your chosen field of employment?" This was my parting thrust, quietly delivered to Crandall, the bully.

"How dare you! I'll have you put on detention," his face suffused, angrily crimson.

"I don't think so." I stared him down and left him flustering. In his fuming, he inadvertently cleared his desk of a stack of papers.

Chapter 4

The boyfriends had guided most of the girls down the hall to the next class, safely away from my exit. An unnatural blonde and her brunette friend, both fastidiously attired, waited on tenterhooks.

"Hi! I'm Kristen and this is my friend, Callie. We're sorry cranky Crandall didn't introduce you." Politely, but practically bouncing, they yearned for my positive response.

"Riordan CatSkill, pleased to meet you," reluctantly, I held out my hand to shake theirs. I'd learned etiquette—somewhere.

The two girls, overly grinning, but blushing an exhibition of pleasant manners, fawned over my hand in turn. I briefly wondered about their opinions of Miss Lance, if they had joined in at her expense. Hold on CatSkill; patience, I cautioned myself. My survey of the hall had not detected the elusive Miss Lance, but her scent lingered and wafted down the hall.

"Sit with us at lunch, I mean, if you want to. We'll tell you all about the school, introduce you around. You know, help you get acquainted," they fumbled.

"Thanks," I shrugged. "But I'm not sure if I'll have lunch today. Maybe I'll catch up with you if I get hungry." I gave them a winning smile- might as well endear myself to someone today. Checking my schedule, I waved as I sauntered off, intent on following a scent. . .to the girls' room. I hoped she hadn't fallen asleep inside. Getting to the next class late didn't concern me much. I leaned against the wall.

"Oops," she stumbled into my chest upon exiting the bathroom. Her head had swiveled to check the hall clock as her body hastened in the other direction smack dab into me. "I, I'm so sorry," she did not look up.

"Hey, no problem. Care to have lunch with the new kid in town?" I urgently decked my inner twinges.

"Uh, thanks. I, I'd like to, but I think I'll sleep through lunch today." Why wouldn't she look up at me?

"And how will you wake up for afternoon classes?"

"Internal alarm clock," she barely whispered and began to move around me.

"How about I eat, watch you sleep and wake you when it's time?"

This raised her head and though the dark circles under her eyes and the pinched features of the overly-tired is what I looked down upon- she was very tiny- 5'to my 6'4"- it was her eyes I dove, no, fell headlong into.

An exquisite, healing shade of green bordered with gold seared me as surely as a branding iron on a calf's hide. That second of contact set all of my senses, and I mean all, reeling.

She broke first, red-faced, and tripped forward. I reached to steady her but she was gone. Separate classes commanded our attendance. No matter- there wasn't anywhere in the universe she could hide from me now I had her essence.

Lunch time I sauntered into the cafeteria, waved at the expectant Kristen and Callie, grabbed 3 organic apples, 4 hard- boiled eggs, 2 bottles of water and went hunting.

It didn't take long. She was curled up outside under a pine tree, head pillowed on her backpack. The sun filtered through the tree limbs and I hoped she was warm enough.

I kept my distance and without tasting my lunch, I devoured it and waited- the backup to her internal alarm clock, which was right on the money in waking her.

I backed off my pursuit of her for the afternoon, though I remained patiently aware. We shared 2 classes but no seats next to each other. It was just as well. She was awake in class but had a glazed look. Talking with a sleep walker is not productive.

I made a number of new friends, a few were complicated. I therefore, use the term 'friends' loosely. Some of the seniors were honest and genuinely interested in me as myself- a person of different heritage from. . . I'll quantify that statement-they appeared to be interested in the self I showed them. I avoided questions by asking more than answering while gleaning reconnaissance. The bullies bided their time and my inner nature smiled in anticipation.

The last I saw of her that first day, she fell up the steps into the bus. Patience is one of my greater virtues, but I was sorely tested not to follow.

That night my grandfather gave me a quizzical look. I ate hurriedly, anxious for the night and a prolonged run. Several times I caught myself poised to pick up her trail, thought better of it, changed mid-stride and flung myself in another direction.

Chapter 5

"Mr. CatSkill, a pleasure. Class, I'd like to introduce a true mathematics aficionado- our newest student, Riordan CatSkill, for those of you who've not made his acquaintance yet."

I nodded to Mr. Gallagher. The pleasantries of the morning continued for she was there, seated by a window, awake and studying an industrious equation on the black board. I ignored hands patting seats to sit next to her.

I took a deep breath, beautiful. "Good morning," I turned to her, my long arms barely brushed her flannelled arm as I sat.

"Oh." I'd drawn her attention from the equation. "Hello," she offered, blushing, with a little, hesitant half-smile, and promptly allowed her lovely hair to fall forward, concealing her features.

"You seem more rested today?"

"Yes, and a good thing, too. We've got gym class this afternoon," she enthused in a polar opposite of the previous day.

"I'm Riordan CatSkill."

"Yes," she flashed a grin and looked away, abashed.

"And you are?"

"B...Bonnie Lance," she blushed furiously.
Her name was Bonnie Lance- apropos!

"Class, please keep your calculators tucked away. On the board I've two, quadratic equations. First one to provide the correct answers, sans calculator, inside one minute, gets extra credit. Go."

I waited thirty seconds. I knew no one else in the room had a shot except, maybe. . .

There it was. Her hand shot up and mine right after.

"Bonnie," Mr. Gallagher's face lit up.

"17 for the first and for the second," she answered.

The non-committal Mr. Gallagher turned to me, "Riordan, is she right?"

I felt the heat of her blush. "Yes, sir."

"Excellent," he rubbed his hands together- a kid at Christmas could not have been more pleased. "I'd like to see the two of you after class. Thank you."

He went on to explain for my benefit that his class would be an independent study. Each one would work through the text book, taking the required tests at his or her, own pace.

"Yes, Bonnie?"

"If we finish the book early?"

"Why, I can give extra credit work that's substantially more difficult or you can use the time as free time."

I watched her. She was pleased and so was I. Who would finish the book first? I wondered, as math, among other things, came easy to me. Ah, I'd probably just wait for her even if she did have a head start- school having already begun when I entered the picture.

Texts were opened and my neighbor dug in diligently. I followed suit, spinning through the beginning chapters Bonnie had already tested out of.

Mr. Gallagher had in mind to convince Bonnie and me to compete in the National Mathematics Competition, as he explained after class.

"Mr. Gallagher, I can't leave home for long spells."

"It's all right, Bonnie. The state exam is in Casper and the national exam will be fed via satellite for the state winners. Please say yes."

"I'll try, Mr. Gallagher," she hedged.

"Riordan?"

"If Bonnie goes, I'm in."

"Capital! Well, you'd best hurry to your next class."

"Have lunch with me today?" I strolled next to her.

"Uh, are you sure, with me?" What kind of reply was this? I was more than determined to find out what she meant as soon as possible.

"I'd be pleased if you'd say yes." I opened all my wild senses to sponge all possible information from her.

She fingered her bag, nervously, but nodded without looking at me. "Meet you in the cafeteria," I said, touching her elbow and stepping into my next class.

We took our lunch outside- windy, but much more private. Contemplative eyes had looked on as we gathered our choices and left the cafeteria.

As if mirror images, we crossed ankles and gracefully drifted to the ground. Silence ensued.

"Are you always so shy or maybe you're just not into me?" I grinned at her, patiently.

"I…I suppose I'm shy. I usually keep to myself."

How to break the ice? "You have a penchant for numbers, too?"

"Yes, they've always come easy to me, kind of fun," a slight shoulder hitched, self-consciously, and the clam-up continued.

"Have many friends?" I didn't enjoy the pulling-teeth

version of getting to know someone, but she was much too restrained and I was heartily intrigued.

"No." A no that would rather not be pushed, I conjectured. Eyes averted, she blurted a question, "Why did you come to this school?"

"You mean instead of a reservation school?" I tried not to get riled.

"No! No, not at all!" Her flaming face betrayed her distressed honesty and simple curiosity.

"Didn't mean to snap at you. I'm used to impolite questions, but I can see you're not that way. I'm here to help out my grandfather- George Red Hawk."

"I know Red Hawk," she gushed, surprised and relieved. "He sometimes shares meals with us. When my dad comes in from the west, he'll pick him up. He's very interesting. I…I like to listen to his stories," she fiddled with her fingers. "He…he never mentioned you. . ."

"No surprise. He'd probably given up on me coming back. You can cook?"

She shrugged her shoulders, "Sure."

"Hmmm. . ." I looked at her intently and it happened. Her head rose to my silent injunction and our eyes locked. A magical moment- very few of those in my life anymore. And not a one of them compared to this.

I sensed her hesitation, but interest lurked there, too; a reflection of the marvel I felt resided in her eyes. Big, dark green eyes with gold glints, a smattering of freckles on a pert nose. Lips I'd swear were innocent of others. Chill out, CatSkill. . .

A half hour lunch flies by, unfortunately. I helped her up, our eyes still locked. I could see what she saw as she continued to look up at me.

I towered over a foot above Bonnie. A half-breed. Lakota-white man cross. High cheekbones, wide mouth, a complexion between white and red man bronze, black-fringed gold eyes and long thick hair- black streaks fantastically framing my ears and the rest- strewn through blonde, light tan and bare, auburn hinted locks. No Indian had ever sported hair like mine. No white man either.

But then, I was not an ordinary anything. What business did I have attracting the interest of a girl like this? Bonnie was a girl/woman for keeps, not for a few laughs.

Maybe I'd better find something else to be fascinated by-good luck with that. I couldn't get her essence out of my mind. I tried- for a minute. Not happening.

"We'd better go." I released her with great effort. "See you in gym class."

She moved off, hesitant, looked back. For a second, she studied me further, hurried away. A good girl who'd not be late for class. I was a different story, but I followed.

Chapter 6

"Alright, listen up," Jack Peak blew a whistle for silence. "Get your running gear on. Today we're timing everyone for a half-mile. Inside a month, I'll expect all of you without doctor's excuses," he rolled his eyes and settled them on a few wimps, "to be able to run a mile within 10 minutes. Everybody out here inside 5 minutes. We'll have a warm up session and then we're off. Get going!"

I stayed put. He wouldn't like my running gear at all, though I was positive several girls would be gaga-thrilled. Probably not mine, though. Not yet.

Did I say mine? Well, why not? First time for everything and I would make her mine. Patience, CatSkill, patience. . .

"Mr. Catskill, do you have a hearing problem?"

"No, more like a clothing deficiency."

"You can't run in those moccasins," he was noticeably appalled.

"Don't intend to. I prefer to run barefoot," I said, matter-of-fact.

"You are excused, Catskill. I don't want any martyrs here," Peak tossed his whistle in annoyance.

"I'm serious."

"Have it your way— but I'd better not get an angry letter from your folks," he turned away.

I pulled off my t-shirt. The air was brisk, but cold never bothered me. Miss Lance and I shared that, too.

"Hey, Road Runner! Beep! Beep!" Cat-calls cackled behind me. Only it wasn't me being addressed, but Bonnie.

Silently, I swore— I'd known she was young, but. . . I gritted my teeth at the hecklers. The girl coming to the track had certainly been well disguised in her old baggy clothes.

Long legs, runner's legs— the thinnest I'd ever seen, were capped by turquoise running shorts, tiny slits on the sides. The latest in Nike running shoes and a white, specially-designed fabric running shirt completed her gear.

Not a hint of breast graced her chest. She could be 12- years old, but I knew that wasn't possible. No girlish frame there; she was like a bud held in abeyance, waiting to flower. It was a damned, good thing patience was my strong suit.

"Beep! Beep," heckled her progress to the track. They were making fun of her. I fell in beside her and watched her try to ignore their taunts. Peak blew his whistle for the calisthenics warm-up.

I leaned down, "Why do they call you Road Runner?"

She bit her lower lip, shook her head, "Because I leave all their coyote hides choking on my dust."

"You don't say," I mulled this over, donned a quelling look and shot it over her head at the hecklers. Those jeering Bonnie got my drift and even the whispers subsided.

They were finding they needed their oxygen elsewhere. Jumping jacks, honestly! Through it all, the girls openly admired my bare chest, which furthered the ill-wishes of the male contingent. Their ghostly white legs were pretty much of a turn-off, I smirked.

"We'll break this group up; guys will start first, then girls, half a minute later. Except for Bonnie— you may begin whenever you like," he actually smiled and bowed to her.

"You like to run, Bonnie?" Wonders don't cease. . .

"Oh, yes," her heartfelt response. Other than her obvious youth, this day kept getting better and better.

Jeans may not be the best running pants but I kicked off my moccasins, dug into the track grit. After Peak's 10 minutes of what I considered non-sensical warm-up, he whistled the guys off with Bonnie leading.

I matched her pace and we ran side by side for a half-mile, leaving a disgruntled group behind us- huffing and swearing.

A half-mile is nothing to me and apparently Bonnie felt the same. As we approached the finish line I said, "Want to kick it up a bit?"

"What do you have in mind?" She glanced over.

"How about another half-mile and turn on some speed?"

"Speed?"

"Yeah, don't hold back on me," I issued a challenge.

"Hold back?"

"C'mon, Bonnie, I think I can keep up." Peak called out our times and my little whirlwind, did I say my, took off.

Her speed caught me by surprise. With a few of my long strides, I was even with her and we raced side by side.

"That all you got?" I challenged.

Unbelievably, she kicked it up again. I usually saved this sort of speed for the night and in a different. . . We pounded down the track together.

Those on the sidelines were now cheering. I put on another burst of speed as we neared the finish but she met my attempt. I wouldn't let her pass. Gentlemanly, I'd not pass her either. We crossed the finish line together.

Peak was blowing his whistle like a band run amok. Both of us slowed to a cool-down walk. All of a sudden, she bent over, holding her stomach and convulsing.

"Bonnie, Bonnie?" I reached for her. "You ok, baby?" As she straightened, I saw she was laughing, her whole body shaking with glee.

Her musical, open-mouth laugh, revealed something else to me- her mouth was full of braces. She'd kept them well hidden in our brief conversation. For the life of me, I started to wonder what it would be like to kiss that silver-laden mouth. Get a grip. . .

My previous idea of finding something else to draw my attention fled out the proverbial window and it slammed in its wake. Bonnie was too interesting to ignore.

"What the. . .?" I floundered.

"I…I never thought it…it w…would f…feel so g…grand to, to run with someone," she gasped, between laughing and sucking in air.

My chest exploded. A rush of emotion cannoned through me-she was right. I'd never felt, never thought I'd enjoy a run like this with any other creature. My nature had always been solitary. . .

Peak descended on us. "You two have got to go to inter-scholastic games. My God, the records you'll set. . . Riordan, do you play football? No, that's about over. Basketball, have you played before?"

"No contact sports," I stated, implacably.

"What do you mean?" Peak's face registered confusion.

"Means he's chicken, Coach," some big mouth offered.

"Means I don't like to be touched," I murmured with a look to back it up.

"Well, come try out anyway, you could always outrun the others. . ."

"No, thanks," I moved through the crowd with Bonnie.

"They won't let you rest without an explanation," Bonnie observed.

"Do you need an explanation?" I taunted my running partner.

"No," startled, she ducked and ran off and I chastised myself.

"You going to the library to do the lit assignment?" I tried to initiate a conversation.

"No, I actually have a copy of that poem at home."

"Care if I borrow it?"

She hunched a shoulder, "Ok, I'll bring it tomorrow." Her tone was curt.

"That's not exactly what I had in mind. Bonnie, I'm sorry if I seemed rude. There's a lot you don't know about me. Forgive my being impolite?"

"Sure, no problem." She kept her head turned from me, which signified there was still a problem.

"What if I stop by and take a look at that poem?" I wanted back in her good graces.

"Oh!" Her tell-tale blush fired up. "My dad's not home. I shouldn't have company if he's not there." That was probably true. She sounded very uneasy.

"Are you afraid of me?" Although, by rights she should be-I was a stranger after all- I didn't want her to be afraid of me.

"Maybe not exactly afraid, more disconcerted, I think," she tried to convince herself.

Disconcerted? I fastened on this- she was cautious, smart, and I, I would have to be very, very patient.

This time, I took the bus home. Our drop-off points were the same. My grandfather's place was a couple miles from the Lance homestead- sweet distance. If I'd allowed myself to travel east the previous night. . .

"Are you following me?" She confronted me.

"Guess so, at least for a bit. Grandfather's cabin, you know. What did the bus driver hand you?" She'd placed something in her back pack.

"It's nothing," she demurred.

"I'm betting it's something. I'm making you nervous- I really don't want you to be afraid or disconcerted or nervous around me," I tried to look harmless, flashed my most winning smile. "Will you let me see?"

She took a deep breath, "It's a gun."

"No kidding?" Bonnie shook her head. "What kind?"

"A 38. My dad doesn't like the long walk to the bus by myself. He taught me how to use it when I was little. I guess I'm the only teenager in the country allowed to carry a gun to school, to the bus anyway." It was no big deal to her. This pleased me for some reason.

"Your father should get you a car."

"That takes money, a license and cars do break down," she was quick to point out.

"This gun, do you think you could kill something?" I wanted to explore.

She abruptly stopped walking. "Wouldn't have to kill, just scare whatever away. I go this direction, see you tomorrow."

She raced off- that disturbed me. I waited a few minutes then I followed her, covertly disguised. Besides speed, Bonnie had another surprising gift- intuition.

Several times she stopped, checked around, waited and nodded as if she knew of a presence. I doubt she knew it was me, but I was not positive. She wasn't as open to me as I'd hoped, but she had her reasons and I'd wait. No other recourse. For as long as necessary. . .

I stayed on point until she was close to home, then I sprinted west to my grandfather's. The mystery of Bonnie, I accepted with alacrity.

Chapter 7

He makes me feel. . .disoriented. No one's
ever paid attention to me as he does, at least no
one in school, barring a few teachers. I was
right the first time- no one- ever, anywhere.

Red Hawk, our Lakota neighbor, used to tell
me stories when I was younger. Mrs. Dyer had kept
me occupied with Disney movies, pencils, paper and
games when she babysat. My dad loves me, but he's
rarely around. I'm more at home, at home. I
guess that precludes my making friends easily.
Always has- I am shy with people.

Riordan CatSkill. Riordan CatSkill. . .his
name rolls off my tongue like a magnetic spell-
makes me want to keep chanting Riordan. . .

This is silly. I'm being silly- a guy like
him couldn't possibly have an interest in me. No
guy falls for a stick who outruns him.

Hmmm, I didn't outrun him. I nearly choke.
He'd encouraged me to go faster- I refused. I
survey my toothpick form in the mirror. He is a
full grown man, whereas I look like a kid.

The girls are keeping him in their sights, but he doesn't even act as if they exist. The way he moves when he walks, gracefully catlike, all self-assured, without arrogance. . .

I mentally pair him up with the prettiest girl in school, Lil Brent or maybe Vera. What a couple. I'm sure he'll eventually fall for her. Yes, she'll get him. After all, who could resist her- perfect face, perfect figure, perfect clothes. They would be beautiful together. I don't resent this, I try not to; it's just how things are. Someday, I'll grow into. . . something. . . Too late for him. . .

It was wonderful racing with him today, almost like having a friend that wasn't an animal. I let it hurt when he was short with me although he did apologize.

What does he want with me? Nothing. Maybe, friendship or a kid sister.

My fairy tale day dreams cast him as a prince opposite my Cinderella. A barefoot prince who can run like the wind with a chest to die for, shoulders broad as a longhorn steer's rack of horns. That dark beard-shadow about his mouth. . . Not to mention his golden eyes and fantastically-streaked hair. Hair that I would love to run my fingers through and put into an even more disorderly disarray.

But, he doesn't like to be touched- no
contact? I wonder what that is all about.
There's an aura of mystery about him, probably
because of his Indian heritage. I wonder why Red
Hawk never mentioned him.

Chapter 8

I played hooky the next day- just didn't feel like going to school. But I was early at the bus stop in the afternoon, waiting in the shadows for Bonnie.

As the bus pulled away, she stood and looked straight at where I was hiding. She remained perfectly still. Thinking I might be scaring her, I stepped out. And was greeted with a smile- a smile gracing a wan, tired face.

"You didn't sleep last night," I concernedly confronted her.

"Hello," the smile answered.

Manners, CatSkill. "Hello, you need to get your rest. What do you do all night if you don't sleep?"

She blushed and began to walk, self-consciously crossing her arms upon her chest. I tried to ignore her natural fragrance- the wind was not helping in this regard.

"Could we just sit somewhere?" I eyed a likely stump. "Hang out for a bit."

"I need to get home. I have chores to do before dark."

"I'll make sure you get home and I'll help."

"I…I don't think that's a good idea."

"Bonnie, look at me. Cross my heart and hope to die, I won't hurt you. I'll stay outside. Hell, put the gun on me," I was nearing exasperation. Not familiar territory.

"It's not that. It's not proper for you to be there without meeting my dad. . ." A good, 'proper' answer. She tried to overcome her uneasiness.

"Ok, Ok, then, talk to me as we walk. Why didn't you sleep last night?"

A moment of silence can stretch unbelievably long. . .   "Sometimes, I don't do well with being alone. My dad's gone a lot. He does farrier work- horse shoeing, and helps out at several ranches." She began to play stone soccer, intently. This was not an easy topic for her.

"Go on."

"I'd bring in one of the guard dogs, but then I'd worry about the chickens and horses. I'd have a cat in, but my dad's allergic. Many nights I drift in and out of sleep," she hunched her shoulders; it was old hat to her.

"Bad dreams?" I prodded.

"Sometimes. Could we talk about something else? Why weren't you in school, today? Oh, I brought the poem," she handed me an old, leather-bound book.

"Didn't feel like it," I answered one of her questions.

"Didn't feel like it," she studied this idea, shook her head, disbelieving anyone could do such a thing. "Well, in case you feel like doing your homework, I've finished my essay. You can take the book with you."

I thanked her. "Tell me, did you hold back on the speed yesterday?"

Bonnie stopped, contemplated everything but me- why was she finding the sagebrush so all-fired interesting right now?

"I never run as fast as I can," she hesitantly admitted. This was a new one on me. A fisherman couldn't have set a mystery hook any better.

"Why, baby? I'll keep up with you," I stated matter-of-fact. I waited her out. She took her time deciding how to clarify.

"I think if I go as fast as I can, I'll become something else, something different- silly, huh?" Her eyes actually glistened with emotion.

"What do you think, that you'll turn into a gust of wind or. . .?" She blushed and fiddled with her backpack. I attempted reassurance- really, I was intrigued as all get out. "I don't think you're silly, but I would love to get inside your head. Can you tell me?" I was positive she had never told this to anyone.

"I don't know. I just feel that I might not be me anymore and maybe, I won't get back into myself." Stone soccer started up again. I would have to slowly digest this and her puzzling sleeplessness, maybe with grandfather's help.

To lighten up a bit, "Have you ever competed? You'd be a shoo-in for the Olympics, if you wanted to go that way."

"Coach Peak talked me into competing last year. He picked the events." I wished she would gaze at me the way she studied the surrounding dirt, evergreens, rocks. . .

"Did you win?"

"Yes."

"All of them?"

"Yes," she admitted, not with pride, but with reluctant embarrassment.

"You should be proud, Bonnie." Her sole response was a shrug of her shoulders.

"I didn't like all the attention. I felt like a freak. The Nike reps provided me with shoes and running gear- clothes. Photographers kept taking my picture. Everyone hounded me with questions," she shuddered, remembering.

"Did your father or a friend go with you?"

"No, Dad was working. He enjoyed the pictures, trophies and newspaper articles. I guess there's something wrong with me. The school principal said I'd put the school on the map. All the kids were congratulatory, but not as if they were glad for me," she broke off. An extremely lonely, little girl, I surmised.

"It would be different, baby, if you had some honest support. Where's your mother, anyway?"

She chewed her lower lip. "I don't know. I never knew my mother."

"Is she passed on?"

"Not as far as I know. I guess I should tell you before the gossips do. M…my mother came out west with her girlfriends after college, a vacation. Met my dad at a ranch where he was a wrangler. She fell in love with him, I guess, at least for a while. I believe he may still love her. They got married against her parents' advice. The romance of the west died pretty quick for her. With my dad gone most of the time, and her left to do all the chores- she was used to people always around. . . She went looking for admirers. I was born and she left. This is what my dad told me."

"She left her baby?"

"Yes." I was dumbfounded. Wild animals behaved better.

"I'm sure she wasn't ready to be a mother. A lady in town, Mrs. Dyer, would keep me with her while my dad was away, until I was 13, then I moved back home permanently. The gossip mill will tell you no one knows who my dad really is. But, my dad is my dad." Bonnie was much too understanding for as young as she was.   But, now I understood some of the looks and bathroom scuttlebutt.

Chapter 9

To distract her, "What kind of chores do you
have to do when you get home?"

"Feed and water the chickens, dogs and
horses; we have a couple broodmares in foal, 2
geldings for riding, clean stalls, chop wood. . ."

"You're not serious," I suggest this to a
girl who is nothing but serious.

"Yes. I cook over a wood-burning stove that
doubles as a furnace- when my dad can get the
wood- it saves on oil," she stated with great
practicality.

"I can't picture you splitting logs." I
checked which century I was in.

"I do all right." A tad defensive, now.

"Sounds like you work too damn much- I'll
chop the wood."

"You don't have to. . ."

"Oh yes I do," I mumbled with finality. As
we approached the Lance homestead, I disguised my
predatory nature. It wouldn't be advantageous to
have Bonnie's animals turn fractious at a whiff of
my preferred self.

I stood patiently, without malice or fear, as two dogs ran to greet their mistress.

"Hi, guys!" She was on her knees, hugging and kissing them. I shook my head. "Riordan, this is Sticker. . ." a pit bull cross eyed me warily. I held out my closed fist and let him come to me. "And Stalker." A border collie remained guardian at Bonnie's side.

"What kind of names are those?" She laughed-a delightful sound. Bonnie was used to this question.

"Sticker loves to pick up burrs and anything else that will stick to his coat and Stalker never barks- he prefers to sneak up on you."

About that time, a nose pushed into the back of my knee. "I see what you mean." I was accepted as being with Bonnie but not as a friend on my own- good dogs.

Sticker and Stalker flanked her protectively as I absorbed the home site. An old cabin, over twice the size of Grandfather's, posed unpretentious, sheltered on one side by a stand of lodgepole pines. A porch, sporting three comfortable wood rockers, ran the length of the cabin.

Some distance away, on the far side, settled a pole barn, bigger than the house, with corrals at each end. Two pregnant mares ambled around idly picking at strewn hay. They nosed chickens out of potential nest-makings. A red-painted chicken coop shared a barn wall and was suitably armored against night prowlers and other chicken despoilers. Two geldings groomed each other in the front corral, their tails swishing in tandem.

Beyond, set low from the homestead ridge, cottonwoods and sycamores belied a creek. I could hear the stream playfully negotiating rock as the waters traveled on their interminable journey. An harmonious setting, I mused.

I spied the wood pile- relished the added workout. "You go on with your other work, I'll tackle this. If I finish before you, I'll help clean stalls." She gave me one of those you've-got-to-be-kidding-me looks, dropped her backpack on the porch and went to greet the horses.

The chickens cackled hurriedly to her, hoping for handouts. A bronze rooster with dark, iridescent tail feathers, strutted, nonchalantly following the hens. If grain was forthcoming, he did not intend to be left out, but like the con he was, he didn't want to appear too eager, either.

"Too early, girls, and Hector, you know better, too." Hector, the rooster- what a name, blew out his chest, flapped his wings and changed directions, pretending to hone in on a bug trail.

It was obvious Bonnie's cadre of friends began and ended with the animals she lived with. Each living creature neighed, clucked and barked, or in Stalker's case, stuck his nose into, the cacophony of conversation. She attended each with a personal touch and or quip. The geldings, a paint and a draft- cross, were introduced as Hoss and Lil Joe. Their kibitzing together was reminiscent of the old Bonanza series- Little Joe and Hoss were always into something. These two, I was informed, would climb into a rain barrel if one was available, not to mention all the other trouble they managed to cause. Bonnie handed out a treat apiece, but I had the feeling the treats were superfluous.

Even the birds perched above seemed to twitter for her and she whistled to them in turn. Bonnie was perfectly confident- truly in her element. Here, outside, among the animals, her face carried a continuous smile. Her body reflected complete relaxation.

Home was a haven to Bonnie, despite the sleep issue. To one who had never called any place home- well, it gave me food for thought.

As it turned out, Bonnie was a faster stall-mucker than I was a wood chopper, but I was able to manhandle some hay bales for her before accepting her thanks and heading home. My brain buzzed with all I had to think about- never mind scholastic homework.

Bonnie's father wouldn't be home until Sunday. I was restless, thinking of her all alone in the house.

"You're like a hen on a hot plate. Want to talk about it?"

"Not right now, Grandfather. I have to go out." I could hear the wheels turning in his head.

I needed something totally innocuous if I were going to visit the Lance ranch after hours. I watched her from a distant tree, facing her bedroom. It was near 1 a.m. and she was pacing- a flannel shirt covering her to long, thin thighs. She kept a night light on; her arms crossed as she moved back and forth.

I had an idea. Tap, tap. Her pacing slowed; she wandered to the window. My night vision picked up her inquisitive eyes. Instead of searching about for the source of the tapping, she seemed to hone in on my exact location. I was positive there was no way she could see me, dark and small as I kept myself, close to the black of the trunk in the black of the night.

I stopped my drumming. Eventually, she turned to her bed, got in, rested her head on her pillow. But her eyes wouldn't close. I picked up the tap, tapping again, soothing and willing her somnolence. Once I satisfied myself that she had fallen asleep, I prepared to leave. But the sleep demons returned and I waited, frustrated, as she writhed amid the blankets. All of a sudden, she bolted upright, breathing hard as if she'd been deprived of air. Her head fell into her hands. I began to tap again. An hour later she gave in and rested peacefully, in a deep sleep, remaining quiet. I would solve this mystery for her own good.

Chapter 10

"Did you bring a swimsuit?"

"You warned me to. Shorts will have to suffice." I handed her book back. "So, are you as good a swimmer as you are a runner?" Dare I hope for an affirmative reply?

"Nowhere close," she mumbled.

"You look a little green around the gills. What gives?" I joked.

"I don't like swimming," she quietly admitted.

"Swimming itself or parading around in a swimsuit?"

"Both."

I chuckled softly. Even though I was amused, I didn't want to hurt her feelings. I suppose many girls were much too self-conscious in swim suits; then I remembered Bonnie's under-developed body. Great going, CatSkill. Her body language told me I had upset her. She was turning in on herself- a different Bonnie than I had enjoyed at the ranch.

"What's up with you and swim class? Don't know how, afraid of the water?" Her posture contracted further. I'd hit the nail on the head.

"Thanks for chopping all that wood. I can't believe how much you did. It was really nice of you."

"My pleasure," I replied with sincerity. "Let's get back to the water issue." Dejected, she began walking. Gently, I touched her elbow, turned her to face me, "Bonnie, why are you afraid of water? Surely, the teacher will help you learn to swim. That's what class is for. I'll teach you, if you want."

She pulled away. "I saw a woodpecker last night."

Ah, the queen of change-the-subject-if-you-get-cornered, but I wasn't biting. "What about me being your swim instructor?"

"Serious?" She was skeptical. I rolled my eyes. She bit at her lower lip, "I don't think you'll be able to. I'm hopeless in a pool."

"Try me. What have you got to lose?" I intended to keep the offer open.

"You mean beside someone to talk to?" She scuffed at the sidewalk.

"C'mon, Bonnie. Give me some credit." I had something in common with Sticker- I wasn't letting go.

"I don't think so." But she was considering
the prospect now, at least. "When?" A fragment
of hope lurked in those green eyes.

"Soon," I promised. I'd been tinkering with
grandfather's old jeep, pondering how it would
come in handy- trips to the grocery store, for one
thing. Grandfather had last used it the past
summer, before conceding defeat to the old
vehicle's idiosyncrasies. If I could get it
running, well, let's just say I wasn't that fond
of Bonnie's long walk to the bus stop, either.
Better to pick her up, if she'd let me, more time
together to figure her out.

"Tell me about your bird visitor. I thought
woodpeckers were done for the season," I inquired
of the safer subject.

"I would have thought so, too." She frowned
a second, then brightened. "I didn't really see
him so much as. . .you'll think I'm crazy. I just
knew he was there, tapping. The sound, it was
nice. Almost like a lullaby. Red Hawk used to
tell me stories, Indian legends of different
animals. One was of a woodpecker tapping out his
courtship song to a prospective mate."

A part of me had forgotten that aspect, or had it? "That bird is also known as a harbinger of storms- it's believed the tapping can even call in a storm. The rhythm of its tap can be a means to meditate, an initiation to shamanic rituals. When a woodpecker appears in unusual circumstances, it may portend a strong force moving into one's life." I sounded like a text book and was treading on thin ice. What was I doing? "The rhythm of the sounds may also put one back in sync— be a call to rest." Ah, terra firma again.

"Or a summons to become a shaman," she whispered this. Before I could begin to get my mind around that shocker, a strident warning interrupted.

"CatSkill, Lance, get to class!" The principal barked an order.

The bus delivered 22 seniors to the YMCA for swim class in the Olympic-size pool. One piece swimsuits were required for the girls, unfortunately. I changed to my jean shorts and watched the parade of the so-called prettiest girls. It was more entertaining to watch the guys watch the sashaying of the feminine parts.

Bonnie and a rather plump girl came out to the pool together- commiserating, I would bet. I read the dismay on both their faces, but for different reasons. The plump one was more concerned with the fit of her suit. Bonnie had the child-like stick figure I witnessed from her running outfit. Patience, Catskill. Her apprehension focused more on the chlorine-infested water than on her looks.

"Girls, line up for the left hand lanes. Boys- to the right. We'll start off with laps alternating breast-stroke for a half lap, side-stroke half and breast-stroke back," the instructor ordered.

I strode over to Bonnie, probably the only one here who did not swim.

"Mr. Kitchener," she approached him.

"Yes," he kept his eyes on the swimmers.

"I can't do this," her voice quivered.

"Can't swim, Miss Lance?"

"No." Her eyes studied the wet tile.

"Sir, if it helps, I'll work with Bonnie," I offered.

"No, go ahead and do your laps, son. There's really no time for a beginner swim lesson." Bonnie stood to the side watching without much interest as the lap work progressed with the coach calling out helpful hints. He set up a relay. Ten pairs formed with a bit of shuffling and trash-talk. Surreptitious glances continued at the girls. Out and out ogling was discouraged when caught by Mr. Kitchener.

"Bonnie," I whispered down at her. "How about you stand in the shallow end, I'll tag you and you tag the finish?"

"You should pair up with one of the others- you could win." Her eyes never left the ground.

"Winning's not everything, baby." I wouldn't give away the fact we'd win anyway. Nothing could touch me on land or in the water.

"CatSkill, you got a partner?"

"Yes, sir, Bonnie."

His face registered surprise, "Whatever. First six pairs get ready. This will be timed. Winners will receive a gift certificate from Rizzoli's Pizza." Kitchener whistled off the first group. The swimmers did a fair job, though several were disqualified for not properly tagging their relay partners. I keyed Bonnie in on our strategy.

"Be ready for my tag," I warned her. She nodded, apprehensive, yet at ease in the shallow water. My springing dive put me far ahead of the other competitors and I immediately relaxed into my best Weismuller-Tarzan imitation. Bonnie was there for my tag. With four strides she smacked the finish. The instructor checked his stop watch several times before announcing us the winners.

"Told you," I leaned toward her confounded smile and got a good whiff of her essence despite the stench of chlorine. Shell- shocked, but beaming, she went to change while the others stepped around me.

"Who is this guy?" I heard their mutterings.

"Thinks he's superman."

"He's super something," one of the girls giggled with her friends as they passed, openly staring at me.

I flashed the gift certificate in Bonnie's face. "If I get us a ride, are you in for pizza?"

"I'm not sure if my dad will be home. I'd have to ask him." We walked to the bus. "You sure you want to go with me?"

"Wouldn't ask if I didn't."

"Why?" She asked.

I swept my still wet hair from my eyes, "What?"

"Wh…why me?"

"Weren't you my partner in the swim relay?" She wasn't offering her face for my perusal but her stance screamed no self-confidence. "Bonnie, let's just say I like the way you smell."

This brought her up short- interrupted three bodies attempting to board the bus. Her face flamed. "I don't understand." And that made two of us.

I changed the subject, for once. "Asking anyone to the girl's choice dance?" I waved my hand in front of her confusion, "Earth to Bonnie."

"N…n…no," she managed to stutter.

"How come? Must be some nice boys in this school."

"I…I suppose."

"Hey, you two! Are you on the bus or what?" This got a rise out of her planted feet.

I sat next to her, of course. "What about this dance?"

"I don't date." She was hiding her gaze from me again. I believed I'd have to see about that dating business.

Wyoming winds play havoc with prey animals' sense of security. The pronghorn antelope, a remnant from 200 million years ago, is a most vigilant challenge. Their large eyes protrude, sweep a wide arc and easily detect movement from up to four miles away. A most worthy adversary for a superb workout, as an antelope can hit 70 miles an hour within 20 bounds. A bit of animal-chess was called for, 70 miles per hour being a hard speed for even my wondrous physique.

But I needed a workout and Bonnie was not available without her dad's permission- the ultimate good girl- so antelope was the distraction of choice. In my preferred nature, I'm the ultimate predator, but it wasn't a hunger for food I was looking for. It was extremely rare for me to kill. Therefore, I stretched lazily and went in search of a good game of tag-the-antelope, sans claws and they in turn would play dodge the. . .

Hank Winch took another swig of beer and nearly ran his truck off the road- something out in the basin was bounding about a herd of pronghorn. It collected the animals and dove into the midst of the melee- scattering antelope in all directions, picking one to negotiate. Then it would spring from one side to another of the chosen one like a reining horse with a steer. A huge paw flicked out, barely touching a reddish haunch, then, it burst in another direction.

"I've had too much to drink," he slurred, shut off his truck and collapsed across the bench seat. Beer dribbled from his outstretched hand as the bottle hit the gear shift. "Nobody will believe me," he belched. "Mountain lions don't play with pronghorn."

Chapter 11

"Hey, CatSkill! Catch!" The near silent whistle of the approaching basketball forewarned well ahead of the human voice. The whistle ignited my instant reflex and I easily caught and twirled the ball. If anyone else had been standing in my place, there would be evident ridge marks on their face from the unavoidable slap of the ball.

"Nice catch," someone snickered. When intuition speaks, it's not wise to disregard it. I had an inkling today would have been a good day not to attend class.

"Mr. CatSkill, any intentions of acquiring athletic clothes?"

"No sir."

The gym instructor eyed my bare feet, "They're your feet, son."

"Mr. Peak, I have to remind you, I don't play contact sports." I could hear the wheels grinding in his thinking cap.

"We're just dribbling the ball and shooting a few hoops. No big deal," he stalked with a shake of his head.

The tallest boy in the class sidled up to me, open, honest face. With genuine interest asked, "What have you got against team sports?"

"Not a thing, I just don't play them." I'd not explain how the receipt of an innocuous touch would be taken as a challenge to fight- pure wild instinct. Someone would get hurt and it wouldn't be me.

"Wouldn't mind playing horse with you sometime. With your speed and reflexes, you could help me tighten my game. I'd spring for a pizza or whatever to compensate for your time. Get a chance to know each other. By the way, my name's Rick Winslow," he offered his hand.

I grinned and shook it, "That's the first decent offer I've had since coming here. Let's do it!"

Rick nodded, "It's on."

"Guys have the floor the first half hour, then girls," the coach specified the routine. I'd read the guy groupings and back and forth whisperings. I knew something was going to transpire, it would not be pretty or routine.

Somewhere in my past, I must have dribbled a basketball. Must not have been a highlight of my past because it wasn't readily coming to mind. Dribble, run, shoot a basket. Hmmm, simple hand, feet, eye coordination- should be a piece of cake.

To start, the guys lined up, each had a chance to give it a shot. I watched Rick, relaxed, very at home in his movements. My turn came and it was actually kind of fun- not as thrilling as running, except for the spring at the end of my sprint when I cannoned that ball down into the hoop. Clapping resounded from the girls on the bench. The socialites were loudest, wanting my attention- their eyes hungry on my bare chest. But it was Bonnie I searched for. Her heartfelt smile and cheer gave me a good feeling.

Rick offered me a high five, "Real soon, man."

The next step was pairing up. Rick and I, without hesitation, played a bit of horse for a few shots before conceding the hoop to the next pair. I'd warned him not to push and though he used his long reach to block my shots, my springs put me above his reach every time.

"Who says white guys can't jump?" Rick chortled.

"And barefoot," I grinned at him.

For the last exercise, Peak put together groups of five. I bowed out, to insulting murmurings. I'd spotted the three main troublemakers and I could have removed myself quicker but Rick threw a last question at me a fraction of a second before trouble number one moved around me. Trouble two and three jostled the ball I'd surrendered, put me in the midst of a triangular formation. A fourth and fifth stumbled around the edge of this action, unsure. Number two had the ball and was about to gig me when instinct or pure bravado took over- I stole the ball from his inept, human, bullyboy fingers, wended through his followers and the bystanders, headed for the hoop. Number three tripped in my line of fire, went down and instead of lying pat, grabbed my foot nearly taking me down with him. This gave trouble one enough time to send two careening into my slightly out-of-balance self. I felt the elbow to my ribs- there wouldn't even be a bruise- but my territoriality, the invasion of my personal space evoked a reprimanding fury. Ball dribbling in left hand, my right elbow shot out forcefully cracking the offender's ribcage.

I felt the imperceptible give and heard the follow-up groan. He was down, gasping. Furious at my resultant action, I dunked the ball and turned. All eyes were on me. Several of the downed one's cohorts started toward me.

Rick shouted, held up his hands, "Not CatSkill's fault. Sam set that up."

"Back down, boys!" Mr. Peak ordered and called 911, kneeling next to Sam.

Angry at myself for being in this situation when I knew better, angry at the troops aching for a battle that would have ended in slaughter, I grabbed my t-shirt from the bench and hastily stalked out.

Bonnie was hurrying across and down the bleachers toward me. She started to say something as she followed me out of the gym and into the parking lot. Her hand reached for me. "Don't touch me," I growled and swept away from her.

I didn't glance back. Maybe, if I'd looked at her- maybe she could have brought me to my senses. But, I ignored her; I was too intent on quitting the scene.

A new silver BMW coupe pulled alongside me. Lil, considered THE prettiest girl in the school by poor human eyesight, stepped out, in all her designer glory. Coquettishly, she waved for me to join her. Her sultry eyes and winning smile kept me from reversing course and racing home. Hell on heels. And with wheels. Why not? I asked myself. Why the devil not? She strutted around, opened the passenger door and blew me a kiss. I threw my moccasins in and joined them.

Chapter 12

"Whew Grandson, you stink!" The obnoxious perfume and other sundry aromatics employed by Lil permeated our small living quarters.

"I'll take a wash outside, Grandfather," I apologized.

"Do that; don't want to spoil my appetite."

After a few buckets of cold water and scent-free soap scrubbing, I took a whiff of myself and was satisfied I wouldn't be a burden to my own or grandfather's nose.

"Was it worth it?" He scrunched up his nose, testing the air upon my reentry.

"Just blowing off steam," I allowed, ruefully.

"Hmmm, maybe you should tell me about it."

I took a different tack, "Why did you want me to come back at this time, Grandfather?"

"I thought you could rehash some lessons here." His attention fastened on his rabbit stew. I knew he was being evasive.

"One of those lessons was today- I didn't handle a situation as well as I should have."

"You let some others pick your fight." He tasted a spoonful of broth, added a shake of salt. I certainly couldn't hide anything from grandfather- his sight and intuition were unparalleled. He'd had years of practice.

"Yes," I demurred.

"What should you have done?"

"I should have stood my ground better, not allowed myself to be drawn in. I should have kept my focus; I allowed myself to be distracted." I remembered Bonnie's cheers and the other girls in the bleachers. How good it felt to sink all those baskets. "I should have checked my strength when I reacted." I pushed my plate away, disgusted with myself for the next admission. "I should not have hurt a friend." This last part was sinking in and more than the other lessons, this one hurt. In hurting Bonnie, I'd hurt myself. Odd. . .

"A good learning day," grandfather nodded.

"Yes," I agreed, knowing I'd take the rest of the night to work it all out in my head. Ah, Bonnie, I hope you'll forgive me. "Grandfather, were there other reasons you wanted me back here now?"

He wiped up the last of his stew with a biscuit. "We'll get to that. You have a question for me," he stated.

"You know Bonnie Lance?"

"Little Bonnie," a warm smile lit up my grandfather's cagey face. "She listens to my stories the way you used to- so long ago. I've not seen her in a while. I'm sure her father has lots for her to do- he's gone most of the time. With the jeep not running it's hard for me to go over there. . ." I laughed at this remark. There was a particular guile in his countenance I could plainly read.

"Is Bonnie one of the lessons?"

"I thought you might like her. She's not like other girls."

"That's very true," I was going to hedge on my reaction to Bonnie and let grandfather play out his hand, if he would.

"Do you like her?"

"She's just a kid, Grandfather."

"Kids grow up, Grandson." The calling and checking of the poker game had begun.

"I must admit she certainly smells good."

"Not like the one you were blowing off steam with, huh?" We both blew up at that. "She makes her own soap with ingredients she finds in the woods and out on the prairie," he informed me.

That explained the completely natural scent on her mingled with her own unique, feminine skin and blood. I closed my eyes, recalling her mouthwatering aromatic delight. When she did finally grow up- when the flowering began. . . I rose, agitated, the chair skidded across the floor.

"If you brought me back for her, Grandfather, that's not fair." I couldn't be there to claim her when she was ready. Bonnie wasn't the girl to feed some fiend's momentary desire. She should be loved and cherished for always. I didn't know her well, but of this I had absolutely no doubt.

"Do you think of yourself as a fiend, a bad creature?" He'd read my mind and exhibited grave concern.

"Grandfather, it's for us to live alone. Isn't that how it's always been- the shaman lives alone to commune with the mysteries in order to be of some help to his people? This is what you taught me. . ."

The beginnings of a disgruntled, dissatisfied passion of uncertainty were hovering. I'd always been secure and at peace with my role. For the first time in my life, questions were vying, invading in a way I wasn't sure how to stave off, except maybe by running. Grandfather rose, he gleaned my disquiet. Why was I here? Was he giving up? Was this the passing of the torch?

Chapter 13

"Grandson, will you please sit with me.
I've a story to tell that I've never told anyone.
A living creature is never too old to learn and
this might be the most significant lesson I've
ever given you." With a deep breath I calmed
myself, this was very important to Grandfather. I
wanted to hear every word he had to say.

He continued after we took our seats again.
"I know the most powerful shamans have always kept
to themselves- apart from the people. In the old
days, wisdom seemed to come to those who asked the
mysteries, the spirits, for aid and knowledge, in
order to help their people. Those seeking the
shamanic way had a hard road to follow, years of
training. If the spirits did not call such a one,
he or she might have to suffice with a lesser
calling. A shaman must have the backing of the
spirits.

Very seldom did one seek answers from the spirits for their own power and advancement. A shaman's role was to aid his people- to ensure their survival. I used to believe I was doing what was required of me, taught by shamans throughout history-become one with the Divine in order to help your people find food, suitable camp sites, succor from cold, strength to win battles, ways to heal sickness. . . As the white men overtook our homes, not one shaman, not one medicine man, was able to find the answer to stem the flood of white man-induced change. This does not anger me now. I've come to accept that change happens- it's within each person to find the means to change and live with new conditions or to suffer. A shaman can only offer his people a reminder of this.

Some 130 years ago, a white, Christian missionary woman and her father came to our reservation. She was not like the ones who came before- she was a blessing, but, in general we were too angry at the time to see her as such. While other missionaries and government officials wanted our children shipped off to boarding schools and to take away all of their heritage, she argued this was counterproductive.

Each child needed to embrace his heritage and with it find inside himself the way to live without suffering in the new and different world of our white conquerors. She didn't shove black books down our throats. Her message of God wasn't bound inside leather covers. She wished for all of our people to be educated, not in some foreign school, and not just for the children, but for all together on the reservation. She was a gentle woman, but with words she would fight the government-sent men who stole our food from us and grew rich at our expense. Her teachings were good for our people- too good.

Her church and the government conspired to remove her from us. She was not a white woman so much as she was simply a good woman. If she were here today, I would do my damnedest to court and marry her. My anger clouded my vision when she was with us. I was not angry with her; I knew what she was about. I could read her spirit. How different everything would have been if she'd remained."

My mind was numb as Grandfather spoke and then raced with the underlying meaning. "You loved her."

"Yes," he inclined his head, his glistening eyes full of emotion.

"Did you ever tell her, give her a chance to respond?"

"In those days, Grandson, an Indian man did not spend time alone with a white woman. The people would not have understood a shaman with a. . . She always had a kind smile, was interested in our history- even learned our language." I could feel grandfather's pain; it lingered after all these years.

He continued, "In those days, if she'd said yes, she would have been ostracized. No white would ever have listened to her."

"So you made the decision?"

"Yes."

"She went on to fight in the halls of Washington D.C."

"Grandfather," I gently asked, "do you think you were right to make that decision, all by yourself?"

"I don't know Grandson, but my time is done." He wiped at his wet cheeks. I began to protest. He held up his palm to stave me off. "I've still a few things to do. . . This is what is important, Grandson. You do not have to be alone. Maybe it was wrong in the old days, but that time is gone. You are here at this time and I say to you: do not force yourself to live alone if you meet your heart's equal in another. I believe two can learn together as well as and probably better than one."

I could tell he'd finished and inside myself I believed he would not give up on life. Somehow. "Grandfather, what was her name?"

"Grace, Grace Esperanza," he reverently whispered. I knew he must say her name prayer-like to himself.

"Thank you, Grandfather." A plan was forming in my mind. Esperanza meant hope- I believed this was providential. "So Grandfather, you think Bonnie and I should kick it?" I grinned at him.

"Grandson, were you not listening? You can play ball with anybody, it's your heart I'm thinking of and hers."

I laughed aloud. He swiped at me, "I'm not too old to take you on for disrespect, Riordan CatSkill!"

"No disrespect, sir," I ducked, "but I think you've been sedentary too long. I'll race you," I challenged.

A sly smile flitted about his mouth. His countenance immediately seemed younger. "I expect you'll accord Bonnie every respect," he warned.

"Take my word for it, she'll give me a run for the money," I laughed again.

Grandfather cheated in the race, descending onto my back as I approached the finish line. His red tail feathers tickled my back and distracted me from really pouring on the speed in the final quarter mile.

That night I began to work on the jeep in earnest. Grandfather also convinced me to assist him with his meditation classes. At the beginning of each season, students, interested parties from all walks of life and from every corner of the world, would attend a teaching session with grandfather. This included meditation under the stars, sweat-lodge rituals and teaching stories. The classes were solely for the stout-of- heart as Wyoming weather did not always cooperate. Grandfather brought shamanism into the 21st century. I don't know if he realized how well he was continuing his own heritage.

"You remember Bonnie is my friend when you start conveying her around in this sorry-excuse-for-a-horse," he reiterated.

I laughed, glad that lightness had returned to Grandfather and me. Heaviness and too much introspection were not for me. "Bonnie can take care of herself, Grandfather. I'll be sure to bring her by if her father gives me the go ahead. And this sorry-excuse-for-a-horse will come in handy hauling groceries and running errands whereas my wild nature would draw too much attention."

"I guess you would make front-page news carting a grocery bag in those fangs."

Chapter 14

"Bonnie," I waited her descent from the bus at the school yard. Head down she hurried by me without the slightest hesitation or recognition of my presence. I deserved that.

"Bonnie," I easily matched her stride for stride. "I owe you an apology."

At this she did stop. "I'm not a financial institution; you don't owe me anything."

I believe wrestling with Bonnie would probably be more fun than anything I'd ever done. A rejoinder like hers was Oscar-worthy with those dark green eyes flashing fire. Yes, I was looking forward to the day when her body blossomed, though I would still need to be extremely careful not to hurt her. Grandfather could be right.

"Come on, baby. Don't hold back, spit it all out." We were attracting an audience which put a stint in her response.

She headed around a corner of the building. "It was presumptuous of me to offer a friendly word," she fumed.

Quick as a cat, she burst away, nearly reaching the side door before I, without careful thought, grabbed her elbow and pulled her back to me. A wince and a stricken look in her eyes struck a nail in my heart. Immediately, I loosened my grip.

"Hey Road Runner, that guy bothering you?" An interfering so-and-so stuck his nose in.

"No," she told him. My glare bid him scram. "We're just talking," Bonnie asserted.

The boy walked off, issuing a threat, "You'll get yours, chief." Evidently he was one of Sam's buddies.

"Bonnie, I'm sorry. Are you OK?" She attempted to rub her injured elbow.

"Nothing a little arnica can't fix," the catch in her voice belied her bravado.

"Baby, I'm sorry." I opened every healing energy I could channel and immediately heat flowed from my fingers to her, encompassing her elbow, forearm and bicep.

"What are you doing?" The wonder in this whispered question told me I was taking away the pain- at least the physical pain.

"It will be better in a moment," I assured her.

"You don't know your own strength," she reproached me.

"Unfortunately for you, I do," I contritely admitted.

"And Sam?"

The corner of my mouth turned up, "Sam had it coming. You however, are a complete innocent. Bonnie, look at me so I can continue my apologies." She refused. I took a different tack. As gently as I could, my left fingers raised her chin.

"Don't you dare close your eyes," I quietly warned.

"Or you'll what?" Almost taunting me.

"I don't know," and I didn't. "Maybe, I'll kiss you." Her eyes flew open and we were close-nose to upraised nose. The most tantalizing meal I'd ever consumed couldn't compete with her scent. My salivary glands went into overdrive. What, I wondered would that sweet mouth taste like? My eyes sought hers and I felt a tremor go through her. Oh yes, she was aware of my thoughts.

Her awareness was profound. I'd been away from class a week but not away from her all that time. Two days ago, I'd come across her. Bonnie's back leaned against a shade-haven tree trunk. She faced an expanse of give-up-the-ghost prairie grass in which I hid silently watching her. A sketch book rested against her drawn up knees and her eyes fastened on my hiding spot.

It was as if she'd been waiting for me,
though that was impossible. Wasn't it? I
remained totally hidden but I sensed her gaze on
me. She began to sketch. Silently, I stayed put,
interested beyond endurance. What was she
drawing? Patience is a virtue of my breed,
luckily.

After an hour, the pencil stilled.
Apparently, she was satisfied. She glanced from
her sketch to my hiding area, a smile gracing her
features. I decided to circle her and see her
artwork. Soundlessly, I evacuated my post, but as
I moved her chin came up and her eyes followed me.
Impossible! I came to a halt. We could have been
playing a staring game- I moved, she pinpointed
me.

As if she knew my intention, she closed the
blasted book, rose, picked up her backpack and
with a nod in my direction, she strolled home.
Unbelievable!

"I'm sorry I snapped at you the other day.
I had no right to treat you like that. I want us
to be friends." Among other things. "You can't
conceive of my mood. . ."

"I thought you didn't like to be touched?"
In a nutshell, here was the crux of her problem.

"I take uninvited contact as a challenge," I
tried to explain.

"I wasn't going to challenge you. I wanted
to make you feel better- Rick and I and I expect
Mr. Peak, too, were on your side. All the girls
were." Her eyes fell to the ground.

"I don't care about all the girls," my teeth
gritted.

"Why did you let her. . .?" She began to
chew her lower lip and then clamped down.

"Continue," I chucked her silent chin.

"Why did you go with her? You didn't mind
her touching you." This last phrase rushed out
with admirable speed.

It took a second for this to sink in. This
time I bit the inside of my lip to keep from
smiling and asking if she were jealous. I
believed I knew the answer but I'd not antagonize
or embarrass her by voicing it aloud.

"Bonnie," how could I say this? "You're too
young to know about the difference between the
touch of a friend," I hesitated now, "and the
touch of a sex partner. At that time I felt too
wild to let you in- maybe if you'd offered to race
me? She offered a particular. . .never mind.
There was nothing to it, don't let it bother you."
I shrugged my shoulders and flashed a boyishly,
endearing smile.

The principal stuck his head out the door.
"Get to class or I'm issuing detention!"

Chapter 15

"Mr. Riordan CatSkill, how nice of you to join us," Mr. Gallagher offered a tongue-in-cheek greeting. "Here I was expecting you to give Miss Lance some competition." He lowered his voice but continued gleefully. "She's already taken six tests to your two."

Bonnie had taken her seat but I was sure her hearing was perfectly attuned.

"I'll see what I can do about that, sir. May I have tests 3, 4, 5, today?"

"But you haven't even glanced at the texts!" The rest of the class was shuffling books, settling into their places.

I opened the requisite book, thumbed through, "Ok, I'm ready."

He shook his head, "If you fail, you'll have to wait a week to take the tests over."

I appreciated his caution. "No problem—there will be no failure."

I accepted the tests, sat down and with a challenging glance in Bonnie's direction, sent her diligently to work to keep her short advantage.

"Have lunch with me?" Outside, Lil batted her baby blues at me.

"Thanks, but I'm having lunch with Bonnie, Rick and I don't know who else- join us?" I knew Rick would be gratified by my bringing Lil to the table- Bonnie, probably, not.

"Sure," Lil answered with the confidence of a coquette. She wasn't yet conceding that we were, in fact, not an item. I disallowed any physical contact and to her credit, she hid her dismay well.

Lunch was an interesting affair. Rick tried to make headway with Lil. He'd already politely approached me earlier about my interest in her. I told him to go for it.

Bonnie studied the scene as an actress cadging the feel for a movie script, wondering about her role, but as I sat next to her, she started to relax. I read the innuendos of Sam and his gang off in the corner. Several other girls, perfume-factory-worthy, hovered about our table of misfits and basketball stars- a court presided over by Princess Lil who drove conversations to her liking.

Soon we were going to need a bigger table. I personally enjoyed myself. Bonnie was keeping her cool and Lil began to fondle Rick's arm. Nothing like being part of a movie, with no line responsibilities, yet knowing your big scene is coming up.

Finishing afternoon classes, I caught up with Bonnie. "Give you a ride home?"

"You have a car?" I enjoy Bonnie's puzzled puss.

"Would you say yes if I offered a piggy-back ride home?"

She mulled this over for half a second, "Yes, I think I'd especially like that. To see if you could do it. I mean. . ." she stumbled and a tell-tale blush fired her pale skin.

"Still haven't forgiven me 100%, huh? Oh well, hop on." I leaned down for her and to her credit she enthusiastically jumped aboard.

I felt her backpack slip to one side. With a push of my shoulder I adjusted all weights. What a misnomer, she weighed next to nothing.

My arms embraced her legs. Her hands tentatively reposed across my collar bone. With my own book bag banging against my leg, I ran out to the parking lot- not too fast, enjoying her subdued squeals. I put her down next to the jeep.

"Though I could carry you all the way home, it would mean I'd have to run back and get my grandfather's jeep."

The old vehicle was certainly a card-carrying-member of antique-rust-buckets-are-us, but it ran fine. Now that we'd discussed all of its little quirks.

Grandfather had cautioned me to fix up the inside to make it more comfortable. I wasn't sure if he had more amorous pursuits in mind or what.

I padded the bereft seats with clean blankets and had swept and washed the interior until, although not quite up to Martha Stewart standards, the old jeep deserved an award for effort and diversity. None of the blankets matched.

Rick waved over at me as he and Lil conversed alongside his new Explorer. Relationships without jealousy are great.

"Wow!" finally erupted from my companion.

"Good wow or bad?" I stood, hands on my hips.

"Definitely good. This will get through muck and snow, I bet." The jeep was set up high on wheels and tires worthy of a war zone.

"If it can make it down our drive, this baby will make it anywhere a wheeled vehicle can possibly go." I opened the door. "Think you can get in?"

She hopped up like a champ, bounced excitedly to check out the seat cushioning.

"Music?"

"I'd rather listen to the wind." She had her window half- way down. A chilly draft hustled in and tangled with her hair.

"You're not cold?"

"No, I rarely get cold."

"And you'd rather listen to the rush of cold air?"

A slight shoulder came up and she defended herself, "I like the Wyoming winds- they keep me on my toes- in tune with everything around me- not in a fearful way like with prey animals. . ." she caught herself as if admitting too much.

Interesting. . . Her eyes remained intent out the passenger window. This surprising take on a new subject had me hoping for more. "Now you won't have to walk so far or take the bus."

"What do you mean?" she whispered.

"I'll be picking you up every day, taking you home." Absolute quiet reigned when I expected jubilation, especially with winter breathing down our necks. "Unless, you don't want me to?"

"I'll have to ask my dad." She studied me. "I don't think he'll mind."

"When's your father get home?"

"Saturday night."

"Good, I'll be over first thing Sunday morning. I'd like to meet him and I've a question to ask him."

"A question?" The puzzled puss returned. I nodded- poker face, non-committal. "What kind of a question?" She persisted.

"You'll see. How's the wood holding out?" I changed the subject before she could attempt to wheedle out. . .

"I can't believe how much wood you split. I don't know if I thanked you enough."

"I'll be sure you always have plenty. I don't want you wielding an axe." That almost sounded proprietary, I mused.

I felt her wide eyes on me and momentarily savored the wonder there before returning to being a careful and conscientious driver.

"You know, I…I didn't think you were coming back. You were gone so long," she whispered, wistfully.

"I wasn't sure myself," I admitted.

Chapter 16

"Today, we're dissecting rabbit fetus," Mr. Sayers rubbed his hands together- the optimum biology teacher. He retained his enthusiasm for every aspect of the biological realm. I liked him- he was on par with Mr. Gallagher in my esteem.

"Proceed to the front with your partner, choose a fetus, pick up your dissection kits, instructions are on the board. Raise a hand if you have questions and I'll be there to help." Bonnie stopped in front of Mr. Sayers, a hand up.

"Bonnie, you haven't even started," he smiled at her, indulgently- obvious, she was his favorite student.

"Mr. Sayers, I can't do this particular lab. I'm s…sorry." I studied her face. The pallor and beads of sweat beginning to surface were not a good sign.

"You don't look well," he empathized.

"I could draw whatever information is required. . ."

At this point, a duo was returning to their seats. The guy was air-hopping his fetus, laughing all the way. Between the chemical smell and. . .

Bonnie went out like a light. Without my instant reaction, she would have hit her head on the lab table as she crumpled to the floor.

A momentary hush of surprise took over the class, then, nervous giggling invaded. Mr. Sayers rushed to check on his fallen student. Hard to believe, but maybe it had never happened in his class before.

A very pale Bonnie rested in my arms. "Sir, I think I should take Bonnie to the nurse's station."

"Yes. Yes, Mr. CatSkill. Thank you. Tell her not to worry. I'll assign something else for both of you." At once concern and gratitude mingled on his face.

With Bonnie cradled in my arms, I squatted, gathered book bags and her coat, rose and effortlessly strode from the parting of the student-lined aisle way.

Outside, I hesitated before going to the nurse. I dropped onto a bench and attempted to revive my lab partner.

She groaned as she came to. One hand rushed to her head and the other to her stomach. A convulsion began in her midsection and she fought to turn from me as she threw up. I gathered her hair and held it back, waited for the tremors to subside.

"What's going on here?" The principal picked this moment to make his rounds. He confronted us, hands on his hips as if we were deliberately skipping class.

"Bonnie fainted in biology lab. I was carrying her to the nurse's station. . ." Her insides erupted again. Unfortunately, the principal's spit-shined shoes were now vomit-spattered, as well as his tweed trousers.

Checking himself, he interrupted an involuntary curse and jumped back as Bonnie remained hunched over.

"I'll leave her in your hands, son. Try to get to the nurse." He wished me luck and fled the scene.

"Bonnie, feeling a bit better?" I soothed and leaned her into my chest. She tried to nod. I picked her up and made it to the nurse's office, laid her on a couch. I found a box of Kleenex, moistened one and wiped her mouth.

"She fainted in the dissection lab and threw up on the way here," I explained to the efficient woman who was taking Bonnie's pulse, feeling her forehead.

"Would you mind getting a bottle of water and juice from the fridge?"

When I returned, Bonnie was sitting up. I presented both bottles to her. The nurse patted her knee, asked if she'd ever fainted before.

"No," Bonnie quietly admitted. I knelt beside her but she wouldn't look at me.

"Did she hit her head?" The nurse addressed me.

"No, I'm sure she didn't."

"That's good. You might still have a headache later, dear. Would there be someone to take you home?"

"I will," I took Bonnie's hand in mine.

"I think that might be best." The nurse presented me with two slips to excuse us and her cell number for medical support.

I helped Bonnie don her coat. "I can walk," she swayed upon rising.

"Forget that," I scooped her up and carried her to the jeep. Once I had her settled in she began to apologize.

"Don't be ridiculous- you didn't throw up on my shoes, anyway. Finish the rest of that juice. We're going to sit here for a few minutes while you regroup."

I closed my fingers on her tiny wrist, brushed her pulse with my thumb and sent a gentle wave of continuous healing energy. The slump in her shoulders waned and color returned to her cheeks and the rose to her lips.

"How do you do that?" she wondered.

"I'll show you sometime. Just try to relax for now, be quiet."

After 10 minutes, she turned to me, a slow smile tentatively spread. "Thank you." This was the signal to still my ministrations.

"Shall I take you home or. . ." I flashed the excuse-from- school passes, "Would you like to play hooky?"

Hooky involved a trip to the library and tag-team efforts to keep a computer and internet access to ourselves.

"What are we looking for?" She asked with great interest.

"Grandfather gave me the name of a white missionary woman he'd heard of. She worked for a time on the reservation around 1870 or so, was highly regarded by the people- the Lakota. Thought it might be fun to Google her and see what became of her."

"Grace Esperanza," Bonnie voiced the name I typed in.

"Hmmm. . ." I ruminated.

"Pretty name. What did she look like?"

Ooh, I almost fell right into that. Surreptitiously, I studied her through my lashes. Her mien was serious- too serious. I was now positive grandfather had been all too cagey on the topic of Bonnie Lance. I remembered how lightly he'd said, "Kids grow up". There was definitely something about this 'kid'.

Most girls were bowled over by my speed- touted how intriguing I was. Bonnie might have been jealous of my encounter with Lil, but she wasn't exactly surprised by me.

Somehow, I knew she knew who or what had been watching her that day while she was sketching. I intended to conduct further tests on this most unusual girl.

"Now that's a girl's question if ever I heard one. How should I know what she looked like?" But I saw her, Grace, through my grandfather's reminisces.

"Well, I am a girl," Bonnie huffed, adorably.

"Look here, girl."

On the screen came an old, sepia, late 1800's photograph. Tall for a woman of the era, thin, dressed in a split riding skirt- grandfather had said Grace could ride any horse better than a man.

A white, lacey Victorian blouse and wide straw hat sheltering a face turned up to the camera, completed her ensemble. Mischievous eyes, high cheekbones, wide full mouth, secretive smile, challenging chin- the photographer caught it all.

Her right hand held the reins of a rangy, Appaloosa horse. The text reiterated grandfather's story. However, the ending lines were compelling. Apparently, Grace rode off one day and was never seen again.

"I'd like to meet her. . . I…I mean I would have liked to meet her." Lovely, now I had two mysteries on my hands.

"Google the name present day," Bonnie urged.

"Bingo," I murmured. A Grace Esperanza worked in Sedona, Arizona. She had more letters touting her expertise than the most prestigious university professor. The woman operated a healing/teaching school to aid the spiritually inclined.

"Riordan?" My ears thrilled at my name finally rolling off Bonnie's tongue.

"Hmmm. . ."

"Let's e-mail her, tell her about you and your grandfather." I had no choice but to comply.

Chapter 17

"I'm starving," Bonnie realized aloud. I was approaching that vicinity myself. Digging out our Rizzoli's gift certificate, my stomach and I hoped the restaurant produced extra, extra large, great tasting pizzas.

"What do you want on your half?" We appraised the menu.

"Just cheese," she asserted.

"Baby food," I teased, looking over the list of toppings-pretty extensive for a small western town pizzeria.

"Lots of cheese and maybe not half, a third will most likely be too much," she clarified.

I ordered my share with everything and anchovies. We made small talk until the waitress placed a steaming pan on our table.

"I forgot; I need some hot peppers," I quipped.

"I'll get them." Bonnie leaned over the counter, accepting cayenne pepper flakes from the busy waitress/pizza maker. Her flannel shirt rode up and I could have sworn there was a definite curve filling the seat of those jeans. What? No one developed that fast, did they? What did I really know about teenage girls, anyway?

"Thanks," I was still puzzling on. . . She gave me a strange look. I brought myself back to food.

"Next Tuesday, afternoon classes are cancelled for teacher conferences. Let's have your first real swim lesson." That ought to confirm what I thought I saw.

Bonnie stopped chewing, swallowed hard. "I bet you've travelled a lot. Why don't you tell me about all the places you've been?"

I burst out laughing. "Oh no, you don't. You are not changing the subject and you're not gonna chicken out on me. Besides, you wanted to know how to run a healing energy. After swim class, I'll show you. Deal?"

I watched a series of emotions play center stage across her face. "Bok, bok. . ." I chicken taunted her.

"Alright," she gritted her teeth. "But don't holler at me if I can't do it."

An enigmatic smile escaped me, "I'd never holler."

"Always a first time," she equivocated. We savored our pizza, quietly for a few minutes, to satisfy the worst of the noisy hunger pangs.

I tried to steer the conversation around her, wanting to know more about- well, everything about her. But she couldn't stem the tide of queries she had for me. The gentleman in me gave her the floor- ladies first.

"Do you remember your parents?" She started with.

"No, didn't know them. Why?" I sprinkled more cayenne pepper on my slice of lunch.

"You seem so comfortable in yourself- I think you are the most self-assured person I've ever met," Bonnie cocked her head and intently watched me swallow several spoons worth of cayenne without remiss.

"Self-assured," I hedged. "You're not comfortable with who you are?" Where was Bonnie taking this discourse?

"I don't feel like I am me, yet. More like I'm still becoming. . .me. When I see you, and. . .you are. . .you are you," she pretended to examine her food as she fumbled through this.

What a tremendous revelation for her to divulge, I realized. And now she was embarrassed. I remained still, refrained from a comment on her youth. Something was gnawing at my guts- I wasn't quite sure what.

"Growing up without a family must have been very hard. You moved around a lot?" she picked up the question list again.

"I was passed around a bit before grandfather took charge of me. Being an orphaned half-breed gives one the opportunity to learn pretty quickly. I've always been a fast learner. In general, I'm easygoing. That incident with Sam was outside the box." I wanted her to feel safe with me, although she exhibited no sign of being wary of me.

"I know Riordan," she was now reassuring me. Fancy that. "It doesn't seem to bother you that some of the guys are out to get you. Please be careful," she cautioned, genuine concern in her contemplation of me.

"They might try to give me a hard time but that doesn't mean I have to take it hard," I shrugged. The operative word was 'try'. Those boys had no idea.

"It's weird hearing you call yourself a half-breed, such an old fashioned term," her little nose crinkled, becomingly.

Bonnie didn't know the 'half' of the half-breed and grandfather- he had some questions coming.

Before Bonnie bounded out of the jeep, I asked about her reaction in the lab.

"I. . .I can't stand to see a helpless. .
.creature suffer. I can't even cut up a chicken
to fry. Our chickens have a forever home, even
when they're done laying eggs," she fiddled with
her backpack, waiting for me to tease.

"Bonnie, the rabbits were dead," I calmly
reminded her.

"It doesn't matter," her eyes began to
glisten. "I still feel for them. I don't know
why I'm not a vegetarian."

"Sorry I brought it up." A sensitive girl;
my heart was ringing with the day's events.

"You can laugh at me on your way home," she
pushed the door closed and ran to the dogs.

"Hey!" I scrambled after her. "Nothing
doing! I'm here to help with your chores. I
don't believe I've ever fed chickens. But I do
have stall cleaning experience. I'd just as soon
you didn't do too much, especially after the
morning you had."

"Riordan?" My eyes descended to hers. "Why
are you being so nice to me?"

Why indeed? Everything about her drew me
inexorably to her. I leaned in and ran my nose
along her neck, right down her jugular vein. No
surprise, she did not back away and we both felt
the tremors.

I took a deep breath, "Could be because you smell too damn good." She giggled- a delightful sound and a great tension breaker. What was this girl doing to me?

"C'mon, kid. Chores are calling."

Chapter 18

Obviously, Mr. Lance had returned. An old dual cab pick-up with a two-horse trailer/living quarter combination still goose-necked to it had been backed into a lean-to shelter. Although it realized some age, the rig was immaculately kept, as was the entire homestead.

I'd arranged myself with more care than attending school. Mr. Lance or rather his daughter, was important to me in ways I'd still not fully defined. Therefore, I hoped to be accepted by the father.

Grandfather, as always, left me to form my own opinions and make my own decisions. He had only spoken of Bonnie's father as hard-working and that Jim Lance loved her- a child of suspect blood only to the mean-spirited. This spoke volumes for Lance's character.

I knocked on the door, eyeing my best pair of jeans and a chambray shirt.

"Dad, my friend is here."

"Ok, honey, let her in." My sensitive hearing heard and predicated misgivings. Bonnie had not exactly told her father about me.

Door opens. In steps every daughter's father's worst nightmare.

"Hi," Bonnie shot me a smile. She nervously bit her bottom lip. Something I'd much rather have been doing for her.

To his credit, Mr. Lance played the scene well- complete composure. He gave Bonnie the once over and extended his hand.

"Jim Lance." His handshake was honest, self-secure. Mr. Lance was medium height, wiry, in shape and had dark brown hair cut short. His face betrayed his work in the sun, but his eyes were young, at the moment confused.

"Dad, this is Riordan CatSkill, Red Hawk's grandson, my friend from school."

Mr. Lance met my eyes without judgment- a fair man.

"It's nice to meet you. Forgive me if you're not what I expected." Yes, he'd been sure Bonnie had a girlfriend coming over.

"Thank you, Mr. Lance." I gave Bonnie a raised-brow query. She hovered; I wasn't totally on my own.

"How's Red Hawk? I've been meaning to visit, but I have to go when and where the work is."

"Grandfather's fine, sir."

"Well, come in, have a seat. I was just catching up on some reading." He turned into the tidy living room.

"Mr. Lance, would it be all right if we spoke in private. Maybe outside?"

This puzzled him. The lines about his brown eyes deepened slightly into worry. He studied his daughter, wondering.

"I…I've got food to fix." She made herself scarce. Mr. Lance grabbed a jacket off the clothes-horse hook and followed me out.

Casually, as if we were old acquaintances, we walked to the nearest corral. He turned to me, latched a boot heel on a fence rail and waited.

Hoss and Lil Joe sauntered over. Hoss began to nuzzle Mr. Lance's shoulder. Politely, Bonnie's father waved the snack- seeker away.

"Sir, I haven't said anything to Bonnie. I wanted to introduce myself and speak with you first. I'd like your permission to date your daughter. We've become friends at school and share several interests, running and arithmetic for example. But conversation between classes doesn't allow for much in the way of furthering a friendship. I hope you don't mind, I've been driving her to and from school. I'd like to take her out for dinner, ice cream, movies, something fun. She's such a studious and serious girl- I'd like to see her have fun."

A patient man also, not once had Mr. Lance made a move to interrupt what for me was probably the longest speech ever.

"You responsible for that stack of wood?" He nodded at the wood pile I'd chopped and constructed.

"Yes sir." I felt good about our discourse so far.

"I appreciate your efforts and your giving my girl a ride to school. You're right. She's a hard-working little girl. I was hoping. . . Well," he checked the cabin windows facing us. I followed his gaze to see a shadow vacate the glass.

Sticker and Stalker had joined us to put in their two-cents. I squatted down and scratched the appropriate areas.

"Son, don't take this the wrong way- I have great respect for your grandfather, but he's never mentioned you. And I'm not so old that I don't remember being your age. How old are you?"

"I'm a senior at the high school," I hedged to remain honest. How to reassure him I was harmless to Bonnie?

"Anyone with half a brain could see you're not a typical high school senior, son," he twirled his thumbs, mulling over his next words.

"What I'm trying to get at. . . I could easily understand you escorting one of those socialite girls at the school. I would have been interested in their curvy wiles, myself. I love my daughter, but she's very, very young and let's face it- she's built like a 12-year old, even though her brain is middle age."

"Sir, I can assure you we're just friends. Bonnie is the ultimate good girl and I've every intention of seeing her stay that way. I'd simply like to spend more time with her. She'd be perfectly safe with me."

He continued his scrutiny of me, "And you didn't ask Bonnie, yet. Why?"

"I didn't want to get her hopes up and have her be disappointed if you said no."

"Hmmm. . . I certainly do admire your manners and. . .axe skills," his eyes shifted to my handiwork. That wood pile- one of the best of intentions harvesting an unplanned fruition.

"I'll think about some rules. If you'll respect them?" There was a direct warning in this question.

"Yes, sir," I held out my hand.

If I didn't know better, I'd nearly swear Bonnie knew what her father and I had discussed. She was practically skipping in place when we reentered the cabin.

Something tasty was cooking on the old wood-burning stove. Caught the interest of my olfactories and stomach.

"I was hoping you might stay for lunch- OK, Dad?" He nodded to her and rolled his eyes at me.

"What are we having, honey? Smells good and I'm getting mighty hungry."

"Potato soup and I've made some homemade bread. . ."

"And cookies, I see," her father reached for a cut-out cookie, still hot from the oven.

"Grandfather is always complimenting your cooking to me." I leaned over to check out the cookies- two different shapes. One of a large bird and the other the outline of. . .

"Hawks for Red Hawk and. . ."

"The ubiquitous mountain lion," her father finished. My breathing stopped. All my senses reeled. . .

"What?" She attempted to decipher the intensity on my face. I'd not mimicked her father in grabbing a warm cookie. "Don't you like cookies?"

"I'm not much for sweets," I managed, my brain caught up in a whirlwind. "Except for ice cream," I amended.

"Oh," she was crestfallen. "Your grandfather will be happy then, he can have yours."

"Wait a minute." I let my sense of smell take charge. The rest of my senses were still in a state of bedlam. "What's in these cookies?" They were enticing me. As was this remarkable, mystery girl.

"Honey and a few other things," she answered, hopefully.

"I believe I'll try one after lunch. Is there someplace I can wash my hands?" She indicated the small hallway that led to the back of the cabin.

There were two bedrooms and a bath. After washing my hands, I got nosy and since neither room had the door shut. . . Bonnie's scent led me to my first choice.

The same Pendleton blankets wound upon leather fasteners acted as curtains on her windows as in the living room. A single desk lamp I'd already discerned from my nightly forays as a woodpecker.

An easel was set up between windows with an unfinished oil painting perched on it. A life-like red hawk soared on the canvas, headed straight for the viewer. What a superb talent Bonnie had! Upon gazing at the painting, I, too, soared with the predatory avian.

Tearing my eyes away, I briefly envied Bonnie's twin bed its occupant. Chill, CatSkill. . . The Pendleton blanket cover was a light tan, black border, with horses racing across and a blue, star-shot sky. Homey, western décor.

Above the wooden headboard- a tremendous jolt shock-waved through me. I nearly pinched myself to make sure I was still in human form.

For there, as if I were looking into a mirror, was an all- too realistic oil painting of me- my wild side- the mountain lion my spirit guide and I shared. The tell-tale bloody shoulder could belong to no other. But how?

Entranced, I couldn't move- even when Bonnie approached, her hand inches from touching my forearm. I realized she was watching me watching me, so to speak.

"Ever since I can remember, I see him as real as. . ."

"You should be more careful of what you put over your head where you sleep," I muttered, shaken. I was about to move away.

"Why?" She asked, perplexed.

Why indeed? I moved around her, discomfited and intrigued at the same time. "You're too young to understand," I gritted.

And then something else caught my eye and drew me to it- no pun intended- the sketch pad I'd seen her with that day I was sure she was watching me watching her. Swiftly, before she could protest, I started thumbing through the pages.

"Wait!" She started toward me.

Her father picked this particular time to use the bathroom. "Look, I know I'm old-fashioned, but I'd prefer you two not be in a bedroom, together, at the same time," he peeked in.

"I was just showing Riordan some of my art work, Dad."

While this interchange progressed, I'd found what I was looking for- a pencil sketch of a cougar, eyes peering through tall, dried grasses. I glanced between Bonnie and the sketch.

Flustered, she muttered something about checking lunch and bowed out. I ran my fingers over the drawing and vacated her room, before losing Mr. Lance's good graces.

Too much to think about. The mystery of Bonnie expounded. Electric currents prickled my senses as if I'd been invaded or exposed or was being led. Maybe I had. All of the above.

Chapter 19

"OK, kids," he looked at me like who was I kidding, but not in a confrontational way. "These are the rules."

This said over the best potato soup I'd ever eaten and bread to die for- the kind a man could sink his teeth into and actually feel like he had consumed something.

"Rules?" Bonnie perked up with questioning brows. I studied my soup and Mr. Lance.

"You still haven't told her?"

"What, Dad? Riordan?"

Casually, I answered, "I asked your father for permission to date you."

"You want. . .to. . .to date m…me?" She whispered, dumbstruck and turned various increasing shades of red. Apparently, she wasn't totally aware of what her father and I were discussing. Her excitement stemmed from the fact I was still around afterwards.

"Yes," I said very simply and returned to my soup. "Great soup, Bonnie."

"Rules," Mr. Lance got back to business. "Bonnie will be home by 11:30 at the latest, until she turns 17. Then, we'll talk about it. No dates on school nights. No dating if I'm out of town. I don't want the ranch left alone at night. I'd prefer it Riordan, if you weren't in the house for extended periods of time while I'm away." A father's worries.

"These rules are subject to change and the possibility exists I'll add to them. I expect you both to behave and stay safe. Deal?"

"Yes, sir."

"Yes, Dad," she continued in whisper mode, disbelieving.

"Good. I think I'll have some more soup. Riordan?"

"Thank you, sir. Mr. Lance, will you be home next Saturday?"

He sighed, a father conceding to a potential rival for his daughter's affections, "I'll make it a point to be here."

I helped Bonnie with the dishes and with one bite became addicted to my first cookies.

"Have you any chores, today?"

"Just night feed."

"Why don't we go for a walk?" I suggested.

"Dad, is it OK if we take a short hike? I'll be back in plenty of time to fix dinner and feed." Mr. Lance waved us off.

I let Bonnie set the pace- a pretty good clip. I figured she probably had a favorite route.

"You want to go out with me next Saturday?" I thought I should formally ask her now that I'd gained the privilege.

"Y…yes," she tripped.

I caught her. Our eyes met and I knew I was in trouble. This might begin as friendship, but it wouldn't reside there long.

Breaking contact first, I took the lead, skirted dried sage and downed sycamores, headed for a stand of pines.

"Riordan?" She was hot on my trail. We had to race- no way around it.

"Hmmm?" I paused.

"I wish you'd quit saying I'm too young to understand."

"Oh?" I was forced to look down at her- she compelled eye contact.

"If you think that of me w…well, why would you want to go out with me on a date?" She rolled her shoulders, part of her afraid I'd back out. "Is there some magic age I'll be able to understand? Won't you try to explain? I bet I can keep up."

Alright CatSkill, you're on. I brushed my hair back. "You're sure?" Hesitant, she nodded.

"That painting over your bed is magnificent. Bonnie you have fantastic talent. I've never seen anything finer in an art gallery or museum for that matter."

How did I broach the more delicate subject she wanted me to explain? "The cougar over your bed is a very potent male figure. For example, if I were a run-of-the-mill teenage boy, I might have a poster of some busty, scantily clad pin-up girl in my room."

"Would you dream of her?"

"I wouldn't, but this other guy would."

"So, what's so hard for me to understand?"

Help me out here, Great Spirit. "Why don't you have a picture of a cowboy hanging in your room?"

"I don't dream of cowboys." She was finding this all too simple, wondering when the hard-to-understand part was going to kick in.

"You're going to tell me you dream of mountain lions?"

"No, not lions- one mountain lion in particular. I've dreamed of him for as long as I can remember."

"Bad dreams- is this the bad dream you have?" I prodded.

"No silly." A wistful gleam lit her dark fringed green eyes. An engaging grin amused her lips. An amusement I was very much drawn to. "All the dreams of him are wonderful and exciting-like being part of a magical world." It was all there on her face.

"You painted that picture from remembering a cougar in your dreams?"

"Yes."

This time I was going to change the subject-this one was getting too intense for me. "Let's race! And no holding out on me."

We raced companionably for some time, took turns surging ahead. Our run covered a couple miles at least, when Bonnie stopped dead. Her head swiveled, seeking.

Like a bottle rocket, she was launched and racing, hell- bent-for-leather. I reacted a split second later, but before I caught up with her, she'd bounded ahead and was veritably springing over a hill of boulders.

Upon my reaching the top, I couldn't believe. . . "Bonnie," I screamed.

She'd foisted herself between two coyotes fighting to get at a meal of fresh rabbit. Opposing, snarling, mangy coyotes were anxious to have it out among themselves. Now they were turning their fangs on this new interference.

Normally, coyotes ran from humans; it was a sign of hunger and Bonnie's complete lack of harm that they dared to take her on. Previous enemies joined forces. She waved and shouted to no avail. The predators advanced on her.

A growl threatened to crescendo from deep inside me. I allowed it to erupt. The coyotes didn't stand a chance against a mountain lion's warning. Ears flicked, tails cringed and they abandoned their sniping and fled.

"What the devil are you doing?" I yelled at her- I never yell. A testament to. . .

She was trembling, though unharmed. Her eyes appealed, looked up at me from what she was kneeling beside.

"Don't holler at me," she quietly implored while examining a wounded brown, white-tailed rabbit sprawled on the ground. A leg had suffered from a hungry coyote. "Help me, Riordan." There was a quiver in her plea.

I knelt to the catatonic rabbit- a female. Gently, I laid a single finger on the lulled body. "It's not so bad, Bonnie. We'll take her back to the cabin."

The rabbit put up no resistance when I cradled her in my arms. As we walked back, I pointed out several plants and directed Bonnie to gather some of each.

I helped her construct a makeshift cage of wire and wood, bedded with straw. One end we covered against the weather and insulated the outside with more straw.

Chewing on the plants, I made a poultice to wrap around the injured leg. No bone damage, but definitely tendon and skin distress. Bonnie provided water and food and admonished Sticker and Stalker to mind their manners.

"I'll check in on her after school tomorrow. If she makes it 'til then, I believe she'll be alright. Rehab may take a bit before she can be released. Now," I began to feel my anger at her foolish escapade building again, "don't you ever get between wild animals and their prey. Not without your 38 or a shotgun. Do you have any idea how you could have been hurt? Coyotes are generally more afraid of you but you got right between them and their dinner- DON'T EVER DO THAT AGAIN!"

I didn't know what else to say. This anger was about the possibility of her being injured. It irked me that a supposedly bright girl born here allowed herself to get in that position.

"I had to save this rabbit," she demurred, dry-eyed.

Something occurred to me through my dissipating ire. "How did you know. . .?"

"I heard the rabbit call for help."

"You heard. . .?" Thinking back, I remembered the coyote yips. They were faint- the distance and the wind would have prevented the normal person from hearing. But the rabbit. . .I hadn't heard the rabbit. "How?"

"I…I don't know. It's like all of a sudden, I have superman ears and. . . Things are happening to me. That woodpecker was prophetic," she appeared all-too forlorn. I backed off, reeling with more startling implications.

I felt her confusion. "Does this rabbit have anything to do with the biology lab?"

Puzzled, but with realization slowly sinking in, she nodded. "Riordan?"

"Don't worry, Bonnie. We'll figure it out," I ruffled her hair as if comforting a kid sister. Right, who was I kidding?

"You brought me one cookie?" Grandfather scowled at me in disbelief.

"How was I supposed to know they are addictive? I ate one on my way home and couldn't stop."

He sniffed, disdainfully, felt the bag and burst into a sudden guffaw. "Ha, she outwitted you."

My brows shot up, "What?"

Grandfather pulled out what I assumed was the last cookie- a hawk shape. Out came a thick dish towel which hid four more cookies. They were light enough, I'd not bothered to check that the towel may have hidden extras and with the extraordinary events of the day, I forgave my sense of smell's dereliction of duty.

Chapter 20

"Do you have your swim suit?" I'd waited for her this morning on the cabin porch. Mr. Lance was out for the week, except he'd promised to be home on Saturday for our first date.

"Hello to you," Bonnie reminded me of my manners with her head down as she walked to the jeep.

"Good morning- suit?" I watched the back of her head nod. "Let's see." I wouldn't put it past her to conveniently forget. My distrust brought her up short and she looked at me with hurt in her eyes- and that wasn't all.

"You didn't sleep last night," I stated, surveying the evidence on her face.

"No," her gaze faltered.

"Bad dreams or just being alone?"

She hunched her shoulders, "Both, I guess."

"Have you ever told your father you hate to be alone so much?" How could he not see what I was seeing?

"No, he has to do what he has to do- work isn't plentiful."

No matter what her father had said about bedrooms and extended hours in the cabin when he was away, I had no intention of Bonnie suffering anymore- even if it meant hanging out in some other form. Come to think of it, this, my human form, would do her the most good here, but the point was moot. Knowing Bonnie, she wouldn't allow my human presence inside, anyway.

"One of these days you're going to tell me about this dream. . .if I have to. . .tickle you to get it out of you," my fingers threatened. She giggled and hastened to the jeep.

"Hey," I followed. "I want to see that swimsuit- cuz if you don't have it, you're swimming in your underwear." I got between her and the jeep door. Reluctantly, she pulled out a towel and the black suit.

"Take a nap on the way to school." I pulled her over 'til her head rested on my thigh. "Comfortable?"

"Hmmm…" And she was out. So this was companionable silence, I mused. Resist the temptation, CatSkill. Keep both hands on the wheel, I remonstrated with myself.

Morning classes dragged. Physical exertion was nearly an addiction with me- being sedentary bordered on torture.

I was looking forward to the pool, despite the horror of the chlorine assailing my senses. Hopefully, I could help Bonnie enjoy swimming as much as I did- the way we shared an enthusiasm for running and numbers.

Luckily, the pool was nearly empty. Three adults seemed to be finishing up, probably ready for lunch- great timing.

"Ok, I'll give you ten minutes to change. If you're not out here," I gave her a sidelong warning look, "I'll come in and get you."

"You wouldn't," her eyes widened, cheeks blushing.

"Try me and see," I grinned.

I dove into the pool in my cutoff jean shorts and struck out. Several laps later, I spied my reluctant student. Surfacing, I swept my hair back and savored her approach.

A large blue towel was clasped like a protective mantel about her shoulders, covering most of her. I walked through the water to the edge of the pool. She stopped.

"Come in, the water's nice."

Her face betrayed several emotions and she was chewing on her lower lip. "I need a new suit," she ducked my eyes.

The black swimsuit, I'll admit, was not the most prepossessing swim attire for her pale body, but it was unlike her to agonize over appearances. It was then I inadvertently dropped my gaze.

Could it have only been a few weeks since a girl with toothpick legs had raced by my side at the school track? These were not the same legs. There was muscle in those calves, yes, but now a sweet curve led up from strong, exquisite ankles.

My eyes followed that mouth-watering curve to a glimpse of thigh peeking from folds of that blasted towel.

I'd have loved to put my hands around that thigh, test the soft expansion I was seeing- toothpicks to Betty Grable legs, even better than movie star legs, because these were right in front of me. I swallowed in anticipation.

"Bonnie, drop the towel," I whispered. The others had vacated and we were alone.

"I...I d...don't think so," she stuttered.

"You're putting off the inevitable. I hope you're not afraid of me. Come on," I cajoled.

"You'll laugh," she nearly cried. The towel clasping intensified.

I smothered a grin. She had no idea. "I can promise you I won't laugh."

Slowly, too beguiling for my comfort, she let the towel sink to the tile floor. I was glad I'd stayed in the pool. The promise of Bonnie's newly developed legs did not let up.

Yes, the suit was no longer 'suitable', except for a 12- year old stick kid. The curves continued enticingly into feminine hips. A small waist begged the circumference of male hands- mine- only mine.

The unsuitable suit rode high on her hips and as for her chest. It wasn't possible for Bonnie to develop into a woman in just a few weeks. Spirits,, help me. . . Her blush extended down her neck and further. Easy, CatSkill. Don't drool; I began a mantra to myself.

"Bonnie, we'll get you a new bathing suit. This one will do for now. Come, let's have a short lesson," I held out my hand.

Walking on eggshells, avoiding my eyes, she progressed. "You look like you're on the Bataan death march. Ease up, Bonnie."

"I guess I'm just. . .nervous."

"Nervous and afraid of water?" I qualified.

"I'm only afraid of deep water, as in, over my head."

"Can you swim at all?"

"I can dog paddle," she replied without much conviction.

"Ok, let's see."

She pushed off in the 3 foot section, paddling and kicking ferociously as if the water were an enemy to pummel without mercy. I swam lazily alongside out of splash range.

"Now we're going to swim back, only with a few changes. I want you to lie upon my palm." I extended an arm, palm up. "I'll catch you. Pretend you're ready to swim, except I want you to lie still, no kicking."

Her discomfort was obvious; I heard her brain cells spinning as her breathing and heart rate competed. "Look at me." Seeing no easy way to break this subtle impasse, I tipped her chin and with my skill of mental suggestion, I mesmerized her, or at least I thought I did.

"What are you doing?" Her brows wrinkled.

"You don't feel anything?" The surprises of Bonnie kept coming. I was puzzled anew.

Still frowning, "No."

Great, CatSkill! Apparently, she was beyond my powers which put her in a select group with one other.

"Humor me, please," I returned to supplication.

She flattened out in the water, head held up. My palm under her abdomen supported her and with the water kept her in perfect balance.

"Keep your legs in the water, pretend you're a fish. Let your legs one at a time glide through the water. Remember you are a fish- you love the water. Breathe. Keep a slow, steady rhythm."

When she accomplished this, I had her add the paddling with her arms. "Cup the water and push it down. Slower, rhythm, breathe." This part took longer. "You're doing fine, keep it up; breathe."

Gradually, as she focused on what her body was doing, I lightened my palm's contact with her body, ever so slowly dropping away. She couldn't detect when my hand left her except that her body began to move through the water.

I wolf-whistled appreciatively. She almost made it to the pool's edge when the wonder of it all caught up with her.

"I did it! And I'm not out of breath!" The pleasure on her face was one of those perfect Kodak moments.

"Sure you did. What did you expect? Try it again, back to me. Remember, if you are tiring it's because you're not breathing. Feed those cells. Breathe."

She laughed, eager to use her new skills. I should have quit with that progress, but I elected to push. I moved into the five and a half foot depth after I felt she had the shallow end down pat. Plainly, I was not under water- I thought this might be a good note to end on.

She started out with a smile, but I knew the moment fear set in. "Breathe," I commanded.

But she began to flounder, fighting the water away. I glided to her before full-blown panic took over.

"I've got you, Bonnie. Bonnie," I demanded her attention. She flung her arms around my neck- all too close, but did not fight as panic- stricken, about-to-drown swimmers will.

"You all right?"

"Y…yes," she stammered, teeth chattering. Her eyes went to my shoulders. "I don't remember seeing this red streak before." No, she wouldn't have, as this was the first time she really looked at my naked chest. The distraction soothed her.

My bloody shoulder, I called it. "My Indian blood coming out," I jokingly smiled at her.

She removed her left hand from my neck, strolled it across the red skin- dark red against my natural tan. My body bristled with her touch. "You smell good," she sniffed.

"What?" I was caught off guard.

"You smell good," her face came closer to my skin.

"How can you smell anything but these chemicals?" Her eyes closed; she breathed in my scent. I broke it off, self- preservation. Spirits help me!

"Try one more time, then lunch before I die of starvation." I moved her back to four foot of water, started her out on my palm until she fully relaxed. Without much ado, she made it to the pool's edge and I swam alongside, content and confused.

"Now back," I ordered and slowed to keep pace with her. That ended our first swim class.

At least five times on the way home, Bonnie thanked me. After checking on our patient's admirable progress and thwarting the rabbit's interest in escaping, I left. Questions for grandfather were buzzing in the hive of my head.

Chapter 21

"Grandfather."

"Yes, Grandson." If you've never tried a conversation with a wise Native American elder, you're missing an experience.

The elders would teach not by answering questions; they presented you with the opportunity to answer your own questions. Coyote learning it was termed- lessons through linguistic tricks, to make you think. Rather unlike the white man's schools.

"Bonnie," I said.

"Bonnie?" He asked. I chuckled. Grandfather would have been a great poker player.

I cut to the chase. After all, I'd been pondering my new friend for a while now. "Is she one of us?"

"What do you think?" I'd known that was coming. Grandfather sat impassive. His black braid rested on his chest.

"It would be too white man presumptuous of me to assume only Indians or half-breeds could be shamans. I would guess the power is there to partake of. . .for anyone. But Bonnie?" This was the hard-to-grasp part. "She seems so unaware of her potential. Yet in front of my eyes, in the short time I've known her. . .she's developing rapidly. Her senses are expanding. Her hearing may be even better than mine. She's picking up scents no human would. And her body. . .she's blossomed into a woman at a speed- as if she were. . ."

"Say it, Grandson," he urged.

"As if she were a wild animal," I whispered. A low whistle swished from me before I continued. "Did you know, above her bed is a painting- she painted it- an oil painting of me as my mountain lion spirit guide? It's like seeing myself in a mirror- it's so real. The portrait is identical- even to the bloody shoulder. For as long as she can remember, she says, she has always dreamed of this particular cougar."

I was awed, but had to continue. "Bonnie has a sense of awareness, yet in some ways she's unaware at the same time. I believe she's premonitory and probably has visions. Is it possible?"

Grandfather cocked his head, remained unmoved while I figured it out. Instinctively, I already knew.

He smiled at my realization, nodded, "Took you long enough."

"But how, why?"

"I suspect it has everything to do with you." This, he floored me with.

"I don't understand," I had to admit.

"When I asked you to visit, Grandson, I only said to come sometime before next summer. But you came immediately. Why?"

"I was worried about you. In my vision you looked tired. I. . ." I rubbed my forehead between my eyes, forcing myself to recollect that vision.

There in the background something came to me. So faint- why had I not consciously noticed the sound then? A young female mountain lion was mewling, calling her mate. . .

I was overwhelmed- a totally new experience for me. "Grandfather, she called me?"

"As you've said, Grandson, the changes she's undergoing right now, never happen this fast. You may share the same spirit guide. I think you're responsible for her siren call. And just like those Greek sailors, you can't resist her. Yet also. . ."

"Our spirit guide is calling her to become," I marveled, finishing his pronouncement.

"And in turn," grandfather continued, "you are the catalyst. Without your being here, I've no doubt her body and skills would have waited in limbo. For some reason the Great Spirit is compelling the two of you to be together and for her to reach her full power in an amazingly short time."

"But, why?" I was enthralled and puzzled at the same time.

"Only the Mysteries know, but you can be sure something is going to happen and all will become clear at the appropriate time."

"What if I left?"

"Left?" He queried, expressionless.

"Grandfather, she's very young."

"So, Grandson, you know more than the spirits, eh? Tell me. Could you leave?"

I thought back on all of her up to this moment: her fears of being alone at night, of water, of bad dreams. The wonders of Bonnie: her open friendship, her total selflessness, that body- Bonnie- as if custom-made for me, and indeed, maybe she was. How gazing into her eyes, like gazing into. . .she'd called it a magical world. I supposed what grandfather and I lived would be considered a magical existence.

No, I wouldn't leave, even if I could, but it would require great patience, thankfully, one of my strong suits.

"Grandfather, have you ever known a female shaman- a white one?"

"No, Grandson. I'm sure Bonnie's not the first. The Celts had their Druids- many of them, women. Bonnie will need our help. She'll need training and soon. We don't want her to feel lost. Training may stem her bad dreams. . ."

"Or lead to interpretations. The dreams may be warnings," I realized. It had been a long time since I'd experienced something new. And nothing as thrilling and stimulating as my Bonnie.

Quietly, my woodpecker guise for the night perched outside Bonnie's window. I was prepared to tap a lullaby if needed.

"Ok, little girl, if it's me you want. . ." Bonnie had gone to bed leaving a tiny night light on for comfort. I would keep my nightly vigil when she was alone.

There would be plenty of time to plan her further education and not just in the pool. My sleep needs were few. I'd use the time to define how to pace myself with her- a full grown man in shaman years and a young girl. I'd study on the divine construct that dictated our communion and the novel feelings expounding in my being.

A shadow moved to the window. Bonnie appeared in a long- sleeve sleeping shirt. She was staring in my direction.

Chapter 22

A totally new scenario for me- going on a date which held the greatest of implied importance. I'd arrived early, respectably dressed, to spend a few minutes with Mr. Lance and hopefully allay any last minute misgivings on his part.

"Good evening, Mr. Lance."

"Riordan. How's Red Hawk?"

"Great, sir. He sure enjoyed Bonnie's cookies." I gave him a friendly smile, hoping to put him at ease.

"I know the feeling. I could OD on those, myself. Have a seat. Bonnie," he called unnecessarily, for I knew she was aware of my presence, "Riordan's here. Bonnie and I were talking. We'd like to invite you and your grandfather to have Thanksgiving with us."

"That would be awesome, sir. Thank you."

Her scent of sage and sweetgrass, so pleasant to my wild nose, preceded her. I stood and had to restrain my facial expressions.

Bonnie appeared clad in a soft, sky-blue sweater, black jeans with way too much allure and tiny, red paddock boots. A blue ribbon matching her sweater was tied in her hair. The sweater's round neck covered the new sweet curves, hugged her rib cage and ended just above the jeans waist band.

I felt her father's eyes swinging from her to me. He was all-too-ready to insist his all-too-young daughter stay home and away from the big bad wolf, me, who he knew beyond a doubt, was not the ordinary teen-age high school senior.

Maintain, CatSkill, I cautioned myself. I was certain Bonnie was seeking approval for the effort she'd put into dressing. I just had to watch my step.

Seconds slid by and she scrambled for words. "I...I wasn't sure what to wear. These...they were my mother's. . . Dad thought. . . I...I could wear my other clothes. I just. . ."

I found my manners and a conservative way out. "Bonnie, I bet your mother never looked better than you in that outfit." I hoped I'd said that with the proper aplomb. Our date depended on it. A relieved smile graced her face.

"Riordan, you'd win that bet. Honey, you look great!" Mr. Lance complimented and shot me a silent warning.

"Thanks, Dad."

"Ready," I asked. She nodded and picked up a red jacket slung over the back of a chair.

"Remember the rules- keep my daughter safe," Mr. Lance's last admonition to me.

"Hold on, Skippy!" Bonnie practically danced to the jeep. "A girl who looks like you shouldn't be climbing into her coach." I opened the passenger door, swept her up and placed her on the blanket-covered seat.

"Thanks," she whispered to my face- too close- move, CatSkill!

"I thought we'd have dinner at the Irma House. I've made reservations, then a movie and ice cream. Sound all right?"

"Yes, wonderful," and the excitement in her voice increased my own for this, our first date.

The ride into Cody started out pretty quiet. I could almost hear her mental confabulations. I broke in, "What is it?"

"Were you angry with me?"

Always a surprise, "Do I look like I'm mad at you?"

"N…no, but you've been awful quiet the last few days since Tuesday."

"Hmmm," I mumbled, "Just preoccupied."

"Is it my fault?"

Let's see, I ruminated; perched on a limb as an out-of- season woodpecker outside Bonnie's window until her father came home- four nights running, trying to catch some shut-eye while keeping a concerned vigil on the girl inside who had turned my world on its axis- not my first choice in the comfortable- resting department. . .

Whether she knew of my presence or not, she only had three restless moments during those nights. Once I started my woodpecker tapping, she'd rested peacefully. And each night she peered out her window before climbing into bed. Bonnie was aware of me- I'd bet.

I didn't need much sleep, but some would have been nice. Welcome to Newness Class 101 presented by a little girl who was undoubtedly a shaman in want of training- one who had probably sub-consciously called me to her.

Ah, well, CatSkill. You were signed up for this. Get your head in the present.

"You give me a lot to think about," probably not the best come-back. "I've never met anyone like you." And that was the crux of it.

"Is that not so good?" Worry was present in her voice.

"Bonnie, you're not going to like this, don't bite me, but you're way too young for me to be this attracted to you. How old are you- sixteen?"

"Yes," she muttered, unhappily.

"When will you be seventeen?"

"Next October."

"Sheesh, you just turned sixteen!" Dismayed, I braked the jeep, turned to look at her. "I want us to be friends. I'm really trying to be a gentleman, OK?" No response. "Bonnie?"

She sighed, near tears, "Are you sure you want to go out with me tonight?"

"Very sure," I maintained. Patience is my strong suit I reminded myself- several times.

"But not after tonight?" I heard her dashed hopes.

I shouldn't have, but I couldn't stave off a low chuckle. "Remember this, I'm not going anywhere." I tipped her chin so she had to look at me and judge my sincerity. "I believe this is only the first- let's enjoy, shall we?"

Her glistening eyes blinked, a smile quavered, "Yes." A bit of hopeful enthusiasm returned.

Chapter 23

"Yes sir, you're a bit early for your reservation. Perhaps you'd care to spend a few minutes in our gift shop?" The hostess welcomed and advised us.

I helped Bonnie remove her jacket and we walked down the hall to the boutique-style gift shop- nicely decorated and stocked with a comprehensive array of attractive leather goods.

"Ever been here before?" I gently pulled my date into the shop.

"Mrs. Dyer used to bring me to watch the gunfights during the tourist season. That was fun. Before the shootout, I remember waiting on the porch and listening to music. They'd pipe out Patsy Cline tunes, Johnny Cash and others. I've never eaten here, though."

"Good, that makes two of us. By the look of the crowd, food must be acceptable." I ushered her around and enjoyed watching her check out the merchandise.

She didn't pick up anything but I noticed where her eyes fell- which items perked her interest. I picked up a small, silver-decorated, black purse with a long, thin strap.

"Here's something your outfit needs."

She turned and I placed the strap over her shoulder. The purse hung at her hip.

"It's awfully cute," she fondled the silver scroll work.

"I think so." I presented it to the woman at the register who'd been eyeing us intently. Long haired, young men were always suspicious. She quickly changed her tune and became sociable when I offered to buy something.

"You're in luck, sir. All of our Brighton pieces are on sale tonight." I handed her two fifties, knowing the change would cover movies and ice cream, but not dinner.

"Oh, Riordan, you can't," Bonnie objected.

"Sure I can, watch me. You should have it- women carry purses."

"But, I…I don't need it," she blushed, prettily.

"My point exactly, I want you to have it. Put things in."

"Things?"

"Girly things- money, Kleenex, feminine stuff," I grinned and Bonnie's blush intensified.

The shop keeper gushed, "How sweet!"

"Do you have any Kleenex?" I asked the saleswoman.

She handed me a box and my change. I pulled out three tissues and put them and a ten dollar bill inside the purse, then placed it in my date's hands.

There was enough admiration in Bonnie's eyes to nearly choke me. Thank the spirits, the hostess called us to dinner right then. Bonnie petted the purse as if it were a puppy on the way to our table.

"Thank you, Riordan," a threat of tears in her voice.

"You're welcome," I'd never spent better money.

The dimly-lit, western-decorated dining area provided a romantic setting. Several longhorns placidly gazed down on us as we perused our menus.

"What are you hungry for, Bonnie?"

"I think I'd like the trout," she smiled up at me. I ordered for both of us. My choice was a big porterhouse steak, rare.

"Please help yourselves to the salad bar," the waitress encouraged.

"How can a girl who likes only cheese on her pizza pile all that stuff on a salad?" I teased her as she kept on building.

"I like all these toppings," she dribbled ranch dressing on an eight-inch high stack of cacophony.

We'd dug into our salads when Lil strode up-hips swinging ardently to attract attention. Fell short with me, but not every other male eye in the place.

"Riordan," she flirted.

"Lil, where's Rick?"

"We're hooking up later. I'm having dinner with my folks." She glanced at my date and did a double take. "Bonnie?"

"Hi," Bonnie managed after swallowing a green pepper slice.

"You look great!" A jealous, honest admission.

"Thanks," Bonnie blushed.

"Well, see you later." Lil moved off without the same surety she'd exhibited on her approach.

My steak hit the spot and Bonnie obviously enjoyed her trout. A woman who could put away the food, run like a thoroughbred plus all of her other goodies- what more could a man possibly want?

"Let's stop at the library, Monday. See if there's a response from Sedona. Now that I'm helping with your chores and driving you. . ."

"Oh, I hope there is. You haven't told your grandfather, have you?" Bonnie twiddled her fork on an empty space on her plate. "You know I appreciate. . ."

"I know you do and no, I haven't spilled the beans," I kept the topics of conversation simple- there were enough subjects to cover in-depth at another time.

"Can I interest you in some dessert?" Our waitress stepped up. I left the decision to Bonnie.

"Are we having ice cream later?" She grinned, hopefully.

"Absolutely."

"I'll wait, thank you."

"Alright folks, have a nice evening," she left the check on the table.

Bonnie excused herself to the restroom. A noisy cavalcade-the football team, had joined the diners, who showed their appreciation by rising and clapping. They were big winners, after all.

Peripherally, I noticed the attention that followed Bonnie. The evening was about to get even more interesting. I paid the check and started to the hall which led to the boutique and rest rooms.

"Hey, Bonnie, Matt," the high school quarterback made his introduction as Bonnie exited the ladies room.

"Hi," she tried to move around him.

"I thought you and I could go out sometime," his lips offered as his eyes fastened vulgarly on her chest. All too sure of himself, he was momentarily brought up short when she curtly told him. . .

"No, thanks." His arm shot out to block her. "Maybe you didn't hear me, I said no," Bonnie reiterated, with more force.

"There's nothing wrong with my hearing. . ."

Bingo, time for me to claim my territory. Yes, I'd decided she was my territory- or rather the spirits had decided for both of us and I heartily concurred.

I have the ability to make my 6'4" frame seem like near 7 feet and by squaring my shoulders can give a linebacker pause for reflection. I addressed him.

"Hassling my girl?"

The jock spun around, "Your girl?"

"Maybe you should have your hearing checked," I retorted. There was a smile on my face but malice in my eyes and tone of voice, not to mention my stance.

This put him on the defensive, "Look here, Catspill or whatever your name is, we don't take kindly to outsiders coming in and playing with our local girls. Got it?"

I'd sensed the cavalry charging to his aid. Three other players posed behind me.

"Ready, Bonnie?" She ducked under the jock's outstretched arm and came to me. I turned and a rumbling snarl emanated warningly from my chest with enough energy coupled with my baring my teeth to startle the opposition. They broke rank and I strode through, guiding Bonnie.

Chapter 24

"Maybe you should take me home," Bonnie
mumbled, head down.

"Whatever for? Are you tired?"

"No, but I think they're going to cause
trouble." A reasonable assumption. Of course,
they did not know the meaning of trouble.
Unconcerned, I changed the subject- I tried to,
but she way-laid me.

"It's OK, Riordan, if we end the night
early. I've had a wonderful time, but you've
spent so much money. . ."

"Are you worried about my financial status
as well as my physical well-being?" I grinned
down at her. Amazing, in all my life I don't
believe anyone other than grandfather had ever
expressed concern for me. I found this amusing
and very endearing.

"Bonnie, Bonnie, Bonnie what am I going to
do with you?" I tilted her chin with the tip of
my forefinger. "You needn't worry about me. I
promise I can take care of myself and I'm far from
breaking the bank."

She began chewing on her lower lip, "I...I just don't want you to get hurt."

I watched those lips for a moment; the idea of tasting. . . Back off, CatSkill, I chided myself.

"Come on, the theater is just ahead." She fell in beside me. I kept a 'friendly' distance.

"Our choices are," I eyed the posters, "robots taking over the world or vampire love story." My raised brows questioned her.

"I'm not big on robots," she shrugged.

"But you like vampires? What happened to my date? Have you seen her? Bonnie?" I looked around. This brought on a spate of giggles.

"Vampire love story it is. Two for TWILIGHT," I handed over a twenty. "Popcorn?"

"No, I'm still stuffed. Riordan, if the movie gets too bloody. . ."

"I'll be ready and willing to pick you up and carry you out, my lady." She rolled her eyes and broke me up.

I kept part of my attention on the screen; way too much lipstick on the head vampire and how in the world did they get his hair to stand up so high? Other than that, he wasn't bad looking.

Most of my regard centered on Bonnie. She probably hadn't been to many movies. The story line seemed to hold her in thrall.

Well, if she had a penchant for Hollywood vampires, what would she make of her own real-life, fairy tale boyfriend? Edward Cullen with his 100 years was a child compared to me and he wasn't as comfortable in his life as I was in mine. All in all though, he was a respectable character. I wouldn't have minded meeting him, if he were real. A race- just the thing.

I could have held Bonnie's hand. It was listlessly placed on her thigh. That would have been the 'dately' thing to do. Other couples, I was certain, were doing more than that in the back row. But, I didn't.

Surreptitiously, I studied her, reading every emotion scrolling across her face. I knew the parts that bothered her and recognized how the romantic ideas affected her.

The last fight scene, I enjoyed. Some of Edward's expressions reminded me of what I must look like when engaged with the opposition. The tearing out of the rogue vampire's throat- finally something I could affiliate with.

Out of 26 flavors, Bonnie surprised me by choosing plain vanilla- 3 scoops in a cup. As for me, the bigger the banana boat, the better.

I had to pause and watch a lady behind us; here was a person who really, really enjoyed her ice cream- she was practically dancing and clapping in anticipation of her moose tracks.

"So, did you like the movie?" I inquired.

"Yes," studiously she focused on her ice cream rather than meet my gaze. "It was the ultimate romance."

"Love with a vampire?" I was incredulous.

"No, love and forever," her response had intensity and more.

"You could see yourself in a similar situation?" I listened, attentively sensitive to every nuance of her reply.

She hunched a shoulder, "The heart has its reasons where reason knows nothing."

I whistled, "Blaise Pascal- the French mathematician. I'm impressed." More than that, I was stunned- the ramifications of that particular quote.

"Riordan, you've dated many girls?" She tentatively asked.

"Let's talk about something else." I'd about swear those lips were thinking of a pout, but no, just her unnerving lip chewing. "Bonnie, you already know the answer to that," I conceded quietly.

Nodding thoughtfully, she asked, "Did you like the movie?" A quick change-up.

"I enjoyed the fight scene at the end."

"But not the romance part?"

"Bonnie, I'm a guy," I grinned at the imperfection of my sex when it came to movie romance. Now, as for the real thing- hmmm. . .

Finishing my banana boat, I wondered if I could handle another. Bonnie had done justice to hers. "Like some more?"

Wide eyed, she shook her head, "I couldn't possibly hold another spoonful. Could you?"

"Probably not," I rethought my position.

"Riordan, have you ever been in love?" Her gaze focused on me.

My life had always been that of a loner. Travel, study, offer aid to those I encountered who needed help. There were always plenty of folks who longed for someone, if only to listen to them for a time.

Then there were others besieged with things beyond their control- I could be very, very helpful. And there had been casual, uh, acquaintances, but in all my life I'd never loved another, never even considered it; never missed the idea of it. The Great Spirit apparently had decided enough was enough.

"No, never." She could have no inkling of my age, yet I got the feeling she was sad for me and at the same time, inordinately glad, too. "Let's get you home."

Chapter 25

The instant we exited the ice cream shop, I saw the enemy forces gathering. In the direction we were headed there was an alley between a sports bar and a tourist gift store. That's where they wanted me. Contrary-wise, I aimed for a section of brick wall before-hand.

"Bonnie, I want you to go back inside, stay there until I come for you. GO, NOW!" She became alert immediately -it was obvious trouble was brewing. "NOW!" I commanded.

The sound of her running, slamming the wood-framed glass door and shouting for someone to call 911 was peripheral. My wild senses geared up. Hopefully, I'd get to have a little fun before the police showed up.

I continued to the spot I'd marked out and waited patiently, nonchalant, without malice, thumbs hooked in my pockets.

The jock quarterback, flanked by four flunkies and two others in tow were all football players, I guessed. The two laggards were ready to drop out at the least provocation. Another was ruminating on how to play it and the three others would go where their captain commanded.

Taking their sweet time, they advanced to me. I dug my moccasins in, felt for purchase, my back expected good things from the brick wall behind me. They'd be better off trying to move a recalcitrant elephant into the nearby alley than to displace me.

"Still hanging around, CatSkill?" Matt started his harangue.

I pretended to look right and left. "At least your eyes work," I politely replied.

Matt checked around at his entourage, smirked, king of the hill, at least in his own mind. "Sam's a friend," he stated.

"Sorry to hear that."

"Yeah, you're sorry all right." Matt and his cohorts laughed and attempted to look intimidating. "Like I said before, we don't cotton to outsiders hanging around our local girls."

"Ain't that a shame," I almost broke out in song- I have a tolerable singing voice and I'm not shy.

Rick and Lil strode into sight, "Hey, Riordan! I've got your back." A true friend wades in when his buddy is severely outnumbered. However, this was not the case.

"Thanks Rick, but gee whiz, there are only seven of them. Do me a favor though, keep Bonnie out of the way."

My date had returned to the potential fray with a wood broomstick in her hands, resolute. I sensed Rick's cautious dismay, but he whispered to Lil and went to guard Bonnie- good luck to him there.

Matt was flapping his jaw again; Bonnie's curfew was coming up. "I didn't know football players engaged in such stimulating tete-a-tete," I sarcastically goaded.

"Are you making fun of me?"

"I don't think so. You're doing that well enough by yourself."

"What?" Matt was riled without complete comprehension.

"There's the issue with your hearing again."

I gave him credit. When he finally threw his punch, he put all his upper body weight into it- fully committed, unfortunate for him. My instincts read his intention well ahead; he hadn't a chance.

I quickly moved my upper body safely left and his right hand crashed into solid brick. I heard the bones in his fist disintegrate. He belted a resounding scream. Wouldn't be holding a football for a while or anything else for that matter.

Cradling his fist, Matt croaked, "Get him!"

Four players closed on me. I dropped and swept my right leg through their ranks. Like a cannon ball taking out bowling pins, there were bodies pell-melling everywhere. I have enormous strength in my legs- I called the shots.

I'd hoped not to completely disable the football team, but I guess their season was over. . . One by one, they regained their feet, their captain encouraging from the sidelines. The two bringing up the rear bowed out and made themselves scarce.

I ducked and weaved through the newly upright. The four bowling pins tried to keep their balance in the close quarters of the sidewalk bordered by parked cars and buildings.

A siren went off in the distance. I maintained my defensive position dancing circles around the heavy-set bullies, throwing the occasional punch and evading potential connections of their fists with my anatomy. Near the end, three of them tripped over each other, forming a dismantled huddle smack on their butts. Number four took a last swing. I ducked and gave a slight push and STRIKE- game over.

"Break it up," an officer demanded. He looked down at four lettered players- the pride of the football team, took in the jibberish-spewing quarterback who required medical attention and the now unobtrusive long-hair still standing. "You responsible for all this?" He asked in disbelief.

"Officer Denton," Rick, Lil and Bonnie started to explain.

"Hold on. One at a time."

"Matt and his friends attacked my date," Bonnie stated with Rick, Lil and an appreciative audience nodding in agreement.

"I think Matt needs a hospital. He hit a brick wall," Rick added.

"You're sure you're not hurt?"

"Bonnie, for the third time, I'm fine. No one landed on me- fist, foot or otherwise," I reassured her.

"That was unbelievable! I hope they leave you alone now."

"One can always hope," I grinned at Bonnie who was still caught up in the reverie.

Pulling into her driveway, I asked, "Would you have used that broomstick?"

"Absolutely, if Rick had given me half a chance. Try to get around a basketball player. I didn't want to hit him but I would have if you needed me."

I was thoroughly amused at her warrior-attitude coming out in my defense. Grinning, I put us back on more placid footing. "Did you have a good time tonight?"

"Very much so. Thank you, Riordan. And for my purse, too," her fingers held the small, treasured bag.

I opened the jeep door for her, lifted her down, escorted her to the lit-up porch. "Good night, Bonnie. I enjoyed your company."

"Riordan?"

"Hmmm. . ." I knew what was coming and I was prepared. I'd kept a physical distance all evening. What a saint, I congratulated myself, while itching to be a devil.

"Will you kiss me?" She tentatively asked. Those big eyes looked up at me expectantly, hopefully. Spirits help me. . .

"No, not tonight." Her jaw dropped as I
turned to leave. "Give you something to look
forward to. Close your mouth, Bonnie and go
inside. Make the curfew. Don't worry your
father."

Chapter 26

"I've got something for you," I handed Bonnie a manila package.

She frowned at me, fondled the thick envelope, hesitated, "You shouldn't buy me anything." Interested, but protesting, how like a woman.

"Just open it." Out came the pale pink, one-piece swim suit with its adjustable halter top tie.

"My goodness," she exclaimed as I laughed. "How did you know what size to get? It's very pretty."

"I have pretty good powers of observation," I downplayed my talents.

Her face reddened; the swim suit lay in her lap. "How much do I owe you?" She was now reticent.

"I figure a couple batches of your cookies ought to do it." I relished the thought of those delicious edibles and the picture of Bonnie in her new suit.

"I'm sure this cost more than a few dozen cookies," her eyes were on me, finally.

"Well, make it four dozen, but not all at the same time." I looked over at her while driving to school and grinned.

"Riordan. . ."

I jumped in to stave off her change of direction. "Let's see. . . Next week's study class we'll swim."

"Oh," she quailed.

"Hey, you did a good job last time," I fruitlessly tried to provide reassurance.

"Until I panicked. . ."

"Nothing to fear but fear itself."

"Yeah, I know. Confront your fears," she rejoined.

"Fear provides the impetus to further yourself," I riposted a comeback.

"Where did that come from?" Bonnie was stifling a giggle.

I shrugged, pulled into the school parking lot, "I just made it up."

"Thank you for the suit. It is very pretty." And Bonnie would look beautiful in it- I could hardly wait for our private swim class.

"Riordan?"

"Hmmm. . ." I wasn't about to like this next topic. It was almost like reading her mind- a meeting of frequencies. I caught her watching Rick and Lil lightly swinging their arms together, fingers clasped, headed for the entrance.

"You told Matt I was your girl," she ventured tentatively.

Maybe it was too soon to admit to her- oh well, in for a dime, in for a dollar. "Any objections?"

"No, not one. C...could we hold hands?"

"Bonnie, I don't like physical contact."

"You touched me in the pool. Your fingers have been on my chin, wrist and I think I remember that first day when I was sleeping in class, I think you touched my leg." Good memory.

"That's right. I touched you when you needed help."

"So if I said I needed you to hold my hand. . ." She wasn't going to let this one go.

"Bonnie," I hedged.

"Can you explain it to me?"

"Not right now, we'll be late." Scaredy cat came to mind as a reproof.

"Fear provides the impetus to further yourself," she came at me with my own words.

"You think I'm afraid of your touch?" This time I stopped and faced her.

"If you say I'm too young. . ."

"Yeah, I know. You'll go all vampire on me." She began to laugh- I joined her. Grow up, CatSkill- if you want her. . . I reached for her hand.

"No," she surprised and frustrated me with.

"No?"

"I want to take your hand." All smiles now and so sure of herself.

I braced myself. For my entire life, I was the contact- initiator. I never allowed any one to touch me out of the blue. Other than moments with a female partner or unavoidable altercations, I usually refrained from physical contact.

Uninvited contact sent off alarms in my system- my wild senses took over and automatic responses were activated. I especially did not want to hurt Bonnie.

But, I was. If the Great Spirit and my guide had meant her for me, they must have ordained a change in my thinking along these lines. Here goes.

She stood there waiting, patiently, until doomsday was my guess or until the principal appeared. I took a deep breath.

"Ok," I dropped my hand to my side, palm held out to her.

Bonnie smiled beguilingly and began to walk. What in the world? "Well?"

"Not right now. Give you something to look forward to," she swung her tawny hair at me. Flabbergasted, I roared a laugh and followed. Bonnie, never a dull moment.

Bonnie's father stayed home Thanksgiving week, leaving me to rest and ruminate and then get really restless at night, all at the same time.

Wednesday night I couldn't stand it and changed into my other self and went running. Then changed again and found myself perched on a tree limb outside Bonnie's window- the vigilant woodpecker on reconnaissance.

And what a sight! If it's possible for a bird to salivate, I was up to it. With her light on, I observed Bonnie studying herself in a mirror. Her hands rested at her waist and then she smoothed her fingers over her hips. What did she think about the changes sweeping through her body in record time?

If she were uncomfortable, she gave no overt indication of such to me. But she had to be wondering. She still wore loose flannel shirts on top of white t-shirts to school.

Sans flannel shirt, she preened before the mirror. Her hands went under her hair and simulated pin-up hair do's.

Suddenly, she stopped her feminine stances and glanced in my direction. I hadn't made a sound- no tapping. Bonnie walked to the window. Her eyes found mine in my bird guise. A chill went through my feathers as if an abrupt breeze ruffled them. In all my life, I'd nothing to compare with what she was doing to me.

Chapter 27

The scents wafting out of the Lance cabin had grandfather's and my own taste buds tripping double time. Mr. Lance greeted us at the door and welcomed us in, enthusiastically recounting the line-up of football games for the day.

Grandfather and Bonnie's father shared a penchant for football and with grandfather manipulating the frequencies, the reception on the old television cleared for a remarkable picture. Those two were lost until the food was served and probably for the rest of the day to boot.

I sauntered over to the prettiest occupant of the cabin. Bonnie had wiped her hands, rushed to give grandfather a hug and then hastened back to the kitchen.

His eyes surveyed the changes in the little girl who used to sit and listen to him for hours-two, story lovers. He gave me a thumbs-up behind her back. I telepathically shot at him, 'Dirty old man'.

She hadn't bothered to try to hug me. My something to look forward to was going to hit me when I least expected it- if that were possible. Knowing Bonnie or beginning to know her more and more, I was certain she'd planned a big surprise.

"Hello, can I help?" I offered, watching her knead bread.

"Hi, Riordan! How are you at mashing potatoes?"

"I'm willing to find out. You're a little nervous?"

"I just want to have everything turn out. . ."

I sidled up to her, "Bonnie with your culinary talents, it's a sure thing." She blushed her thanks.

Today she sported a white cable knit sweater and new jeans. "New clothes, huh?"

"Yes, my dad took me shopping. I…I needed some things." This time her face rivaled the old fire engine red.

"We have a break in the action," she covered the bread for its last rise in the bread pans and turned to me. "You're not interested in the games?"

"Not a contact sports fan," I shrugged.

"Unless it's you involved in a fight?"

"I don't start them, but I am a guy. We like a good rumble now and then. If there's time, show me more of your art work."

"I...you wait here, I'll bring a few paintings out. They're in my bedroom." I recalled Mr. Lance's admonition about both of us in Bonnie's bedroom.

She returned with five canvases, three oils and two water colors. One of the water colors depicted two frogs squatting on a pond side rock. Cattails and dragonflies abounded with pale blue sky above and story-filled water below. You'd expect those frogs to jump in any moment- they were that realistic. The other water color was of a nest of robin's eggs.

For the oils, she'd done a study of Sticker and Stalker, a painting of the geldings strolling about their corral and, I gulped, a woodpecker perched on a familiar limb. "When did you do this one?"

"About six months ago. Do you like it?" Was she smiling at me conspiratorially?

Grandfather had wandered to the art show on his way to the bathroom while I was stuck plundering the mystery of Bonnie. He grabbed a peanut butter filled celery stalk from the appetizer tray and admired each picture.

"You have a great gift," he admiringly mused.

"Can you believe my daughter drew these?" Mr. Lance proudly gloated. "They're so life-like, makes you think twice about petting the dogs or waiting for those horses to nicker."

"Bonnie, have you ever showed these to a professional?" I asked.

"No," she hitched a shoulder.

"You could have a career as an artist. These are phenomenal. I've never seen any to better them." We males all concurred on this point.

She blushed at all the attention focused on her and gathered the paintings together. I silently advised grandfather to check out the cougar above Bonnie's bed as he walked down the hall.

"Bonnie, would you like to take commissions? I'm betting the Buffalo Bill Museum might allow you, as a local artist, to display some of your art in their gift shop- maybe earn you some work."

"I guess I could try. I'm not sure about pricing. . ."

"We should look into that, honey. Good idea, Riordan, Bonnie's father hugged her and went back to catch a much vaunted play.

"I'd need to personally see the animals to know about them, understand their quirks, their personalities, their expressions," she attempted to explain. "I wouldn't take a commission from a picture."

"For this quality, you could ask for anything- no reservations," I assured her.

I removed the turkey from the oven. Bonnie put the bread in. We stood together in the cozy, scent filled kitchen.

"How do you make the paintings so real?" She studied her shoes, reluctant to answer. I lifted her chin, "Tell me."

"I…I see what I'm drawing as if, as if I were the living beings I'm drawing. As if my body becomes theirs. I feel their emotions. I read their thoughts in pictures. It becomes like…like a self-portrait almost. I wonder sometimes if I'm supposed to be human." She'd never revealed this to anyone before- that's how much she trusted me, but confusion reigned on her face.

"It's OK, baby. It's OK. You are," I swallowed, gulped more like, "You are very, very special."

If we'd been alone, I probably would have kissed her right then. It was all I could do. . . "The potatoes!" Good save, CatSkill. Burnt potatoes are not edible.

I whispered to her, "We've a lot to talk about- soon."

Bonnie asked for the TV to be turned off during dinner. Her father had a momentary rebellious reaction to this, but he acquiesced.

Grandfather and I were all eyes and salivary glands fastened on the feast laid on the table. No over-cooked vegetables or dry turkey here. Absolutely the best meal I'd ever had and we three males moaned and complimented the chef- took turns at it.

I'd not appreciated stuffing before Bonnie put her fingers to it. For dessert, she'd made a pumpkin and an apple pie. These didn't last long either.

"Am I going to have a turkey sandwich tomorrow?" Bonnie's father asked hopefully, spying the remains.

"Yes, Dad. I reckon there's one for me too. Next year I'll get a bigger turkey," she shook her head in wonder at all the empty plates, bowls and pie pans. "This must be what it's like feeding an army."

Grandfather and Mr. Lance rose much more slowly than they'd originally come to the table, rubbed extended stomachs in satisfaction and headed back to the TV.

"I'll help clean up." Not one used to the 'good' dishes, I was careful about clearing the table and drying. In the close quarters of the kitchen another scent begged recognition.

"You made cookies."

"Yes, the installment plan, remember?" She grinned up at me. "You can have them when you leave."

"Not if I find them first," I boasted.

"How can you possibly consume another bite?"

"Hey, I'm a growing boy," I made myself look as tall as possible.

"Well, you better watch it. We don't have a skylight to open in here. I wouldn't want your head going through the ceiling."

Chapter 28

"Tell me about your cougar dream." After clean-up, Bonnie had suggested another of her passions- star gazing. The two of us were lying side by side on the cabin roof.

"It's not the same dream all the time," she opened with, pondering how to continue.

"I'm in no hurry and the 'boys' are still busy watching football." All my senses were up for the latest surprise I'd come to associate with my Bonnie.

"The first time I saw the mountain lion- it was sort of peripheral to the rest of my dream, like he was patiently waiting for his big entrance."

"How old were you?"

"Maybe ten, I don't really remember. Perhaps he was there before, but I didn't notice. About a year ago, he began to take a more visual role in whatever I was dreaming of until he eventually became central and it was him- the mountain lion, I was dreaming of."

"You say 'him'?"

She laughed lightly, "Oh, it's very clear he is male. He's not there every night, but when he is. . ." Bonnie went quiet on me.

I wasn't going to let her off that easy. "Tell me, what does he do in your dream?" This was better than a movie any day- not that I'm into movies.

"He watches me. Sometimes, he thinks he's hidden. For example, I'll be drawing- bringing a potential idea to life. I must sound crazy. . ."

"No, not crazy- maybe a little idiosyncratic, but hey, you're an artist," I elbowed her gently, very gently.

"He'll watch me draw. I can hear him make suggestions. I'll dream I'm running and he'll accompany me, urging me on. He'll rest on a tree limb and watch me take care of the animals here, but he's not interested in them as a cougar would be. I come across a cave nearly hidden by boulders- he's reclining in the entrance. He goes inside and then reappears- I know I'm supposed to follow him. . ." Her voice had softened to an awed whisper.

I was on tenterhooks with her providential descriptions. "Do you. . .follow?"

"No, I always wake up first," she admitted, resignedly.

"You're never afraid?"

"No, he would never hurt me." This she said with the utmost surety. "You're not laughing?"

"I'm too intrigued. Go on."

"The last dream repeats but with different aspects taking center stage. I'm sitting in a cave, it's not dark; my hands are wrapped around my shins. And he's there, sitting opposite me. In pictures he shows me places he's been: lakes- he loves to swim, mountains- he loves to climb, forests and now, don't laugh, you wanted to hear. . ."

"Go on," I think I heard myself say.

"He shows me cities." I was very still. Was I even breathing at this continued list of revelations?

"Imagine a mountain lion loose in New York City- at least I think it was New York. Venice, Italy, I recognized right away."

"Did he show you what he's doing in those cities?" Once more I heard myself as if from a distance.

"Yes. In New York or whatever city it was, he helped a tourist who was surrounded by bad guys. Oh, I remember, he showed me San Francisco and saving some poor folks from an earthquake. In Venice, he pulled a. . . I never thought of this before, but some of these pictures were not present time. The earthquake was a long time ago-there were no cars. The young man he pulled from the canal was dressed in costume or," her forehead crunched as her brain sought explanations.

I could feel her recalling more and more and the inherent confusion. "He showed me a group of young Native Americans he was working with-helping them to regain pride in their culture, overcome. . .," she shrugged as words failed. "There was a little dog, hurt and lost and an older woman crying. He was very happy about returning the dog to the woman."

"A mountain lion returning a dog to its owner?" I couldn't put disbelief in my questions. I couldn't feign it- especially not with her. "Did he show you how he managed this?"

"No, only the results," she reclined comfortably, hands crossed at her waist while her words spun me into a vortex.

All of her scenarios were very familiar to me- the cougar was me. The young man I'd pulled from the canal had been robbed, beaten and pushed into the Venetian waterway, left for dead. I rescued him, reciprocated his attackers and carried the insensible fellow home. I'd reaped a great reward for that. He'd been a wealthy duke's son.

The great San Francisco earthquake, yes, I was there. I remembered a group huddled in an alley between brick buildings. If I'd not moved them out they would have died, crushed.

I regularly visited my acolytes on the reservation. It wasn't hard to gain their attention after Red Hawk, their shaman, recommended me and I 'helped' them with an issue or two. All of these represented a tiny fraction of my history.

"Is there more, Bonnie?"

"Too many to tell. Every time I see him, he shows me something new." I wanted to get up and run, faster than I'd ever run, but the surprises didn't stop.

Chapter 29

"Oh, look! There's the Pink Lady!" An excited Bonnie pointed into the sky. A pinkish-cast star was moving about in the vibrant road map above. "My dad said I was seeing things. If so, I like seeing them, that's why I come up here. But, only when my dad's home."

"Do you see any others?" I quietly asked with the greatest of interest.

"Oh, yes!" Like a kid in a candy store she went on. "There's the Green man, Mr. Blue, Nearly Yellow. . ." She broke off, wondering if I wondered if she were long gone on the crazy side.

"How do you differentiate between lady and man?" I wasn't certain what to say or ask first because another, distinct Bonnie-inspired-moment was presenting itself and the ensuing thrill engulfed me. Something else new in Bonnie's class of Surprise Me 101.

"Do you see them, too?" Her hushed voice inquired.

"Yes."

"Then I'm not making it up?"

"No."

"Why can't my dad see them?" Her confusion sparked me.

"Most human eyes need special night vision scopes to observe what you are seeing," I explained the easy part.

"But not yours?"

Here's where it got really interesting-Spirits help me with this explanation. I surely did not want to frighten her. "No, our eyes are different." Did I slip? Well it was all going to come out anyway. "Tell me about the Pink Lady." That ought to distract her, hopefully.

"I call her an art nouveau star because she travels in arcs and flowing lines. The others must be male- art deco stars. They only move around in straight lines, angles. . . Am I amusing you?"

I'd begun to laugh. When was the last time a laugh had gone completely through me? "Bonnie, Bonnie, Bonnie," I rolled over on my side, my right arm about her waist, my weight resting on my left elbow. "I'm not laughing at you. You thrill me no end. I get the biggest kick out of you. What do you think those stars are?"

"Souls that have passed?" She speculated.

"Aliens?" I ventured.

"Maybe, guardian angels."

"There are cultures that believe the departed join the stars, become the stars."

"Maybe all of these are the same," she hedged.

"UFOs= departed souls= angels?" I was still chuckling.

"Could be," I felt her shrug against me.

We both laughed over our little repartee. My eyes gradually locked on hers and the laughter faded. Ah, Great Spirit, such a wonderful gift you've presented me with.

A tapping engulfed my heart- I couldn't escape that damned woodpecker, providential woodpecker- ordaining a great change not only for Bonnie, but for me, too.

"If you have no objections, I'm going to kiss you." I heard her rapid intake of breath, felt her body blush.

"Yes," her lips curled sweetly into a smile, her eyes half-closed after popping.

"Yes, you object or yes, I should kiss you?" My body knew an unfamiliar fever.

"Yes, kiss me. Please?" Her hand gently settled on my chest.

A shockwave vibrated through my bloodstream. I'd already discovered some of the extraordinary depths of her other senses, physical and extra-sensory. Now on to taste- to taste those inviting lips. Prolonging the suspense, until I could endure no more, I lowered my mouth to hers.

Tender communion of souls. A feast more savory than water to the deserted. If the mysteries and my spirit guide had meant this delicious surprise for me, then it would be the height of folly, misguided ingratitude, to do anything other than accept and be thankful.

Earthquake and hurricane forces besieged my body at the meeting of our mouths and I fell into the heavenly vortex of what could only be love. This is what poets sing of, I thought.

With the greatest of reluctance and use of will, I gently pulled away as her arms wound around my neck. Untangling her, I stood and offered my hand.

She was breathless and disconcerted at my departure from her side. "You could teach me how," chagrinned, she whispered and rose into my heaving chest.

"How?" My lips were twitching.

"How to kiss. So we could keep practicing." I felt the heat of her blush and heightened embarrassment.

Throwing back my head, I howled with delight. This really miffed her and her eyes glistened. "Bonnie, Kitten, do you know what a shotgun wedding is?"

"Yes," she scowled.

"I'm going to do my best not to be a participant in one. Let's go down now."

I hurried down the ladder, giving her a minute alone to understand what I was telling her. Waiting at the foot of the ladder, I gazed up at her, thoughtfully resting several rungs above.

"You liked to kiss me?" There was a glint of awe resident in her appealing voice.

"Way too much," I avowed.

Bonnie pondered this heartfelt admission for a moment and the biggest smile lit up her face- definitely, an art nouveau face. She was a complete masterpiece- mine.

"Bonnie, look in my eyes. What do you see?" I felt the dawn of her realization as it broke the darkness and rayed upon me.

"Love forever," she whispered after a lifetime.

"Yes," I committed and escorted her into the cabin.

"Grandfather, she has the sight, too."

"Of course," he nodded.

"She is mine," I laughed, pure joy. "I love her."

Grandfather was very still and all of a sudden he groaned and doubled over.

"Grandfather!" I shouted, stopped the jeep and put my hand on his wrist. His face was pained and white in the moonlit cab.

"I'm alright, Grandson.   Take me home.   I know why you are here," a stricken whisper.

Chapter 30

"Riordan, glad you're here." The worry
lines about Mr. Lance's eyes, the relief in his
voice, the hastily saddled gelding, the shotgun in
its scabbard- didn't take my innate powers to read
this.

"Where's Bonnie?" All senses on guard.

"I don't know," he grimly admitted. "Last
night, a friend stopped by. Apparently, a
mountain lion has been spotted some fifty miles
northwest of here. Not the sort of sighting to
soothe ranchers with winter coming on. He told me
a hunting party's getting up. You know Bonnie has
this thing about cougars. . ."

"I'll find her, sir," I vaulted away, honed
in on her scent.

In my reconnaissance of a sizeable territory
the previous night, I'd caught a whiff of a young
male lion, probably displaced and seeking a new
hunting ground- his own territory.

As I hurried through high desert brush, north of the woods-supported hidden springs of the Lance homestead, I recounted some of last evening's conversation with Grandfather. We were up late discussing his revelation in the jeep on Thanksgiving night.

A vision had assailed grandfather along several sensory fronts. "Do you remember Chac?"

"The jaguar man?" I was puzzled. Grandfather nodded. "I never met him on my travels, but I remember you had made his acquaintance."

"A good thing, too. He is disillusioned, distraught and extremely angry over the destructive changes in his world. Once he was revered as a god by the native peoples of the South American and Latin American jungles. With the onslaught of encroaching civilization, the old ways are dying out and he is now more reviled than revered except by conservationists. He has seen Bonnie in a vision and has an idea of her potential. For an aboriginal shaman to have a white woman shaman. . .he seeks her as powerful medicine. He believes he can change the circumstances of his life by joining with her-enslaving her if necessary. To him this bond will create a potent magic which will bring back his previous god-like stature."

"He thinks he can just come and take her?" I asked in disbelief.

"Chac knows he can," Grandfather grimly stated.

"Well, he's got another thing coming," I bristled.

"Chac is sly and even though dissolute, he still has tremendous strength. Grandson, for all your experience and strength. . .I fear."

"No one will take Bonnie from me- hasn't the Great Spirit put us together?"

"I believe her spirit guide has called you as her protector and your being here compelled the quickening of her body's maturity and the advancement of her supra-senses all at the same time. A lesser person would go insane at the rapid changes she is undergoing. No wonder he wants her."

"He'll not have her," I vowed, ready to battle. "Does he see her now?"

"Did you tell her you love her tonight?"

"Yes, what of it?" I felt the frown forming.

"Your declaration for her has propelled his interest, hence my vision. He only knows a man is circling her, not who you are. It's important to maintain your stealthy fog about you always. He can't penetrate your reclusiveness, and we should monitor some-such for Bonnie. The less he knows, the better."

"Won't that make him come here immediately?"

"No, Chac hates the cold, bless the Wyoming winters. He is so sure of himself, he'll wait until summer. Innately, he knows Grandson, nothing can withstand him."

"And if he finds she won't go with him?"

"He'll put her in a trance and escort her away," Grandfather shrugged as if a chill sidled down his back.

"She can't be mesmerized; I've tried in our swim class and Grandfather, you know I can weave an hypnotic web."

"He may drug her."

"We have time to teach her. I'll keep her under constant guard. He'll never get near her," I began to formulate plans.

"It may come to a battle."

"I welcome it," I gritted with relish.

"Do you think she's ready to accept who we are- who she really is?"

"I think she's more than ready; either way, she has, or her soul has, made its choice. I've been in her dreams as my other self for quite some time," I assured Grandfather.

"You must also prepare yourself, Grandson. No one has ever beaten the jaguar," Grandfather bowed his head.

"I'll be ready," I could feel the unsheathing of my claws- bring it on. . .

Grandfather mulled something over. "It may still come as a shock when you change for her." I'd worry about that later.

So many of Bonnie's remarks were hitting me from all sides-her becoming, not being able to get back to herself, not meant to be human. . . How dare anyone, shaman or no, think he could take her from me!

"Without knowing who you are, he'll believe she will keep until summer- an ordinary man is a joke to him and that is what he surmises you are. It's a good thing you regularly sustain your stealth- his whiff of her did not include the truth of you- our advantage, Grandson. Her lessons must begin now."

I agreed. More important than swim class, now other lesson plans were running through my head.

"I know Chac, Grandson, in his younger days he was truly frightening. I would not have been able to defeat him. In believing Bonnie will restore to him. . .I think you understand."

The mountain lion-v-the jaguar. Let him try- no one would take Bonnie from me.

Miles away, as the ground swept up into rocky hills, I found her. My senses warned me to go slow- she was not alone. I checked my smothered scent and stealthily worked my way closer.

Bonnie was sitting, arms wrapped around her legs; a tumbleweed swayed at her back. Opposite her, reclining above on a rocky ledge was her potential nemesis. An elk carcass lay under his paw.

Unbelievably, they were actually conversing- the young male lion was showing her by means of pictures, the journey he'd made to reach this point. He'd feasted the night before on part of his kill, a disabled elk and was content- for the moment.

His tail languidly rested then slowly moved as a breeze hastened up to him. From his repose he started to rise with a snarl of agitation, but Bonnie inclined her head and he resettled.

As if I needed more proof of Bonnie's spirit guide and her powers, here it was. A human girl- a true spirit-called shaman without any training was communicating with. . .

Did she believe this was the one in her dreams? This cougar's picture story would have disavowed her of that by now. Plus, there was no blood-red streak and this specimen did not begin to approach the size of her painted dream.

Although her spirit guide provided some protection, this was a foolhardy position for her to be in. The cat might pounce at any moment- the Discovery channel or a blood-thirsty survivalist show would make a fortune off of a film with this scenario.

A squirrel barked from a desiccated pine and the cougar renewed his alert, rose, and a rumbling issued from his throat. The cat growled and I poised, ready to strike, but once more Bonnie soothed him. He cocked his head at her, listening.

'Bonnie, don't move', I telepathically warned her and by the slight movement of her head, I was relieved and amazed to discover she'd heard.

A young cougar completely gets the idea when a bigger, more powerful and more experienced male issues a get-lost command. This youngster wasn't ready to try me.

From deep inside me I brought up a very clear rumble and growl that let junior know he wasn't up to messing with me. The tone of my 'voice' gave him a vibrant picture of just how formidable an opponent was near and also an unmistakable indication that this territory was taken.

I also warned him to seek a safer home to the northeast to avoid the coming hunters. The cougar bounded up the rocky ridge and disappeared without a backward glance.

"What the devil do you think you're doing out here? Do you even have your pistol? Have you any idea how worried your father is? Do you not understand, that animal could have severed your neck from your body and had you for dessert?"

I railed at her- my fury bursting out from my concern for her safety. Her father wasn't the only worried one. I swore, something I never do- self-control momentarily forgotten.

"He wouldn't hurt me," I barely heard her say as I ranted.

"Don't be stupid! That was a wild animal, not a dream, not a cuddly stuffed animal from a store, a wild animal. . . This is not a Disney movie," I broke off as her lower lip began to tremble and those glistening eyes threatened to overflow.

"I thought you would understand," her ragged voice cried and she ran by me. At least she was headed home. I kept pace, but stayed behind her. The run would cool me off, I hoped and as for her. . .

Mr. Lance reined in Hoss. "Bonnie!" he shouted. She stopped dead. "Where have you. . .? Are you all right? I've been worried to death, young lady." He dismounted. "Are you OK?"

I stayed back. "Y…Yes dad."

"Why are you crying?"

"Riordan h…hollered at me," she choked, forlorn.

"Hollered! Hollered! He should have turned you over his knee and blistered your butt. Get home! Now! I'll deal with you later." Now there was a pretty thought- the sight of Bonnie's butt, not the blisters.

Bonnie took off, racing for home. My anger had melted and allowed me to feel her hurting. Wow- I was totally unprepared for this immersion into another's soul and for sure, it would only get more intense as our relationship progressed.

Mr. Lance turned to me as I walked forward. "Where did you find her?"

"A few miles north of here."

"Any sign of the cat?"

Here I gave some protection to Bonnie and the cat. "Some recent tracks heading back northwest. I think it's gone."

"She's never done anything to make me worry like this before. I'm not sure what to do here. Thanks for finding her, Riordan."

I nodded to him. I also felt sorry for Mr. Lance. He was out of his element here- way out.

"How do I punish her? There's nothing to take away from her; she never asks for anything." He fingered his reins, upset and lost, as Hoss nuzzled him comfortingly.

"You could suspend her dating privileges?" I offered.

He looked at me quizzically, "That would affect you, too." I knew he wondered about me. This would add to that score.

"I've an idea, Sir, I think might be just the ticket."

Chapter 31

I couldn't help myself. She was still in
pain- my fault. I had to see her.

Early nightfall found me outside her window
in my human form. Bonnie was curled on the bed,
only a nightlight for company. Silent sobbing,
trembling shoulders, fingers clasping and grinding
the hapless pillow.

Hang the rules about us being in her bedroom
together. Mr. Lance dozed in front of a noisy
television. I saw the lock fastened on the window
frame- a simple exercise and it was free. I
lifted the glass and entered without a sound.

"Bonnie, Kitten?" Her body went quiet,
feigning sleep. In another instance, I would have
chuckled at her acting.

"You can't pretend with me." I picked her
up, sat on the bed, her curled form on my lap. I
would break the uneasy barrier between us.

"I'm sorry I yelled at you. I've never
yelled at another person in my life- discount the
rabbit incident. Your father's not the only one
who was worried about you. Now that I find myself
caring for someone. . . Knowing that I love you.
. . If anything happened to you, I'm not sure I'd
want to go on. Bonnie?"

I lifted her chin; her tear-streaked face
kicked me in the gut. Kissing the trail of her
tears to her lips, I resisted her mouth and kissed
her forehead instead.

"I didn't mean to hurt you. . ." The
stillness of her body was replaced with reinforced
trembling. "Bonnie, you have to talk to me. You
can tell me anything, absolutely anything. Yell
at me, but quietly, if you want."

"My father might hear us. You shouldn't be
here." She put her head in the curve of my neck
and shoulder and began to cry once more.

Lifting her, I carried her to a radio I'd
seen on a bookshelf next to her desk. I turned it
on, to static of course. Sending out a frequency
reminder, I achieved a station emitting soft
music.

"How did you do that?" Great CatSkill,
finally, you incur her interest- not in the fact I
had entered her room by means of a previously
locked window, but that I tuned in her radio.

"I'll tell you if you spill your guts to me. Why are you still crying?" Silence snoozed by until a low wail of submission dwindled to a sniffle.

"I don't understand what's happening to me. Every time I see my reflection I wonder who's there. I don't recognize myself. I've never caused my dad to worry before. You were late this morning. . . When you didn't come at nine, I…I thought maybe the hunters had found you. I thought it was you." The sobbing broke out again.

My own heart threatened to crack up and bleed. This precious bundle had not been unaffected by the relentless course of changes roiling through her being.

I put out a peaceful energetic veil to enclose us both. On some level, she knew I was the one in her dream- her painting. Bonnie had been concerned for my safety this morning.

"Bonnie, are you unhappy with your looks?"

"N…no, but I don't like the way the guys at school are looking at me."

"Do you mind the way I look at you?" I smiled into her hair.

"I only feel comfortable with you," she sniffed.

"I wish you had a girlfriend to talk to about. . .girly things, body changes. But I'm happy to listen- be a girlfriend and boyfriend in one if you like."

She glanced away from my searching eyes, twiddled her fingers. "It's not normal for a girl to develop this fast, is it?"

"No, for most girls it's more gradual. But you are not an ordinary young lady. Bonnie, don't be afraid of what's happening. You are. . ." I hesitated. Should I wait for grandfather to tell her?

"I am?"

I wrapped my arms about her. "You know grandfather is a healer, a medicine man- sometimes called a shaman by white people?"

"Since I was a little girl listening to his stories, I've wondered if he were magic; he made his words live. I could see the ceremonies, the spirit guides, the legends come to life as he spoke," the tears were drying.

"That is one of his gifts. There is magic in the spoken word if the intent is there. Bonnie, you have a great gift also- your paintings. Your drawings glow with a life force that you give them- that is more than artistry. Call it magic, if you wish. You are a shaman, Kitten, a very rare parcel and your gifts are begging to be recognized and used. As for your body's fast maturation. . ." Watch your hands, CatSkill- I reminded myself. "Grandfather and I have a theory about that, too."

"Tell me," her hoarse whisper.

"I'm not scaring you?"

"No. Riordan, you also have special gifts?"

"Yes," I answered, knowing or believing she already knew the answer on some level.

She curled more comfortably, for her, into my arms, while my body flared with tremendous desire.

Her eyes sought mine, "You are the one in my painting. You are the one I've been dreaming of. The red patch on your shoulder- I saw at the pool, is just like his."

I nodded, gauging her reaction every second. "Grandfather believes our spirit guides have designated us to be together and that on some level, you have called me here. My presence, as a male, has hastened your. . .feminine attributes." Great wording, keep it up, CatSkill.

I swallowed with effort. "The cougar you were talking to today, did you think he was the one of your dreams?"

"Only as I hurried to find you, once I saw him, it was plain that he was not the one."

"Did you enjoy the conversation?" I nitpicked.

"Yes, I've never…never realized. . ." enthusiasm replaced her unease. A green flair of jealousy was poking its head into mine.

"What did you show him to make him snarl at you?"

"I pictured you," she smiled.

"Huh, as a human?"

"Yes."

"So, he knew of my wild nature," I pondered. Bonnie frowned a question. "He'd not protest as a cat would if he saw me as an ordinary man."

"Oh," she was intrigued and fascinated. "I want to know more. I want to know everything about you. Where. . ."

"Hold on. We'll get to all that. I promise. Do you talk to other animals in pictures?"

"Yes, I sing to the birds sometimes. Once, I helped my dad with a horse no one could do anything with. The horse had a back problem nobody recognized. My dad bought him after I talked to the horse, brought in a chiropractor and solved the problem. He was a kind and worthy horse. My dad made a nice profit and the horse went to an understanding owner who promised regular chiropractor check-ups. The other ranchers gave my dad a lot of ribbing, but once the money changed hands, what could they say?" Bonnie was regaining herself.

"Do you always talk to every animal?" I pursued in this vein.

"Well, no. I guess you wouldn't talk to every person."

"But you could?"

"Some people are interested in making acquaintances. In my case, more animals are interested in talking to me than people," she shrugged, tears all forgotten. "That's OK with me."

"It's a beautiful gift, Kitten," I kissed the tip of her nose.

"I know I should express my gratitude more often."

I took a deep breath and plunged, "I love you, Bonnie. You are mine, Miss Lance." The fog was now and would remain in place from any of Chac's incursions; my identity was safe- I could protect her.

"I'm happy to be yours," pain had disappeared. She leaned in to kiss me, but I courageously staved off her attempt. Like a woman, she changed direction without missing a step, but she could not hide the slight. "Do you not want me to talk to other…other animals?" She inquired.

I fondled her cheek. Was it fair for one so young to commit herself without dating other boys? My spirit guide growled in my ear.

"You're so young, Kitten."

"If you tell me that one more time, I WILL bite you."

"Like a vampire?" I chuckled.

"Like a. . .I. . .oh, like a cat," she actually licked my neck and grasped a bit of skin with her teeth.

"Ow! You little vixen!"

"Wrong species. Remember that," she smiled mysteriously at me. "I love you, Riordan." Our eyes locked in their own sonnet and my temperature soared.

"Call me CatSkill," I murmured teetering on an edge, my nose on her jugular vein.

"I don't like the 'kill' part," she whispered and trembled.

"Silly, it's Cat Skill," I chuckled.

"I love you, CatSkill." An all too alluring voice- heaven help me.

"And you're not afraid of our destiny together?"

"I'm not afraid when I'm with you," she sincerely replied and her nose vacuumed my scent.

"And you'll ask me whatever, whenever you have a question?"

"Yes, Riordan. Will you kiss me?"

"One kiss," I almost groaned "and then I want you to go and get something to eat, talk to your dad and then get some sleep-you have Sunday school tomorrow."

Chapter 32

"Consider this a placement test."

"A what?" Bonnie looked puzzled and a puzzled Bonnie is the cutest thing.

'Riordan, focus,' Grandfather shot me a telepathic telegram.

I was still enthralled, like a parent on his kid's first day of school. I'd picked up Bonnie early Sunday morning after her chores were finished. She'd skipped out the door her father held open, to his wondering consternation.

Mr. Lance shook my hand, hardly hiding his state of confusion. "Study hard, honey, and learn something useful."

So, there's my charge, protégé, child, girlfriend, one day lover-to-be {couldn't wait for the last one}, dressed in her uniform baggy- not too baggy anymore- jeans, over size flannel shirt that so deliciously hid Bonnie's curves, jacket over an arm and a notebook with sharpened pencils to boot.

"Probably won't need pencil and paper, Kitten, it's not that kind of class," I grinned at her.

She was ahead of me on this point, "I have to have something to show my dad; otherwise he might think we're disguising a date as a class." Bonnie smiled conspiratorially up at me.

"Hmmm. Aren't you the smart cookie? Speaking of cookies?" I sniffed.

"Here's another installment," she handed me a bag from under her jacket.

"I knew I loved you for more than one thing," I set up her sweet blush.

And then it went quiet in the jeep- too quiet. "What are you thinking of?"

"The rabbit got loose. I tried, but I couldn't find her. I hope she's all right," dismay trembled in her voice.

"Hey, cheer up. That's a good thing. I'm sure she knows when she's well enough to be on her way. What else?" Being privy to all of Bonnie- a new and exciting state for me, I knew when to force the ball rolling.

"Just wondering what I might learn today and. . ."

"And?" I felt her mulling over whether or not to continue.

"Nothing." She'd decided not. I was also anticipating what might be accomplished today.

"Grandfather has never met a female shaman, nor heard of one in recent memory." That was saying something. "In the old ways and in some tribes today, women were sequestered during their time of the month so as not to disturb the males' power with their own. A woman gained her own special power through rituals surrounding her coming of age- the power that comes with the ability to bear children. She was taught the virtues that are associated with being a good woman."

Bonnie intently studied her shoes and then the bare trees out her window.

"You are cycling now," I tossed into the mix. Her face turned a furious red. "Don't feel embarrassed; you are mine just as surely as if you were an extension of my own body. I can sense what your body is doing," I left it at that.

"Does that mean you can read my mind?"

"Only if you leave it open to me, Kitten." The disconcert that came with that revelation curled sweetly in my gut- ah the lovely holistic Bonnie I was privy to. . .

Would grandfather follow the old ways? What if a woman had power to use, regardless of the time of the month, that did not interfere with a man's strength? I did not feel depleted by Bonnie- in fact, she spurred me to feel invincible, especially for the coming. . .

"I can block you from reading my mind?"
Had I opened a can of worms?

"Yes, Bonnie, it's simply a matter of
intent. I hope you aren't going to shut me out,"
I glowered at her.

She changed tactics, darn it. "I know
something of the life ways of the people, but
Riordan, I'm not of the people's blood. I have
other roots- Celtic ancestors."

"I know, Kitten. You are as white as they
come," I kissed her hand. "The Celts had their
shamans, Druids, many of them, women."

In order to distract her from her quandary,
I continued along the lines of female shamans.
"Grandfather has met female healers, medicine
women and heard of many others- also women
warriors, women chieftains. One in particular
interesting woman was a Cheyenne healer- Mary
Standing Soldier. She carried the claws of a
bear. You know bears are famous for healing
propensities?"

Bonnie nodded, all ears. "Well, it was told she killed this bear when she was very young. The Divine had a purpose in mind. In the late 1800's she would heal warriors fallen in battle with the U.S. cavalry. As she removed bullets, she would growl like a bear- gave her patients the strength to heal and rise. In general, she scared death right out of them. It was said as she grew older, she came to resemble a bear. Now that would have been a sight to come home to."

I began to laugh, Bonnie joined in- picturing a true bear hug welcome.

"Whether or not she actually did, who knows? Grandfather never…here we are." I was certain Bonnie didn't realize a lot of things, yet. I didn't want to spill the beans before their time, about ages.

I opened the passenger door for my apprehensive, but eyes-full-of-excitement student. Side by side we walked toward grandfather, when an unfamiliarity. . . Bonnie's fingers laced through mine.

"Surprise!" If I'd had my hackles on they would have been straight-up. She felt me bracing and started to disengage.

"Don't be mad, Riordan," she cringed.

Get with it, CatSkill, I mentally kicked myself for hurting her again, and refused to release her hand.

"It's alright, Kitten. You warned me." I brought our entwined hands to my lips and kissed the back of her hand. 'I love you,' I telepathed to her upturned face and the blush, but more important, the cognition in her eyes told me she'd heard.

Standing by a creek which together with an underground stream meandered down from the hills and eventually fed a sizeable lake (one of the reasons grandfather had acquired this piece of land long ago) Bonnie waited the explanation of her task.

"Prehistoric shamans considered where land meets water to be a liminal place- a means to go between worlds- a portal," Grandfather opened with. "Tell us what happened here."

Bonnie turned her head and then her body around, surveying the evergreens, cottonwoods, the tracks in the fading foliage and ground cover, the clouds above, tested the wind. I knew all her senses were engaged as if they were my own.

As a tracker, I could read the physical clues of a site for a certain period of time. Grandfather read a scene in visions throughout time, past and future. I wasn't as good at reading the distant past as I was more proficient in the here and now and prospective future in a particular location.

"When?" She asked.

Grandfather's eyes met mine and a smile lurked there. "How far back or forward can you go?"

"We disturbed a squirrel and a pair of ravens as we approached. The ravens flew east, the squirrel ducked into a cavity there," she pointed up a lodgepole pine. "This morning four deer single-filed through here to drink. Last night a weasel carrying a mouse tried to reach safety under those roots before an owl above and a trailing coyote could intervene. Before that. . ."

She went on to recount past exploits of coyotes, rabbits, antelope, squirrels, for a whole minute. Grandfather held up a hand.

"Well done, Granddaughter," he gave her the honorific, recognizing her as family. Silently we checked all of her points were in the past, no future predictions- but that might still come.

"In the time long before the cave painters were travelers between worlds- the worlds of spirits, the people communed with plants and animals and the Divine themselves. As groups of people grew in numbers, specializations developed. Soon communion with other beings, other worlds, was left to those called holy men. I prefer to call them shamans. These men, no offense, Granddaughter, it is presumptuous of me to say men," he shrugged.

"These men were supposed to use their divine-given skills to help their people- to locate animals for the hunt, plants for food and medicine, find the lost, heal the sick, pray to the Great Mystery for power to win battles, send good weather- help the people with whatever was needed. Many continued this for the good of all. Some became power-seekers for their own designs," grandfather sighed.

"The history of humans is filled with movement, usually not peaceful movement. I came from the east with my people to settle after many years in the west as Lakota. It has not been an easy task to put my peoples' needs first. But I have tried, except for one small period of time."

"As white men- missionaries, soldiers and assorted miscreants brought violence and forced changes on us, it became more difficult to retain the old shaman ways. We didn't seem able to help."

"My grandson had to continually hide to avoid being forced into a boarding school where a complete elimination of all 'Indian ways' was beaten into the young. All suffered for this-the loss of the young destroys the old."

"I did what I could to preserve, teach and heal those who suffered at that time. My training came from many holy men I met along the way-healers, shamans and the spirits in my vision quests kept me to my path."

"Riordan has studied and experienced around the world- his training is more cosmopolitan than mine. He has a most powerful guardian spirit. You know this."

Bonnie solemnly nodded. "For this guardian spirit to call you so completely to be together with my grandson. . . We believe you share this guardian. We know some of the purpose, too. But, not all. It will be revealed in good time. The spirits direct and call as they deem necessary. Not everyone listens. Grandson?"

"Yes," I stepped forward.

"Recently, you have begun to communicate silently with my granddaughter." I inclined my head in acknowledgement. "It is important you expand on that." And class was over for the day.

I knew Bonnie had snow-balled a monolithic pile of questions. She didn't know what to ask first.

"There's something you're not telling me," her first effort, and it was monumental. Go blank, CatSkill.

"There's a lot I'm not telling you. Look, just because you're a sixteen-year old genius doesn't mean you can have all the information at once."

"It's not that, it's something else important." She hinted again, much too canny for her own good.

"All your lessons will be important." Keep it up, CatSkill.

"I always like to learn ahead," she cajoled.

"Well this time you'll have to trust your instructors are giving you what you need when you need it- same as the spirits." I didn't think I'd phrased that quite right. Come on, CatSkill- you're dealing with an intuitive sprite here, remember?

I gave her a cockeyed grin, "There aren't exactly any good books out there on how to be a shaman." I could feel a 'but' coming on. To ward it off, I hastened on.

"Bonnie, you can't learn everything at one time. It takes years. It's a miracle your senses have developed as fast as they have without any training. The spirits must have designed you for something very special." Maybe that would hold her.

"Do all shamans change into. . .?" On eggshells, here.

"No," I admitted reluctantly. She wouldn't like that and I felt her apprehensive yearning.

"Look, Kitten. I'm still learning as old as. . ." Cut it, Catskill.

"As old as?" She relentlessly pursued.

"We'll leave that for another time." I felt like I'd entered a chess tournament, unprepared.

"Ok, then. What could you possibly still have to learn?"

Finally, I got a break- an easy question. "About love, for instance," I braked the jeep, shut it off and pulled her to me. "About loving you- a totally new and exciting prospect for me."

I kissed her lips, nuzzled at the fragrant skin over her jugular vein, licked up and down her petite white neck and then softly blew on the trail before another onslaught of questions from Bonnie, the over-achiever erupted.

"No fair," she barely whispered, returning my ardor.

Chapter 33

From the look on her face I was about to get hit with a big one. She didn't disappoint me.

"When will I get to see you change?" Bonnie gazed at me with great expectation.

"Change?" I hedged.

"Into my dream."

"So, you don't dream of me?" I quizzed as my mind buzzed.

"Nearly every night, but usually in another form- the male lion above my bed."

"Should I be jealous?"

"No, it is you," her green eyes glowed with love.

"Patience, my pet," I was very unsettled about approaching this conundrum.

At the school parking lot, I opened her door. She bounded out and began walking. I waited. She turned.

'Are you going to take my hand? I need the practice,' I telepathically communicated.

Her whole countenance lit up and she hurried back and grabbed my hand. As we walked to school, she began to swing our arms together. I gave her a rather firm no, in reproof.

She smiled in reply- 'just testing.' Great Spirit, help me, I implored. 'I heard that', she broke out laughing.

We did have two classes apart and when I was bored without her presence I checked in with her. Silent communication. A short distance, but nevertheless I saw her practically fall out of her chair the first time I sent a message.

"Perhaps, Mr. CatSkill, you could tell us what's so amusing?" The instructor asked.

I didn't hold back. I went on a short diatribe about how the English language was changing so fast, what with texting and such, that it seemed a shame to continue to analyze Latin and its effects on other languages.

'Meet me by the water fountain in the hall before lunch', I silently asked Bonnie after I was excused from Latin.

'Ok, Riordan', and as if she were next to me, I heard not only her but a couple girls who were walking with her. Ah, Kristin and Callie.

"Are you and Riordan hooked up. . .er, going steady?" Kristin was bursting for information.

"Well, I see him all the time." No lie there, I grinned, sure I'd enjoy this conversation between girls.

"Tell us. What's it like having the strongest, most attractive guy in school looking only at you?"

Yes, Bonnie, do tell, I thought to myself.

She was hedging a bit. "Hmmm. . . It's like, for the first time in my life, I have a best friend." I should close her off, this was almost an unkind eavesdrop. And what did those girls think about the 'best friend' part?

"Wow, I'd take a friend like him any day. I heard about the fight outside the ice cream parlor. To have a guy fight over you. . ."

"He wasn't fighting over me. Matt and his football goons were pushing their weight around-they started it," an irked Bonnie spit.

"Maybe so, but if there's a girl in the equation. . ." Callie trailed off.

Kristin broke in, "Lil's friend, Vera, is telling everyone she's going to take Riordan away from you."

Vera was one of those 'hell on heels' like Lil, correction, like Lil had been. She seemed happy with Rick now, and he was over the top.

"I…I guess." I felt Bonnie squirm.

'Kitten, I'd like to see her try,' I silently sent my vote of encouragement. Bonnie had just turned the corner, stumbled and dropped her books. At the same time, Vera sashayed to me.

I made sure to stay out of her arm's reach as I winked at a blushing Bonnie. 'After you called my name, Kitten, you didn't close yourself off,' I silently explained.

Scooping up Bonnie's books, I rose to, "Riordan." A seductive whisper and a murder of perfume assaulted me.

"Hey, Vera. Met my girl, Bonnie- we're going steady- in case you were wondering." I said this loud enough for everyone heading to the cafeteria to hear.

Putting my arm around my girl, I asked Callie and Kristin if they wanted to join us at our table. Rick and Lil, trays in hand, slowly sauntered over, winking and touching hips. I kicked up some chairs and they sat down.

"Hey, Riordan, Lil and I are going to Yellowstone for a weekend picnic and hang out around Old Faithful. Want to come?"

"You know, that sounds like fun- I guess I'll have to take a rain check, though, Bonnie's grounded." Every ear attached to every head within hearing distance honed in on us.

"Come again?" Rick was incredulous, positive he'd misheard.

"My girl's grounded," I stated and waited for the fun to begin.

"Not Miss Goody-Goody, straight-A student?" Lil chipped in, aghast. "What did you do?" She fastened her painted face on Bonnie.

"I was in the wrong place at the wrong time," Bonnie choked and blushed incriminatingly.

I winked at Rick. Bonnie put down her fish sandwich before she seriously choked at my antics. Callie and Kristin hankered for details, futilely.

Something else caught my drift. My eyes scanned the cafeteria. Matt, sporting a cast on his injured hand, was debating with his cagey clique.

"I say we go visit his girlfriend when her dad's away, maybe he'll get the message then," I read his lips, unnecessarily, for I heard every abhorrent word.

"Look, Matt. You need to chill out. No one wants to hurt the Road Runner." This sensible fellow's advice was shared among the rest.

"You guys are wimps," Matt snorted.

"No," I chimed in. I'd stealthily gained attendance on them. "It would seem your friends are actually achieving an education in this hallowed institution." I eyed the sensible ones, who respectfully nodded and skedaddled.

Every eye in the place was on us and I saw a teacher making his way in our direction. I leaned into Matt's personal space.

"If Bonnie suffers a single indisposition-anything from a split end to a lost button," I looked at him meaningfully, "I'm coming straight to you. It would behoove you to pray for her continued great health. Now, pretend you know the gist of good sportsmanship and shake."

I proffered my hand. The bright boy must have had a light come on in the dark, empty recess of his cranium. We shook.

"You shouldn't have given Rick and the others the impression. . ." Bonnie broke off, embarrassed.

"Impression?" I knew what was coming, but hey, I'm a guy.

"They'll think we're. . ."

"We're?"

"You're impossible," she grumbled, red-faced and moved away. A single long stride put me right next to her.

"Do you really care what they think?" I forced her to look at me. "Do you love me? I guess it's totally unfair of me to ask if you love me. You're not even out in the world. You're too young for this. . ."

"Riordan, I've been in love with you for as long as I can remember- you or the wild part of you has always been sort of an anchor in my life- a solid, good thing for me to hang on to."

"I know, Kitten. I feel what you're feeling. I was just being a guy. . . At some point in time we will be lovers, so, who cares if they believe it now? Do you want a ring from me to prove I'm serious?" There's an idea- I wasn't into jewelry, but maybe this was important to Bonnie, especially after the fiasco of her parents' marriage. I'd have to think on it.

"Do you believe I love you and that we are destined to be together?"

"Yes, Riordan," she quietly avowed with those intensely-verdant eyes.

"Then that's all that's important."

"Riordan?"

"Hmmm?"

"When?"

I kissed her, "When the time is right, Kitten."

Tuesday morning. "Hey, Gloomy Gus!"

"Hi, Riordan," she tried to smile. The dark rings were evident.

"Bad dreams, again?" I swore at myself. I should have checked on her last night. Grandfather and I had talked long into the night. But even distracted, I should have known. Something about swim class, I now realized, brought on a nightmare.

"Bonnie, do you only have this nightmare the night before swim class?"

"N...no, not always. I mean, yes, the night before swim but there have been other times." She sounded confused, the confusion of the exhausted.

"Think about what brings it on. We need to talk about this," I kissed the top of her head and ruffled her hair.

The only improvement to Bonnie's second swim lesson was the fit of her suit and that was a superb, mouth-watering improvement. She managed well in the shallow depths, but anything over four and a half feet disturbed her greatly.

"We'll have to address this dream and the source of your fears so you can progress. Even if you don't want to."

She nodded, anxiously agreeable. "All I remember after the dream is blackness. I'm afraid, and then there's nothing. I won't be at school tomorrow."

"Why not?" A day without Bonnie?

"My dad knows a rancher who's bought the horse of his dreams, except this stallion is not responding as the man wants him to."

"And you're going to 'talk to the animal'?" I broke out in the Doctor Doolittle tune, did a little shuffle step. She cracked up and joined me in a chorus.

Chapter 34

Here I am pacing on a limb, as a starling this time, above a round, pipe-gate corral, watching a furious black heathen proclaiming his superiority to all and sundry.

Mr. Lance had pulled up in his truck, escorting the horse trailer. Intros were made. The disillusioned rancher and his wife thanked him for coming.

They weren't sure what to make of my girl, but apparently her reputation preceded her. The rancher wasn't too pleased at having a tiny female on his ranch to 'address' his latest acquisition. His wife was a different story- what have you got to lose, I heard the good woman whisper to his disgruntled face.

Peter, the ranch owner, was ticked off at himself because he hadn't been able to decipher the stallion. Two lackadaisical ranch hands pretended to be busy even as they kept sneaking glances at the action.

"What do you want to do?" Peter grunted.

"I'll go in with him and just stand," Bonnie replied calmly- she understood the man's frustration.

"I'm not sure that's a good idea, Miss," Peter rubbed his chin.

'Bonnie,' I ventured in. She looked around, a smile playing about her lips. 'Up here, Kitten.' All silent communication.

'Riordan,' she nearly said aloud but checked herself and giggled slightly.

'You be careful. Talk to him outside the fence first.' She seemed to think over my suggestion. 'I mean it,' I warned, silently.

Bonnie walked the perimeter of the fence until she was away from the group of onlookers. The stallion retained her in his field of vision- which is a remarkable range and typical of prey animals.

She greeted the beast. 'I'll talk to you little person, but not your friend.' The horse tossed his head in my direction.

'Riordan, I'm closing you off.'

I telepathed, 'I'll be watching.' The rest she recounted to me later.

'Why did you not want him to listen?' Bonnie asked.

'Why is he so important to you? You could be dreaming of me.' There were no words to hear. Mr. Lance was used to his daughter's way with animals. The others just wondered what was going on.

'I've always belonged to him. I've never seen you in my dreams.' Bonnie cocked her head.

The horse stomped his foot. 'Come inside then, you'll be safe. It will be nice to talk to someone who understands.'

Bonnie climbed the rails. "Bonnie," her father called.

"It's OK, Dad."

"You going to let her in there? That beast has tried to trample me," the rancher fumed, worriedly.

"I trust my daughter. I've seen her work miracles. You've heard of her successes or you wouldn't have called," for all his acceptance of the situation, Mr. Lance carried his worry well.

Bonnie stood inside the fence rails. She told the stud her name. He preferred to be called Handsome.

'The man who owns this ranch has always wanted a horse like you- you are magnificent.' She eyed every facet of his physiognomy, long trained in judging horseflesh from her father and their small broodmare operation.

'He doesn't want a black stallion. He wants a black slave. He thinks I'm the run-of-the-mill nag who'll put up with rowel spurs, a saddle slapped on my back, a curb bit yanked in my mouth while his weight slams into my kidneys. Not to mention he stinks.'

'Has he ridden you?' Bonnie interrogated.

'Are you kidding? I've seen how he works his other slaves. He tried once- not happening again. Now you smell nice,' the stallion slowly, peacefully walked close to Bonnie. 'You're friend is lucky.' The horse extended his muzzle, 'Real nice.' He nuzzled Bonnie's shirt tails.

I felt like an expectant father pacing and watching from my limb. If that wise-ass horse made an untoward move, he'd end up as 'cat' food.

'May I touch you,' Bonnie asked. The stallion agreed and came closer, rested his head at Bonnie's chest. The rancher was scratching his head, his wife sighed and smiled. I felt some better, though I preferred he wasn't that close to Bonnie's curves. But he was a misunderstood being, after all.

Bonnie's right hand rose to caress his huge jaw, then up to his ear which he lowered for her. She stroked under his mane, down his neck. They broke contact; she moved to his other side and scratched his withers. He nuzzled her in reciprocity.

'Why don't you take me home with you?'

'I could never afford to buy you from him- he'd probably not let you go. He not only wants to ride you, he also wants to bring you lots of girlfriends,' Bonnie assured.

'I'd be better off with you,' the stallion whiffled.

'I'll talk to him.'

The rancher balked and kicked up a fuss as Bonnie reiterated what the stallion liked and disliked. "He's very spirited and proud- the reasons you wanted him to begin with," she attempted to reason with the male brick fence.

"No spurs, no curb, be easy saddling. . .you telling me I bought a pansy for a stud horse? And what's this, he doesn't like the way I smell business?"

"Handsome. . ."

"How did you come up with that name? We call him by his registered name, Stark Nite."

"He prefers to be called, Handsome. I believe it's your cologne and laundry detergent that he's objecting to, he has a sensitive nose."

"Bull, I'll show him. . ."

"Peter!" But the man thought he was being made fun of- a joke at the expense of 'his' horse. He pulled a rope and whip from the top fence rail and made to enter the corral.

The stallion began to pace, snaking his neck, laying back his ears and baring his teeth. Bonnie scrambled over the rails, dropped into the ring and put herself between the angry rancher and Handsome. Her father was close behind.

"Get out of my way," Peter seethed.

"No, you're not going to touch this horse with those weapons." I was considering a change of body styles, when all at once I knew what she was doing. The stallion did, too. He quit pacing and stood behind his champion.

The rancher, on the other hand, was perplexed. Mr. Lance stopped his progress. Bonnie's eyes never left the rancher's but, yes, she was entrancing him without a single lesson in that department. I was in awe.

The man instantly calmed- good thing, too. Mr. Lance's frown and my alert self were quite ready to run a rescue at Peter's shenanigans.

"Listen to me," Bonnie intoned, magically. "What did you pay for him?"

"I should have known the price was too good to be true- they must have had him drugged. $4500."

"Let's go back outside the gate and talk," Bonnie soothed. And as if he were sleepwalking, the rancher exited the ring.

Outside, he seemed to wonder how he got there. His wife put a hand on his arm. Bonnie waved her father out of hearing. I saw Mr. Lance roll his eyes, study his daughter and feel his chest pocket.

"Peter, I'll give you what you paid for him, write a check right now."

Still under a 'spell', the rancher eyed the rope and whip in his hand as if he'd picked up a snake. "Jim, I'd feel responsible if anything happened."

"If I ride him, will you sell?" Bonnie ceased the mesmerizing- the man had to decide of his own accord.

"Yes," said the wife and Peter nodded, at odds with himself.

'Bonnie, I wish you wouldn't.' But she wasn't listening to me.

Back in with the shiny, black stud, she went. She asked permission to sit on him and maybe, go for a ride. The beast seemed extremely pleased with his savior. Bonnie climbed to the top of the fence, away from the bystanders, and beckoned the horse close. He stood perfectly still as a gentleman while Bonnie eased herself onto his back. Her fingers twined in his mane.

She pictured a walk and he set off. Bonnie was beautifully balanced and at ease with Mr. Pompous- I had to admit they made a splendid couple. After getting a feel for each other, she pictured a trot. They circled the ring, floating. Mr. Lance wore a huge grin, proud of his daughter. The rancher was abashed and his wife totally relieved.

The stallion picked up a smooth canter, once around, then a flying change of lead and the opposite direction. Showing off, he collected himself for a transition to halt. Bonnie praised the big fellow and he ate it up. She slid to the ground, scratched his withers, took a peppermint from her pocket, unwrapped it and offered the candy. His ears perked, arching his neck he politely accepted the morsel.

Mr. Lance handed over a check. Reluctantly, the rancher took it.

"Do you have time to talk to…er, see about my cat, Miss Priss? She's inside. I'll make sandwiches and coffee," the wife hopefully inquired.

"Bonnie, I nearly fell off my perch when Miss Priss suggested they bring some mice in the house for her to hunt," I was laughing uproariously, picturing that rancher doing such.

"Riordan, she doesn't like the cold," Bonnie snickered, too.

"At least she doesn't mind the rancher's smell. . ." I went off again.

Chapter 35

It made good financial sense, I equivocated with myself. With four and a half girlfriends, the stallion would pay himself off. Bonnie could prove he was promotable and the Lance homestead had an extra corral to keep the beast away from the other horses.

Except for one thing, well, two. I was spending Saturday building a run-in shelter (the beast didn't like stalls, either) with Bonnie's father, and now she'd have to spend extra time with the beast- time away from me. I wanted her to use her talents- heck, maybe I'd cadge a ride.

After all, we had a common interest. And I had to remember, whereas I could change into other forms, he remained a horse. I wasn't jealous.

Bonnie provided stew and homemade biscuits for two hungry construction workers. "Any cookies, Kitten?"

"My dad's beginning to complain that you get more cookies than he does," she joked to me and her father grinned ruefully.

"Riordan, you're a god-send. Can't thank you enough for helping me."

"You're welcome, sir. I do smell something- not cookies?"

"I made pies today- lemon crème and banana crème." And they were both fantastic.

Night had settled before we finished dessert. I suggested a little sky watching from the roof. The Pink Lady and her courtiers weren't out initially, so we lay side-by-side companionably, waiting the show.

"You were fascinating to observe- the way you handled everybody. Did you realize you were entrancing the rancher?"

"I knew something was happening, coming through me to help. I thought it was you, Riordan."

"No, Kitten, you were on your own, totally in tune with your guardian spirit."

"I couldn't let him hurt Handsome."

"Your guide beat me to the punch- literally."

"Would you have gone at him as a starling?" She giggled.

"Didn't get that far. You're being taken care of by more than grandfather and me. I don't think you realize just how in tune you are." We stayed quiet for a while. I felt Bonnie recounting the events of the other day.

I know I'd asked this before. "Are all animals as easy for you to talk to?"

"I've not spoken to all yet. Most seem happy to talk. Probably, like people, though, not everyone cares to. Riordan, will you kiss me?"

"I thought it might be nice, if you come over here." My hands were under my head. I wanted her to initiate first contact. Check my reaction.

Mountain lions are solitary creatures, except for the male-female mating interlude. In general, I'd always settled for solitude, venturing into company to help someone or if I were called upon. Or a brief episode with a willing partner. Otherwise, I was a free spirit- never felt lonely.

Discovering Bonnie had changed this for me and I would be with her for always- gratefully with her. I didn't want to hurt her feelings by drawing away if she reached for me. This left practicing as a most enjoyable option.

Bonnie hesitantly leaned over me, rested her hands on my chest. My bracing reaction, I noticed, was shrinking. My hands found her waist and pulled her on top. All senses were raring to go, firing tumultuously as her lips lowered to mine. Her sweet mouth, with a hint of lemon, sent me reeling into another dimension.

I opened my eyes. The Pink Lady bounded about in flowing approval. Reluctantly, I ended our embrace. "You need to get to bed, Kitten. Sunday school, tomorrow, remember?"

"Granddaughter, I differentiate medicine men and women, holy men, healers, from shamans this way. The others can commune with plants, animals, spirits and the Creator. A shaman extends his expertise by traveling across space, time, dimensions and between worlds. A shaman can adopt a body to suit a particular situation. Riordan takes many forms. He is very comfortable in those, but he has a preference." Grandfather studied Bonnie, waiting her reaction.

"My guardian spirit is the red hawk; I am at home communing in his body. The training for this transformation generally takes years with an older, more experienced shaman advising, chaperoning vision quests and interpreting dreams. Your talents are coming out by virtue of your own guardian spirit. You are at home with animals. I want you to extend this talent to understanding people around you on an innate level. You can offer healing energies as you see fit."

"I don't understand, Grandfather," Bonnie said.

"Give me your hand," Bonnie placed her hand in his. "Feel as if you are part of the sun, earth, the air and water. At one with all plants, rocks, everything about you. Allow yourself to feel the energies surrounding you. Once you are comfortable, channel what you feel to my hand. Open yourself up and allow your body to be a conduit."

I began to feel Bonnie's body experimenting. She tried too hard. 'Don't try, Kitten, allow,' I encouraged. I knew when she had it. I felt the stream coursing through her system.

Grandfather smiled and nodded as his palm tingled. "Increase the power," he instructed. As the flood gates opened, his eyes widened imperceptibly. It was a fusion of hands- a powerful welding together.

"Now, less." Within seconds, she stemmed the tide. "Now, cease." And she did.

"You can set with your intent how this will most benefit the patient you wish to help. Come spring, we will teach you the healing plants," Grandfather released her hand.

He allowed her a moment to assimilate and we enjoyed the wonder on her face.

"Your homework is for both of you to practice communication over greater distances than neighboring class rooms. It is very important you excel at this without any interference. We haven't time to send you on a vision quest, but you can practice meditation- complete stillness and receptivity. Listen for what the Divine may be telling you- it doesn't matter if you don't understand- remember, and we'll discuss. It is now time for you to see the transformation."

I cautioned grandfather; I was not ready to expose Bonnie to the potential danger of my wild side. We followed him to a clearing and he moved off to stand alone. Bonnie trembled in anticipation.

Instantaneously, grandfather transformed the cells of his body into his namesake. A red tail hawk soared. The rustle of his wings, dancing on air, ascended as the hawk rose higher and circled the clearing. He banked, keeping an eye on the two humans below.

Bonnie's face was aglow, unsurprised, but thrilled. The red hawk hovered before us and then faster than a blink of the eye, grandfather was standing with us again. Bonnie clapped her hands, laughing.

"I'd like you to join us for our winter solstice group- if only for the evening session."

"I'll ask my dad. Hopefully, he'll let me come after chores are done. School will be out for Christmas."

"That reminds me, Granddaughter. Riordan and I want you to have Christmas dinner with us." She promised to ask her father.

Grandfather admonished me to answer all Bonnie's questions-a monumental task. He also reminded her to jot down scenes from meditations or dreams that she didn't understand and to expand our communication distance. Sunday school was over.

Her interrogation rained in earnest on the way home. "When do you think I might be able to change? Are you sure I will be able to?"

"It will happen when it happens." A cryptic response.

"Do I have control?" She badgered.

"Usually not so much the first time- it's important to listen to grandfather and me. Be patient. We will help you to be ready."

"Does grandfather transform into other creatures?"

"He prefers the red hawk," I acknowledged.

"But you?"

"I'm content in and enjoy other forms– a good thing, too. Can you see a mountain lion prowling around your home with Sticker and Stalker on guard?"

"Ooh, and the horses and chickens. . ."

"Exactly."

"When will you change for me? When will you show me the cougar?"

"I don't know," I hedged. But, it would have to be soon.

"There it is again," Bonnie's forehead wrinkled.

"What, Kitten?"

"I can sense there is something you're not telling me." An understatement.

"All in good time," I promised her frustration. I parked outside the Lance cabin, escorted Bonnie to her door and kissed away the remaining questions.

Chapter 36

"What do you sense?" We had stopped at the library to check grandfather's web site for a final count on who was coming for his winter solstice class and to see if there was a response from Sedona concerning Grace Esperanza. Fourteen for the first and nothing from Sedona.

I felt Bonnie's examination of the few library inhabitants. "Pretend they're animals outside if that helps, eventually you'll be able to read those who are in need."

"The librarian." Bonnie looked up at me.

'Silent Kitten, we are in a library after all. What about her?' Bonnie frowned slightly. 'Don't try, allow,' I instructed.

'She twisted her ankle. The doctor says she should stay home, rest, prop up her foot, but she needs to work.' A fairly easy surmise- the woman was limping and pain decorated her features. So I intended to make it more difficult.

'Where did she fall? How? When?' No response initially, then Bonnie's eyes heralded her success.

'She fell two days ago from a step stool trying to reach a can. . .a can of peaches pushed to the back of the cabinet over the stove. As she stepped down, it was wrong. Her ankle almost broke, but she caught herself- a bad sprain. She's taking ibuprofen sparingly. She's against pain medicine. I'm right, right?'

'I guess I'll take you out for ice cream before going home. How are you going to help her?'

'I can do this across distance?' My student asked.

I grinned encouragement, 'It's the same principle- intend and allow.'

Bonnie's body opened to the energies around her and she swept the librarian with a gentle frequency that gradually increased. Two minutes, five, the flow of energy came through my girl unimpeded. Remarkable focus of intention for a first attempt on her own.

Bonnie's spirit guide recommended a break and slowly she brought the healing energy to an end. The pain lines on the librarian's face eased and she was tentatively moving as if something too good to be true had happened.

'Is it all better, Riordan?'

'You tell me, Kitten.' I loved watching her concentration.

'N…no. I'll work on her again tonight and.
. .tomorrow morning, at lunch,' she crunched her
features listening to the inner voice. 'After
tomorrow night, she'll be fine.'

I kissed the top of her tawny head which
earned a reprimanding frown of disapproval from
the same librarian.

On the way out, Miss Inquisition started.
"I'm not invading personal space by doing this, am
I?"

"How do you feel about pain?" Coyote
teaching.

"I don't want anyone to hurt."

"If your intentions are good, how can you go
wrong?"

"It's not necessary to be asked? Do you
often help those you see?"

"Yes. I'm called to remedy some situations
by the Divine-as I stay open to that power and to
my spirit guide, always. Who's to say that those
I help without being asked aren't put in my sphere
to aid of my own accord?" I shrugged.

I hesitated to confide another aspect, but she needed to know. "There are those who wear pain like a mantle because they are averse to change. They prefer to receive others sympathy and to be catered to ad infinitum. If you try to help a person like this, it's possible your energy will be thrown back at you. If this happens to you, don't be alarmed or think you're doing something wrong. Recognize it for what it is and let it go."

"That's sad," Bonnie shook her head.

"Everyone has their own path to walk- don't be sad."

"Are there shamans who do not have good intentions? Who use the energy or spirits to harm others?"

"Yes," I grudgingly admitted.

"Have you ever met one?"

"No." Not yet.

We enjoyed ice cream cones on the way to Bonnie's. "I will be away for a time."

"Away," she almost dropped what was left of her ice cream.

"I've been called north."

"How long?" At a loss.

"I don't know." There was never a set time; I stayed until I'd finished whatever needed doing.

"Will it always be like this, Riordan? You receive a call and must go?"

"I'll be back, Kitten." I took her hand, squeezed very gently- she was still fragile to me and would be until. . .

"I know. I'll miss you," she studied her shoes.

"Someday, when you've learned to travel and we're married, you can go with me."

"M…married?" I chuckled; she'd completely overlooked the 'learn to travel' part.

"You can always reach me. Practice communication over distance as grandfather advised. I'll return before the winter solstice class. Grandfather will take you to school and probably conduct Sunday school without me."

I chucked her under her chin and lightly kissed her good-by. "This will be a nice opportunity for you to focus on your classmates. Have lunch with our group. Find those who might need help- in any form. Call me."

I winked and left a dejected Bonnie at the cabin. Handsome nickered for her. 'Take care of my girl,' I told him.

'Gladly,' he snorted.

'Bonnie, are you awake?' I slipped into her dream.

'Riordan, where are you?' I felt her stretching. She'd been napping, but not seriously.

'I'm at the Lakota reservation.' We'd been three days apart. I was surprised just how long those three days were. 'Did you try to call me?'

'Yesterday, but I didn't get an answer. I thought I was doing it wrong or you were busy.'

'Very busy.' I didn't apologize. I knew she did not expect one.

'Can you tell me how it's going?'

Why not? 'I'm working with a group of young people and some adults who aren't interested in drugs and alcohol; they would like to purge their lands of these substances. This is hard, similar to city kids, because many of their peers have succumbed. The elderly aren't always given proper respect; youth ignores lessons. I'm seen as someone more their own age. My white blood doesn't help, but my other talents more than compensate. Medicine men and women have also made inroads by advocating the 'Sun Dance'. You know of this?'

'Yes, a renewal of faith with the earth and Creator through a powerful ritual.'

'It's a very potent ceremony. Those who join in pledge to keep their bodies clean. Encouragement is needed by those preparing and those too young to participate, but who are looking forward to joining, and those in-betweens. Then, of course, there are circumstances beyond their control- drug dealers.

The Lakota, historically, have never believed in killing cats. Cats are thought to have especially powerful magic and to possess the ability to cast spells. Harming a cat invites a curse. You can imagine the respect I accrue here.

Now and then I appear and wipe out the current drug pushers- usually an appearance suffices to drive them insane. My group is at peace for a while. My greatest confidence lies in that the size of this group continues to increase. They can help each other through the maelstrom of indignities of those high and drunk around them.'

'You sound tired. Rest, Riordan.' The comfort in her tone had me wishing. . .

'You make me feel lighter. I intend to find a quiet place to sleep. Bonnie, don't worry about me. . .too much.'

'Grandfather says I should not trouble myself over you. I love you, Riordan. I'll always worry a bit when you're away.'

I laughed softly into her dream. 'Get some rest, Kitten. I'll call, no, you call, soon. I want to hear what you've been doing.'

'Is there a better time to call?'

'Early. Good night, Bonnie.'

'Riordan, I'm very proud and grateful to have you in my life,' she whispered.

'Ah, Kitten. I love you.'

I'd managed to get a few hours of rest and woke to an intriguing idea. 'Bonnie, don't be startled.'

I watched her feet stir under the covers- a smile curled those delicious lips. Her arms hugged her pillow tighter. For the first time in my life, I considered the pros and cons of transforming into a pillow.

'Kitten, open your eyes.'

'I can see you with my eyes closed.'

I laughed. 'Then open your eyes for a nice surprise.'

She squealed. 'Bonnie, your father,' I warned.

'He's gone.' And she was out of the bed, flinging herself into my arms. I had no choice but to catch her or she would have flown over her desk and out the window. I expected the bristling reflex from the force of her initiating contact. Instead, a warmth flooded me as I realized I wasn't bracing, no hackles rising. My body was recognizing its own. At least as a human.

Being close to a female never felt so good and this wasn't just any girl- Bonnie was mine. My hands gently clasped her as close as I could. I felt the soothing warmth of her naturally scented skin. Her pajamas consisted of a t-shirt which had ridden up as we hugged.

"How did you get here?" We spoke aloud.

"It's a type of travel you'll learn about," I grinned into her face.

"You mean you came right from the reservation?" She gazed back at me in wonder.

"You might say in the blink of an eye." Her eyes brightened with the implications of my 'traveling'. I'd thought she'd known, apparently not.

"Are you here to stay?"

"No. I have to go back. I just thought to surprise you."

"This is a wonderful surprise," she threw her arms around my neck- got her fingers tangled in my hair and we both laughed.

A few kisses later, our breathing patterns headed into race mode. I pulled away.

"You better get some clothes on, Kitten. This is way too dangerous."

"Dangerous?" She began to blush and pulled her shirt down, to no avail. Don't look, CatSkill, I warned myself.

"Bonnie, you're grown up enough and I'm in love enough to want you," my eyes bore sultrily into hers. Discomfited, she hastily pulled on some jeans.

Chapter 37

"Red Hawk is early." I heard Bonnie say to her father just as she opened the door.

"Your bus driver awaits you, my lady," I bowed.

"Riordan!" And she was in my arms as I straightened, laughing and holding me tight- well, as tight as a tiny girl could. Again, there was no detonating reprisal from my body, but a recognition of Bonnie as part and parcel of me.

I was careful of my hand placement and the strength of my holding her. I welcomed the time-to-come when she changed into my mountain lion mate. Her ability to change would herald an increased strength in her body. Although she would always be tiny, there'd be less chance of my inadvertently cracking one of her ribs.

I greeted Mr. Lance and saw a momentary flash of pain in his features- not just a father about to lose his daughter. Our reunion was much more exuberant than when he returned home. I intended to approach this with Bonnie at some point today.

"Chores all done, Kitten?"

"Yes," she beamed whole-heartedly.

Mr. Lance shook my hand, "Successful trip, Riordan?"

"Yes, sir." He wasn't one to pry, but I felt he'd be interested in the edited version of my trip to the reservation. "I'm working with a group of young people who aren't into substance abuse. They'd much rather become independent and educated in their history and participate in their own cultural ceremonies. Grandfather thought they might be more amenable to me because of my age." Don't laugh, CatSkill.

"I'm trying to bring a happy medium between age groups. Help them learn to listen and support each other. As in the old days."

"Sounds like a challenge," Mr. Lance offered.

"Very much so. The light hair doesn't help."

"Hmmm," he rubbed his chin. "I guess you could always dye it, but on second thought, with those eyes. . ." He shook his head, rested a hand on Bonnie's shoulder, "Study hard, honey."

"Your father misses a closeness with you even if you've never been real close. I know it's hard with him being gone so much, but it makes good sense for you to attempt to spend quality time together when he is home. He really loves you; he's also a fair enough man to see I'm not a threat to him."

Bonnie clammed up, slightly embarrassed. Not meaning to, I'd come across a little too parental. And she read my thoughts.

"I've always known my dad had to work sometimes far from home. I don't think he's aware of how lonely I get when he's gone. I've never told him- didn't want to burden him further. Itinerant ranch hand, blacksmith, farrier jobs- he works hard."

I took her hand, gently massaged it with my thumb. "I know, Kitten. It's time now to tell him these things- explain to him just as you did to me." Her eyes were glistening; she didn't trust her voice, but she annoyed her bottom lip and nodded.

To brighten her a bit, "Tell me about school."

"Oh." The tone of that 'oh' spoke volumes.

"C'mon, cough it up."

Exhaling loudly in protest, "The conversations at school were: Where's Riordan? What's he doing? When is he coming back?- constantly."

I laughed- to be expected, I knew. "No problems with Matt?"

"No, he did ask me out, but I told him you'd be back and I wasn't interested in anyone else. After the second week, everyone began to look at me kind of strange." She fiddled with a notebook.

"Why is that?" I knew; I wondered if she did.

"Kristin, Callie, Rick and Lil, I think they felt sorry for me. They thought you weren't coming back," her shoulders rose and fell. In opening herself to others, Bonnie was learning to read the subtle innuendos that a coterie of people were often rife with. I patted her knee.

"I helped Kristin and Callie with homework problems. Another girl at lunch, Sandy, was having headaches- you know, I think she realized I was taking away her pain. She's at our table now and her brother, Carl and cousin, Char."

"Sounds like we have a bigger table. You knew I'd return, right? You didn't let them get you down?"

"I coped." So their comments had bothered her some. Wait 'til Monday.

"Granddaughter, do you see yourself in your dreams?" Class began.

"Sometimes, but not in another form," Bonnie wasn't too thrilled with this confession.

"Nothing you need interpreted?"

"No, Grandfather. Usually, I'm watching Riordan. . .er, the cougar, and lately, the red tail hawk is often in my dreams, too, sailing high overhead."

'Her protectors,' I telepathed to Grandfather.

"Grandfather, when will I be able to travel as Riordan does and transform into my. . ." She eagerly sought the answer to this question even though she felt hesitant in asking.

"You will have to wait for your guide to tell you- it may take a long time or. . .perhaps you have fears that interfere with these changes. Perhaps the appropriate time is awaited. There is no forcing if the Great Spirit asks you to be patient."

Bonnie's contrite gaze fell. "Don't be discouraged, Kitten."

"How long, Grandfather, before you. . .were able to transform?"

"Everyone is different, Granddaughter." He listed the progress of Bonnie's talents- the awakening of all her senses, the strengthening of her healing, the rather abrupt feminine changes in her body.

She was half-heartedly listening when something occurred to her. "What if I'm not a shaman? Maybe I'm a medicine woman."

Grandfather smiled indulgently, "Granddaughter, I've seen you as a shaman."

"Really?" This brightened her, until another question popped into play. "Grandfather, how old are you? Sometimes the way you say. . ." Grandfather and I exchanged thoughts. "Something I've been missing, isn't there?"

"How old do you think I am?"

"I'm not good with ages. Maybe 45, it seems as if you've never changed- I remember you the same as when I was little." She tilted her head, studying grandfather.

"I'm not good with ages, either. Near as I can figure," he hesitated. "Near as I can figure, I'm 300 years of age in human counting."

Bonnie was very still- almost to the point of not breathing still. "Do you live forever?" She whispered.

"My life span is completely up to me at the behest of the Great Spirit. My people came from the east- driven by stronger tribes until we eventually called the Black Hills, Paha Sapa, and the northern plains our Lakota home. I allowed my body to settle on the age I seem to you now. I can become older if I choose, but I cannot become younger."

"Do your powers increase as you age?"

"Not necessarily. Age is not important. It is what I, you and my grandson do with our lives to improve other lives- that is what is important. You have a fear lurking inside of you-this bad dream. . ."

But Bonnie had completely tuned out. She was staring at me. "Y…you're not 17? Are you?" I shook my head. "18?"

"No." Before she swooned and hit the floor I was on my knees before her, steadying her.

"Breathe, Bonnie," I placed my hand on her thigh. Her whole body began to tremble; her face paled and tiny drops of sweat appeared upon her upper lip.

I picked her up and carried her outside the cabin. Found a sheltered copse to be alone with her and I rocked her on my lap.

"Bonnie, if you're OK with my being- becoming a mountain lion, traveling through time, why does my age bother you?"

It took a few minutes, but the calming energy through my body contacting with hers, the rocking as if she were a baby, and actually, compared to grandfather and me, she was a baby- rooted in her system. Bonnie's tremors dwindled.

She pulled away and with great reluctance, I let her go. She scrambled to sit opposite me, to watch me as her questions formed and as she asked- to judge my response, as if I could lie to her.

"H...how old are you?" She finally managed.

"I've no concrete evidence of my birthdate. Probably between 150-170 years. My body has rested in the prime of manhood, somewhere between 18-25 years," I cast nonchalantly.

"You're not really a high school senior?" Her blanched face whitened further.

"No, but you knew that?" As much as I wanted to engulf her in my arms, I had to allow her space, time to come to terms. . .

"I don't know what I know," she grimaced. "Grandfather said I called you here. Why did you sign up at school?"

I smirked, "I think Grandfather arranged that. One, to meet you and two, to renew interesting lessons. My life is not restricted or defined by human years. In your dreams, you've seen me in different places. Somewhere inside you, there was a glimmer that I was not exactly 17 or 18. I remember you thought it was ultra-romantic in the movie. . ."

Her head fell into her hands and she plied that lower lip- something I ached to relieve her of. On the one hand, she was still stunned. On the other, she was processing, trying to fathom an age mystery.

"Bonnie, if your perception of me has altered, I'm still a man- the same man who's kissed you, befriended you, fallen in love with you," I put all of my boyish appeal on.

"Are you a man, physically. . .?" She blushed.

"Very much so. I wasn't joking about wanting you," my eyes donned what is termed 'bedroom eyes'.

"You can marry and, and have children?" The blushes intensified.

"Children are important to you?" An aspect of loving I'd not considered.

"N…not now, but m…maybe someday."

A relief, she did see us together in the future. She was not denying that. "I can make love with you and we can have children together. It's all a matter of intent and the design of the Great Spirit, of course. Not all couples have kids."

Had there ever been a male-female shaman couple that produced children? I was quiet for a moment- my mountain lion guide was addressing me. I smiled at Bonnie. "That is a decision we must make together. After we're married."

I watched her speculatively. The wheels in her brain working hard, digesting unexpected information. "It's time to get you home, Kitten. You know, most girls enjoy the attention of a somewhat older, attractive male," I tried to bring a bit of levity into the proceedings.

"I…I'm sorry. I seem to be overreacting. I…I never really, didn't think. . ." she broke off in confusion.

"Don't apologize," I extended my hand, "C'mon. I need to get you home or your father will have my hide." She wasn't having any of my levity. What now, spirits?

Bonnie slept fitfully that night; the woodpecker kept vigil as she tossed and turned. I ruminated on whether or not I'd have a girlfriend to take to school in the morning.

The unlooked for prospect, miracle, of being in love with her had made my life more fully enjoyable in so many ways I'd never imagined. I couldn't understand why my age unnerved her. An idea came to me near morning as I saw her father drive off.

"Good morning, Kitten." She wasn't running into my arms, but she wasn't running away, either.

"You don't perchance think of me as a father figure, do you, with this age business?" Please say no, I prayed. I put all my young male, rico suave into the look I gave her. My eyes swept her curves, longingly, lovingly.

"No. I'm h…having a hard time with the idea of you wanting me- as young as I am. Even in physical appearance you're quite a bit older than me," she tentatively replied.

"Is that all? You think I won't. . ." A relieved howl (wrong species, but what the heck) burst from me. "Bonnie, Bonnie, Bonnie you gave me such a fright."

I picked her up and swung her around in pure delight, set her down, tilted up her chin and into those glorious green, gold-glint eyes, now wet with about to overflow tears, I professed my unwavering, undying love and followed my declaration with a kiss that vouchsafed my integrity and desire.

Chapter 38

It was time. Although grandfather's reassurances were echoing in my brain, my misgivings refused to give up center stage. Bonnie wasn't pressing me, for which I was thankful, but my spirit guide was eager to meet his future mate. Time to let the cat out of the bag, so to speak.

I mentally rehearsed his words. "She needs to know everything. She must be prepared for Chac's coming."

"I realize that," I grimaced.

"Grandson, do you think she'd be less afraid if the jaguar simply sneaks up on her? She needs to see and believe in all that you are."

Considering the girl sitting next to me in the movie theater, the one who thought falling in love with a vampire was the ultimate romance, well, let's see, I also needed to know what she thought of her own personal fairy tale and not some Hollywood artist.

Our small group of friends had snowballed in my absence. It seemed most of the students were helloing, nodding, high fiving and jostling to find enough chairs to pull into our lunch sphere. Bonnie's new aura of openness attracted all and sundry-having the local bad boy as her returned escort was not a hindrance, either.

Even the designer kids were expressing interest. I was sure their parents would not follow suit. Vera had ceased her claims of stealing me away from Bonnie and she and Lil were the leaders of the society section of our table.

The entire basketball team sans Sam tossed out suggestions about double dating and group excursions- as soon as Bonnie was no longer grounded. I guessed it would be beneficial to see if Mr. Lance was ready to release my girl in the name of propitiating friendships.

When she wasn't at my side, Bonnie walked the halls with a new semblance of self-assurance, of being part of the senior class- no longer the pseudo-outcast walking with blinders on.

The lunch group questioned me about my meetings with the Lakota youth, even wondered if there was some way they might help. Many of our new friends wanted to meet the Native Americans, too. I'd study on this seriously, because unlike the government or most missionaries of the past, these high school students had no ulterior motives.

They listened intently to the problems on the reservation. A lot of the issues coincided with their own lives in one way or another. Questions were shot at me about culture, history and how some of the problems started. I left them brainstorming as I escorted Bonnie to our next class.

"My dad will be away most of the week of the 21st. He's taking off the week of Christmas and New Year's; he's arranged his schedule, provided there are no emergencies."

"Think he'll be home on that Saturday?" I asked.

"Maybe not until Sunday."

"If he is back by Saturday, maybe you can join our sweat lodge. Be good for you. And if not, we'd better arrange one just for you."

She squeezed my hand, "I'd like that experience."

"A sweat lodge can open one to interesting messages from Spirit, if your intent is to listen."

Bonnie nodded. Yes, a sweat lodge ceremony seemed like the ticket for this shaman-in-the making. In traditional shamanic or medicine training, sweat lodges- purification rituals and vision quests were de rigueur.

Bonnie had missed so much, yet her progression was remarkable. But, hey, the spirits were in charge, after all. She was so accepting, eager and anxious to progress further and never complained. I never doubted the spirits knew what they were about.

"I'm going to suggest to my dad that we do something together, just the two of us."

"Good girl. Remember you're having Christmas dinner with grandfather and me. Dessert's on you," I challenged.

"I figured as much," she grinned up at me.

"Race you to that ledge there," I pointed to what seemed an unsurpassable rock-strewn cliff.

"Somehow, I don't think that's a fair race- I bet you've been up there many times," Bonnie baited me.

"OK, I'll give you a head start," I rolled my eyes in concession.

"What about lessons today?"

"I'm the instructor for the day."

Bonnie spent about a minute divining the best route up and then without a get ready, get set, she bounded off. I stood rooted, watching her graceful, slender body negotiate and then click onto my own covert path that wandered up.

When she was half way up, focused and intent on reaching the finish line first, I put my long legs to work and silently fell in sync with her, guiding her in between and around the last few obstacles to a hidden crevasse.

"A cave," she murmured, excited.

Turning sideways, I made my way through the narrow entrance. I held my hand out for her and she easily breeched the opening. I pulled her along for several steps until the outside light was completely blocked.

"You OK?"

"As long as you have my hand. It's awfully dark."

"Just a little further," I encouraged and pulled a lantern from a recess and by feel and use of my night vision, I opened the glass, lit the wick. A soft, warm glow caressed the cavern.

"This has always been a sacred place to grandfather and recently to me. It's one of the reasons he has a cabin near." Through Bonnie's eyes, I saw this place of magical wonder anew. I would never tire of coming here.

This was now my favorite spot to be alone and commune with other worlds- in which case it was a misnomer to call being here, being alone. The old adage, in solitude one is least alone, was apropos on many levels. Was that really Lord Byron's surmise?

Bonnie was immediately drawn to the cave's art work. I released her hand to let her explore. Where four hand prints in red pigment were lined up, she raised her own hand to test for similarity of size.

I hadn't thought of this- the prints were way too small for grandfather or me. Bonnie's right hand fit perfectly. If I weren't so accustomed to spirit ways, I would have had chills up my back.

"Riordan?"

"What do you make of the prints, Bonnie?"

"It's as if I could have done this, but. . ." she stopped, puzzled. "How old are these?"

"The age business, again," I chuckled.

"I'm glad I amuse you. I'm serious, tell me about them."

"I can't say how old they might be. I know they were here when grandfather first found this cave- he told me. Picture this, Kitten. What if the prehistoric cave painters of Europe-the shamans, what if they were able to travel here and these are their prints?"

"Is it so, Riordan?" Her eyes were avidly interested.

"I can only speculate. Not every question asked is answered. Some questions are better left to mystery, don't you think?" She acquiesced after reverently touching each print.

"Come." With my hand at her waist, I drew her deeper into the sacred space. I lifted the lantern and she gasped.

Above a table top boulder, near the ceiling was the most mysterious, intriguing art work I'd ever encountered. No museum or cave in Spain or France had ever drawn me as this simple, yet absolutely beautiful, beguiling picture had.

Traced in yellow ocher with coal black highlights was a full grown male cougar. On his right shoulder a red patch streaked down. Before Bonnie, I'd never given a second thought to what this mountain lion was facing. Great Spirit, forgive my blindness.

A small replica mirrored the male- only the small lion was a female. Much lighter in color, the artist had had to experiment with pigments to attain the lightness of ocher for her body.

She was looking up at the male, who had inclined his head to meet her eyes. Above the pair, and it was now obvious to me that they were a pair, was the outline of a hawk in full flight.

Chapter 39

"Bonnie, Kitten?" She'd not said a word-all her attention on the drawing. I held the lantern high and to the side, the side of the male; decided to shift it, gain a better appreciation of the female and. . .I heard her stifled intake.

Her fingers caught in my shirt sleeve, clutching. I focused on what she was gazing upon-literally putting myself inside her eyes. Usually I did not use a light when I came to this sacred cave.

Perhaps it was the lack of light, perhaps the Great Spirit had chosen for us to be together for this reveal. The two lions and the hawk formed part of a circle- but only part.

To the right of the female cougar was a. . .lizard? Bonnie read my mind.

"Riordan, I…I think it's a dragon."

"I guess that makes sense. If the ancients left this drawing, it's likely they'd not seen a dragon-representative before." The figure appeared stilted, kinked, with a long tail, long snout and long feet.

At the bottom of the circle was a black morass. I assumed caused by smoke from a torch that the artist used. Something else occurred to me- more likely the black represented Chac, the jaguar man. Why wasn't he drawn as a cat? I could only speculate, blocking Bonnie from these particular thoughts, maybe the black represented chaos, period. Other theories were also clamoring for attention.

Just above the blackness was the faint outline of a pronghorn antelope head or. . .

"Riordan, I don't think it's an antelope head" -she had been allowed to read me again. "I think those are ears facing left. What's really interesting is that this is a two-headed creature. The head facing right. . ."

". . .is some kind of bird," I finished for her.

"There's no body," she wondered.

"I don't believe the artist ran out of space, either."

"The blackness is part of the story. . ." she barely whispered.

I was afraid of what she might intuit; not time for the revelation of evil coming. I sensed her vibrating with fear.

"Bonnie, don't be afraid," I calmly said.

"I thought I remembered something. . ."

"Tell me, Kitten."

"N...never mind, it's gone, now. The rabbit- do you think?"

Ah, the rabbit we rescued. Yes, I supposed the figure to the one side could be a rabbit. How or what grand design did the two-headed creature serve, though, rising phoenix-like from the black lake? The creature completed the circle, but why?

"Bonnie, you are the center of the circle, the others including me, surround you. You have a very special purpose Kitten, and I'm betting somehow, someday, these others- the dragon and the two-headed creature, will put in an appearance, here. Maybe, they've not heard your call, yet."

The entire panorama was near three feet by three feet. The male cougar was the largest figure and his mate drawn lovingly, beguilingly, was central. You could especially feel the artist's endeavors in the body of the female cougar. Why?

"Gives us food for thought, Kitten," I pulled Bonnie into my arms. "You OK?"

She rested her head on my chest, eyes turned to the archaic painting. "I could listen to your heart forever."

"Good thing that's what I had in mind." I massaged her back, soothingly, until the trembling brought on by the drawing and its potential ramifications subsided. "I'll discuss this with grandfather."

I turned her face to me so we were eye down to eye. "Are you ready to see me as in your dream or should we wait?"

Her pulse jumped. This would certainly provide a distraction from whatever fear the painting had brought on.

"Are you sure, Riordan?" Her wide eyes expressed their concern for my feelings on the subject.

"It has to happen sometime," I put on a smile.

"You really don't want to. I can feel your resistance," she stroked my chest- a distraction in itself.

Try to hide something from Bonnie- good luck- full time job. I'd need to be extra careful about a few ideas until. . .

"Listen carefully," I led her away from the artwork-endowed ledge. "I want you to sit here. Don't say a word. Don't move. I've never transformed in front of anyone- ever- not grandfather, not anyone. When I'm the mountain lion, I'm me, but I'm also a wild animal. I can't predict with absolute surety how I'll react. SO IT'S EXTREMELY IMPORTANT YOU DO AS I SAY. Agreed?"

Solemnly, she nodded. "Sit here and stay," I ordered.

She huddled with her back to the cave wall. I left her and went toward the boulder below the drawing.

"Can I look at you? I mean in your eyes?" She asked.

"In order to avoid a feeling of confrontation with my wild nature, look away after a split second. Think submissive. You must not antagonize. Got it?"

"Y…yes. Will you have to take off your clothes?"

That got a laugh out of me. She was good at making me laugh. "Will that bother you?" I smirked.

"N…no. I'll just close my eyes." She put her head down, then quickly glanced up- not wanting to miss anything.

"Chicken! The same energies that change the cells of my body will take care of my clothes. However, when you change, I'm wondering if your braces will stay on," I laughed, picturing Bonnie- my lioness, with braces on cougar fangs.

She giggled, apprehensively, "I'm amusing you again."

"Here goes, Kitten." I called to my spirit guide, intimating his future lioness mate was here; beseeched him to stay benign.

The power coursed through each cell, energizing and rearranging. I felt my muscles lengthen and supple, my fingers sprout immense claws from human nails.

My human body dropped to all fours. I couldn't conceive of a time when this metamorphosis wouldn't thrill me. Woodpecker and starling medicine were good in appropriate situations, but the mountain lion- lions were rightly named the king of beasts. When I took my preferred nature, I felt as a king should.

My cougar head took stock of my surroundings- his nature was now prominent. A mountain lion always knew his environment; his life depended on his awareness and reading every nuance of his surroundings. My human side lurked within the depths of his system- I would call the reverse change if needed.

I felt his/my huge golden cat eyes light on Bonnie. A snarl rose from my abdomen. I turned fully toward her. Bonnie's eyes were dish-plate size in response, but no sign of fear. Remarkable girl.

The lion paced to and fro, seeking to achieve a level of comfort to the presence of this new scent- this vision of his betrothed via the spirits ordination, his bride-to-be. The rumbling of his nerves from being placed in this totally intense situation echoed about the cavern.

After several minutes of reconnaissance, he/I sat on our haunches. Bonnie gazed in fascination over her arms clasped about her legs. She caught herself and looked away. If her eyes locked too long on mine, a snarl of warning issued.

I was close to ending this first session when all at once Bonnie abandoned her promise, rose and came straight to the cat. Instantaneously, the wild one vaulted with a defensive hiss and scream- bounded right at the fearless, foolish girl.

Chapter 40

I summoned every ounce of power within me to reverse back to my human body, praying I'd not be too late. I felt my jaws open wide, saliva dripped from huge cougar fangs. The mountain lion's head lowered. . .

I found myself, my human self, straddling Bonnie, on my hands and knees, my mouth at her throat. Her body was completely motionless- if she'd moved an inch under him/me, the lion probably would have had her.

The remaining scream of the cougar dissolved into my own voice railing at her. Hastily, I scrambled off of her, pulled her to her feet.

"Wow!" She whistled.

"Wow? Don't you ever listen? Didn't I tell you to stay put?" I screamed at her, berating her for all I was worth.

"What's wrong with you? This isn't some Disney fantasy- no Hollywood vampire movie. There are no retakes. I could have killed you," I'd never been so frustrated.

"No, I don't believe you could," she all too calmly stated. Was I not getting through to her?

"All right, Miss Know-it-all," I tried to regain a semblance of composure, fighting for each breath. When what I really wanted was to tan her hide and run until the fear of my worst nightmare ran out of steam.

"Riordan, Riordan CatSkill," from somewhere I heard her trying to reach me. I was sure my face showed every smoldering emotion. And there were plenty of them all stuck on a roller coaster racing rampant through my blood stream.

"I don't believe God would bring us together for you to kill me," she was so at ease, as if nothing potentially deadly had transpired.

"You don't believe? You don't know. You don't know. . ." I shook my head. "How easy it would have been for me to hurt you- do you think I could live with myself if I hurt you, killed you. . .?" My voice trailed off. I didn't know what more to say; I felt completely enervated.

This could never happen again, at least not until she was able to become the mate. "This was not a good idea. Come on, we're leaving."

She blocked my path, "No. Look, I apologize. It was stupid of me, I realize that. I…I just wanted to touch you. You, you can't conceive how much I wanted to touch you. All the years I've dreamed of this, of you. . . Please, Riordan- just once more. I swear, I swear to you, I won't move- you can tie me up if you want. . ." She pulled baling twine out of a pocket and presented it to me.

"No! No way," I tried to displace her.

"Please. Please, Riordan," her fingers were on my forearm. "Please, once more."

"Are you insane? Do you think I'm insane? How would I explain to your father? Well, you see Mr. Lance, I turned into a wild animal and ate your daughter" -a Grimm's fairy tale come to life.

"Please," her eyes begged.

I was wavering. How does a man resist when the woman he loves pleads? I needed an answer to this one and fast. But, I wanted this to work, too.

"I should be locked up. No." Once more I attempted to move around her, but she stood her ground.

"Please, you can call it my Christmas present."

Christmas present- gift exchange. Oh. . .
There were many aspects of caring for a person I'd
not considered. I needed to get on the ball.
Though my age, my old-fashioned age, had thought
of a ring. As I recall, I was supposed to ask a
father's permission first on the ring business.

She sensed my hesitation and the 'pleases'
rolled off her tongue along with the vow to be
absolutely still.

"I should be committed and you should be
placed in a padded room so your self-destructive
side is denied. Thank the Great Spirit you didn't
approach that young male lion that day."

"I knew he wasn't you when I saw him," she
hid the smile beginning to form on those
irresistible lips.

My hand attempted to run through my tangled
hair-frustration and longing competing for king-
of-the-hill. "Go sit down," I capitulated.

"Thank you, Riordan."

"Save the thanks for when you leave here
alive and in one piece, unharmed," I grumbled.

She tiptoed up to kiss me- barely reaching
my jaw. "Thank you, Riordan," she released the
smile.

Once more I called upon my spirit guide. I
whole-heartedly relished the flow of power through
me. If I didn't embrace this surge, the change
would not take place.

In the blink of an eye, I stood opposite
her. The mountain lion and the girl. My tail
twitched, anticipating. But Bonnie remained
steadfast. I/he tentatively sat.

The lion's eyes fastened on her still form.
She cast furtive looks in his/my direction. Waves
of calm energy emanated from her and embraced me.
Smart.

'CatSkill,' she was telepathically calling
me to her. The tail went quiet. The rumble from
inside of me turned to sort of a purr- a very loud
purr. We remained this way for a lifetime,
seeking the communion of mated souls along a
knife's edge of possibility. Magic and
spirituality, together.

The mountain lion/I rose and calmly, slowly
padded over to her, my claws retracted. The
curious cat contemplating a harmless, juicy morsel
before us.

Within arms' reach, Bonnie kept her arms
wrapped about her legs. I, the lion, moved
closer. We were gaining a semblance of serenity-
the three of us.

My head approached nose to nose with her.
She was reluctant to hold our gaze. I purred and
told her to look. Eyes became eyes- mirrors of
each other. The doorway to the future opened
wide.

"Beautiful," she whispered- a singing breeze.

I couldn't resist. My tongue lapped her face- the pebbled house cat tongue magnified. I lathered her pretty good and she began to laugh- wind chimes musically baptizing the sacred space.

Her hands slowly reached to touch my chest. I leaned into them and she scratched. What cat doesn't like to be scratched under its chin?

"CatSkill," she murmured. I chose that moment to return to human form. End on a good note.

"Magical," she insisted, hugging herself with delight and then she flew at me, arms reaching for my neck.

I seemed to be getting used to this, as a human anyway. I pulled her head to my chest and kissed her tawny crown.

"Welcome to our future, Kitten."

Chapter 41

"You're so much better looking in real life," Bonnie enthused. And enthused.

"Woman, you are a trip." Secretly, I was proud of myself. I/we had done it. A successful introduction. Now we could explore further-induce Bonnie to follow suit, become what she was born to be- a lioness inspired shaman.

Her aversion to the black mass I countenanced with great speculation. Along some level she was afraid, and this needed to be dealt with, the sooner the better. The mystery of the painting would unfold as the Great Spirit ordained, but I was anxious to talk with grandfather, too many ideas racing through my mind.

"Thank you so much for my Christmas present, Riordan," she placed her hand over mine on the gear shift. I heard her mental desire for the next episode and telepathed something about surprises. And patience.

"You're welcome." I knew she'd be happy if that were my only gift to her, but, hey, everyone should have a gift on Christmas day, too. Seems I remember that tradition from somewhere. Right, I had to get with the program. I'd pulled off a pretty good first date for us. An idea came to me about the approaching holiday.

Mr. Lance waited as I pulled up in the jeep. I opened Bonnie's door for her. My hands went to her waist and I lifted her down.

"Hi, honey. How was class?"

"Dad, it was fabulous- the best class I've ever had," she regaled her father.

'Tone it down, Kitten or you'll not be able to explain what you did today,' I silently warned her.

"That's great, honey. I'm sure no one's ever enjoyed being grounded as much as you. Seems to me there's something wrong with this picture," he faked a cough and tried to hide his smile.

Bonnie gave her father a hug which surprised him to the point his eyes registered his emotion. He cleared his throat, regained a semblance of composure.

"Well, well," he patted her back, kissed the top of her head. "You have some phone calls to return. I wrote down the numbers by the phone. Girlfriends?"

"I bet Callie's having trouble with math again. I don't know who the others are."

"Go on, make your calls. I'd like to talk with Riordan a few minutes." We watched, both of us, with proprietary looks as Bonnie went inside the cabin after greeting that noisy black beast and distributing hugs to the dogs.

"Do you have a few minutes, son?" He turned to me.

"Yes, sir. Then I better help grandfather with this week's preparations."

"Right. How many are coming?" Mr. Lance leaned against a fence post, inadvertently inviting Handsome's attention. After hugging her father, Bonnie had snacked the big boy, but snacks aren't considered finite in the minds of horses.

"Fourteen folks from all over the U.S.- including one from Germany. I'll be busy picking them up from the airport Monday night."

Mr. Lance leaned back, a little on edge, I sensed. Whatever bothered him, he was having trouble finding the words.

"Son, I, I guess I need to thank you. I like the way you treat my daughter and more. . .I hardly recognize the quiet, keep-to-herself-kid-before-you-came as the upbeat 16-year old girl she is now. She's beautiful, happy. . .I. . ." he broke off and avoided my eyes.

I knew he wondered why he'd not had this effect on his own daughter.

"Mr. Lance, you've raised a great girl. . ."

At this moment, Bonnie burst out of the house, "Dad?"

"Yes, honey," he softly surveyed his bouncing girl.

"The girls want me to go Christmas shopping with them," she clasped her hands, excitedly.

"Girls?" He inquired with a smile.

"Lil, Vera, Kristin, Callie- Lil's dad is flying all of us," she looked up hopefully as she said 'us', "to Jackson Hole for the day, on Tuesday. No school. They want to buy gifts for family members and boyfriends, too."

"What about school?" The 'father' asked.

"No school on Tuesday," we chimed together. The three of us laughed.

"Who's the father?"

"Justin Brent," Bonnie answered.

"Ah, I remember him; we shared some classes. I'll want to speak with him. . ."

"I've written his cell number down," Bonnie interrupted. Daughter knew father more than father knew daughter.

"I'll give you my answer after I talk with Justin. What about chores?"

"I'll get up extra early, Lil said she'd pick me up and they promise I'll be home before dark."

"Ok, honey. How about starting supper? I'm getting hungry."

"Coming up. Riordan, are you staying?"

"Much as I'd like to I need to get home. See you in the morning for school." I gave her a special look.

"Dad, does this mean I'm not grounded anymore?" Being grounded had put Bonnie on par with the rest of the girls at school- an unexpected good turn of luck.

"Riordan, you think she's learned her lesson?" Tongue-in- cheek, Mr. Lance eyed me.

That question had too many nuances to it. I didn't hurry my answer as Bonnie began to fidget. Keeping a poker face 'til she practically danced, I finally answered, "I'd say that's a pretty good bet, sir."

Her eyes twinkled at me and she left. "Sir, just a minute, please." I caught up to Bonnie on the porch.

"You know better, I hope, than to buy me a present."

"You don't want me to get you a gift?" Her face registered hurt.

"It's not that, Kitten. I don't want you to spend money on me. You are the gift of a lifetime- I don't want anything out of a store." My fingers caressed her cheek. The resultant rocketing of her heartbeat echoed mine.

"Riordan, you do so much for me, I don't feel worthy. . ."

"DON'T YOU EVER SAY THAT," I enunciated each word, and earnestly, I repeated, "You are the gift of a lifetime."

"I guess I'll just have to use my imagination," she put her thinking cap on.

"That would be perfect, but not necessary. . ." I finished to a closed door.

"Now where were we," Mr. Lance had watched our interplay.

"I was telling you what a great girl you've raised, sir."

"I'm thinking she's pretty well raised herself," he replied ruefully.

"Not true, sir. You've instilled in her proper virtues and a smart way of thinking- she doesn't shrink from what needs to be done and she's not a complainer," I hastened to reassure him.

"Y. . ."

Once more, Bonnie burst out of the cabin and came running over, "Dad?"

"Bonnie, I'm trying to talk with your young man. . ."

"Sorry," to her father. "Sorry," to me. "Dad, I had a great idea. I want to invite some of my friends over- say for a cook-out."

"A cook-out? Honey, it's cold out," he frowned, perplexed.

"I know, Dad. The fire will feel great. Just a simple grill out- hot dogs, marshmallows. Some of the kids want to see the stallion. Two of them have broodmare operations," she applied convincing logic.

"An ulterior motive?" He grinned at her zeal and business smarts.

"Never hurts to think ahead," Bonnie replied.

"All right, I'll spring for hot dogs, buns. . ."

"I'll provide the drinks- no alcohol," I added quickly.

"I'm sure they'll bring snacks, marshmallows. . ." Bonnie suggested.

"Hershey's for S'mores," Mr. Lance added. "I wouldn't mind having a few of those now."

"Great Dad. You can meet the kids. We'll need a suitable fire pit, it's been awfully dry," Bonnie eyed a likely site.

"Do you have a mouse in your pocket, honey?"

"Huh?" Now Bonnie was perplexed.

I grinned at the two of them, planning a fun event. "I'll build the fire pit, Mr. Lance."

Bonnie clapped her hands, "How about the day after Christmas?"

"Whatever you want, honey. Am I ever going to get any supper tonight?" He rolled his eyes as she scampered off.

"See what I mean," he turned back to me. "She's become normal since you came here."

Boy, was that comment way off the chart. His 'normal' daughter- a shaman in the making, the center of a powerful Divine plan- as far from 'normal' as you could just about get.

"Riordan, Bonnie and I are going to spend quality time together the week between holidays. I…I'm not sure what sort of activities to plan. I want us to have some fun."

"How long has it been since you've ridden together?"

"The geldings haven't had a good workout since last summer. It's fairly cold. . ." he mused.

"Cold doesn't bother Bonnie, sir."

"Can you think of anything else?"

"Do you bowl?" I tried to be helpful.

"I used to. Used to be darn good at it, too."

"Teach her how to bowl."

"That's an idea- you don't think she'll be bored?" He rubbed his chin.

"No. The Buffalo Bill museum is always a great time."

"I haven't been there in years," Mr. Lance's eyes were alight with possibilities.

"You might want to speak with the one in charge. Take some of Bonnie's paintings. She has a definite talent and potential career as an artist. I bet the museum would be proud to display a local student's artwork," I pointed him in the right direction.

"Thanks, Riordan. I'm going to feel like an ass, now, but you're the only boy, no young man, Bonnie's ever been out with and. . ."

"Mr. Lance, no problem here if Bonnie would like to go out with another guy." I could say this with absolute surety. Bonnie was mine and I belonged to her. No ifs, ands or buts.

Chapter 42

"What did Riordan get you for Christmas?"
The girls were hovering and clamoring over Bonnie,
dying to compare presents from their boyfriends,
and those without boyfriends were still supremely
curious.

Rick and the rest of the male force were
helping me with the final touches on the fire pit
and the subsequent building of a bonfire. Guys
naturally gravitate to fire- no discussion of
presents with the male contingent.

My first Christmas celebration after, oh,
150 years or so- I enjoyed myself immensely. We
all did. I discovered I love to give gifts,
especially to a certain someone, but holidays
would not confine that enterprise.

Bonnie had presented my grandfather and me with a smaller replica of the painting in the cave. With her innate eye for detail, she'd recreated the simple lines and matched the colors of the animals with uncanny perfection. The ancients would have approved her talent. Like as not, they'd stood at her shoulders and guided her brush.

Grandfather's first holiday gift brought tears to his eyes. We were both impressed and touched. I kept my tears to myself, but sent Bonnie a silent message.

She'd also created a basket full of braided sweet grass and dried sage for grandfather's rituals and several of her hand-made soaps, which I adored. My salivary glands turned from the scent of roasting wild turkey to layers of Bonnie's cookies, nestled in a towel. I couldn't wait for the next holiday- what I'd been unconsciously missing throughout my life until Bonnie!

Grandfather laid a finely woven blanket in Bonnie's arms. "You'll need this for that new horse of yours," he winked.

"Grandfather, it's beautiful," she traced the colors of sky, water, fire and earth on the tan wool- the colors of the four elements.

"I have a friend who's an artist on the loom," he said while reaching into his wooden chest. He brought another saddle blanket out for Mr. Lance. "I hope you can use one, too."

Way too much emotion circling about. Bonnie's shining thanks showering grandfather, and Mr. Lance struggling with the expression of his gratitude. Not to mention my grandfather's and my own eyes continually sneaking peeks at Bonnie's painting.

I played nonchalant as if the gift giving were over. Grandfather wasn't having any of it even though Bonnie was truly not expecting a second present.

"Here, Kitten," I put a small wooden box in her hand. Telepathically she told me, 'Riordan, you shouldn't have.' Her eyes threatened a flood before she even lifted the lid.

"Open it," I whispered.

Grandfather and Mr. Lance peered over her shoulders as she lifted the lid. I held up a lantern, the flame would enliven the gift. Her fingers shook and I placed one hand under hers in case she dropped it.

"So beautiful, beautiful," she intoned a
mantra as she lifted out a sizeable tiger's eye
that I'd carved into a cougar head. The colors
shifted in the fire light- the cougar seemed
magically alive. I'd had a gold suspender
fastened on the back of the pendant and the cougar
now hung on a gold choker chain.

"Well done, Grandson."

"You made this, Riordan?" I nodded keeping
my eyes on Bonnie and her trembling admiration.
"I see my daughter's not the only artist here-
abouts. This is amazing work."

"Would you like me to put it on you,
Bonnie?" Her fingers played on the carving,
tracing the lines with admiring pleasure. I took
the piece from her and walking behind her, asked
her to lift her hair.

Our guardian spirit fit perfectly in the
hollow at the base of her throat. She turned into
me and the flood flashed as her arms wrapped
around me. Grandfather and Mr. Lance made
themselves scarce- went to check on the turkey.

With a pineapple-glazed ham punctured with
cloves that the Lances provided, grandfather's
wild turkey, roasted potatoes, carrots and
Bonnie's blackberry cobbler, we feasted as a
family in an old-fashioned setting- no Christmas
tree, but evergreen clippings placed in the middle
of the table sufficed.

Bonnie's girlfriends couldn't take their eyes and thoughts off Bonnie's present and once the guys heard I'd carved it they were quick to voice their fascination. Too much male attention directed at my girl- I suggested we admire the stallion before dark and then roast hot dogs.

Handsome had a few potential girlfriends lined up after Kyle, one of Rick's cousins, dialed his father on his cell and began extolling the virtues of the black beast.

Mr. Lance came out to indulge in introductions and hot dogs. Then he hung around for S'mores which Lil and Vera, in a factory-like manner, turned out to expectant, waiting hands. No I Love Lucy back-up messes here.

Everyone sated, we settled convivially around the fire, conversing under a brilliant parade of stars.

"Riordan, I've been thinking about your work with the Lakota. I'd like to hear more- whether it's history or, anything you can tell us."

"It's not the happiest tale, Rick."

"All of life isn't happy, but it's important to learn. How else can one help?" Lil patted Rick's thigh and leaned into him.

"What are you looking at, career-wise, Rick?" I asked.

"He's going to medical school, to be a doctor," Lil's gaze fastened glowingly, lovingly on her beau. She had really settled down and Rick was a good man. "I'm so proud of him." She tickled under his chin, made him laugh until he kissed her.

"Are the rest of you wanting to hear more, tonight?" The head nodding prompted me.

"Mitakuye oyasin," I spoke in a Lakota dialect which immediately made me the center of attention. "This is a basic greeting and tenet of my native people. It's held as a belief of aboriginal people worldwide. Simply put, the phrase means all my relations or we are all related. Native people have known this for thousands of years before today's physics super stars are proving that it is true. Destroying one aspect of a culture or meadow or forest etc. is not an act without consequence along some level.

Teenagers today suffer stress usually related to family problems, school stuff, keeping up with the Jones'. Some of the young on the reservation suffer from a loss of identity that reaches far back.

When the white men took away the plains tribes' major food source, the buffalo, and then the use of the land which was held sacred, and afterwards tried to take religion, language, ceremonies, well, think how you might feel. A pride of place and resultant self-esteem were endangered. Children were forced into schools far from home and were not allowed to speak their language or wear native clothes.

Today's people move from country to country, farm to city and vice versa without losing their self-esteem, they've been doing so for hundreds of years, but the Lakota way of life revolved around a particular land- the northern plains and the Black Hills. They hunted, they weren't farmers. A whole self- sustaining culture developed from the beginnings of these peoples.

The new white religion was embraced by some, after all whose God was stronger, the conquerors or the conquered. Alcohol sales became prevalent- anathema to native bodies. There was no resistance to white man's diseases. Shamans and medicine men had helped with cures and rituals since time immemorial, now they seemed helpless. Some of the native healers were castigated by whites, even institutionalized- all in the name of 'civilization'.

Today there is a revival of renewed interest in Lakota heritage. My work involves putting groups together to listen and support each other, relive pride in their ceremonies. This is necessary to defeat the use of toxic substances- drugs and alcohol, provide hope for the future. It's very difficult, but the least inroads, I know, will gather steam and reinvigorate my people."

Quiet reigned for several minutes.

"If you think of some way we might help. . ."

"My family visited Pine Ridge as part of our vacation one year. My father was especially interested in Wounded Knee. One of his ancestors was with the cavalry. He'd left a diary telling of the horror and his disillusionment with his position. I remember a tiny church and a grave yard. There were two girls sitting on the steps of the church, making dream catchers to sell. They told us the story of the massacre. I felt an overwhelming sense of sadness. I was just a kid, but it affected my stomach horribly- I couldn't wait to leave. How does one live with and rise above such sadness?"

"That's a question for people everywhere," I murmured.

"Riordan, I don't mean any disrespect, but aren't you half white? I mean your parents. . ." the question trailed off.

"I didn't know my parents. I was pretty much passed around," I acknowledged.

"How did you survive the sadness?" One of the girls asked.

"I was never one to indulge in gloom and I did have help." Thank you, Great Spirit.

Bonnie's arms stole about my waist. I pulled her to me and kissed her forehead.

"Now for a lighter topic," I reached behind me and pulled a pair of night vision binoculars into our circle. "I suggest we head to the far side of the cabin and do a little sky watching with these."

I winked at Bonnie. We didn't need them. I'd already spotted the art deco stars; our new friends would get a kick out of using the night vision scopes to see what came naturally to Bonnie's and my unenhanced eyes.

Chapter 43

"Hey Kitten, do you like '50's music?" My a.m. greeting.

"You mean like Elvis?" She had heard of him, I wasn't alone in left field.

"Yeah, and the Everly brothers, Chuck Berry, poodle skirts, pony tails and jitterbug?" I could rhapsodize along these lines, but. . .

"I guess. I've not listened to much music. What's a jitterbug? It's not a creepy crawly, is it?" This from my outdoor girl.

I laughed, "I forget sometimes how much I've got to teach you- it's a dance."

"I've never danced," she admitted without expression.

That floored me. I enjoyed the heck out of the 50's dances.

"They're having a 50's sock hop for Valentine's day in the school gym, actually the Friday before Valentine's day. There are prizes for best outfits, the best twisters and the boppinest jitterbug couple. I want you to go with me."

"But I don't know how to dance," she tucked her head away from my enthusiasm.

"I've an idea it won't take you any time at all to learn." I'd made up my mind we were going.

"You're pretty good at these dances?" Now she was studying me.

"Yes," a simple affirmative. The plain truth is I'm a very good dancer.

"OK, I'm willing to try- don't count on winning any prizes, but it sounds like fun. Tell me what to wear." That was an easy acquiescence but hey, Bonnie is my girl. What did I expect?

"It so happens I counted on you to say yes. I've rounded up an outfit for you. It's in the bag in the back seat." Complete even to organic red, red lipstick.

"I feel an installment plan coming on," she gave me a crooked little grin.

"The installment plan," I chuckled. "It's the Great American Way. Maybe I can keep you indebted up to my eyeballs in cookies."

She played with the bag, began to open it. "Seriously Kitten, you don't owe me anything. Only make cookies if you want to," I tried to placate her apprehension and found unkind thoughts I wished I could send to her faithless mother.

Looking into the brown paper sack, "Riordan, you're too good to me. I feel. . ."

"Bonnie, I'm going to keep on being good to you. I've never felt better than when I do something for you even if it's only," I leaned over to kiss my girl. Somehow I needed to convince her she was everything to me and break the whole 'abandoned child no self-esteem construct' that was still ardently part of Bonnie's make-up.

"What have you done to your hair?" Bonnie exclaimed, aghast.

"I believe he's greased it down, honey," Mr. Lance wore the biggest grin.

"You put grease in your hair?" What an expression!

"My hair's a little too long to put in a perfect DA, but I did OK with what I've got." I'd left a curl hang down my forehead- that piece, I trimmed.

I wore the typical bad boy gear- tight Levi's, biker boots, white t-shirt with sleeves rolled up, the right one over an empty cigarette pack. Slung over my shoulder was a biker's leather jacket- scarred enough to be from the 50's.

Bonnie was deliciously fetching in my selection of pink cashmere sweater with a darker pink scarf tied at her neck above the cougar pendant. Her peg leg jeans were lovingly tight about her now curvy legs and turned up at her calves to show off bobby socks and saddle shoes- these probably original to the 50's also. Her hair had grown long enough to be fastened in a high pony tail that bounced as she walked. And those lips. . .mmm mmm, I couldn't wait 'til later to taste those red, cupid bow lips.

"Hang on kids. I want a picture of both of you," Mr. Lance had dug out an old camera. "Have fun," he flashed a few pics and waved us off.

The school brought in a band of older musicians who knew not only the best 50's dance tunes, but performed them with gusto and used original lingo- like cool and hip daddy. The dancers hesitated to take the floor until a chaperone couple of teachers began to show off the dance moves.

"Hey, CatSkill! What are we doing here?" Rick's parents or grandparents must have coughed up some geeky clothes, floods to penny loafers, though Lil in a poodle skirt made him look good.

"I can't believe I let my mother put this gunk in my hair," he pseudo-wailed.

"Quit complaining. Let's dance," I harangued him. Lil pulled him along to the dance floor in our wake.

"You've got to be kidding. I'm not much for dancing- even line dance moves are beyond me," Rick stalled, dug in his penny loafer heels.

"Just watch Bonnie and me." Bonnie's jaw dropped. She shook her head at Lil who was laughing as a glob of Dippity-Do slid down Rick's cheek.

"Riordan. . ." Bonnie started.

"Bonnie," I replied to her flustered self.

"I don't know what to do."

So I showed her. Telepathic dance lessons straight into the real McCoy. She picked up the twist to a Fats Domino tune easily and with a little coaxing and my showing off beside her, she got creative.

Those on the side lines got a load of us and joined in, filling the gym dance floor. The band played Rock Around The Clock and I pulled Bonnie into my arms for a jitterbug.

Being part of another sure helps in dancing. As the guitar lead took over, I swung my girl up on one hip, then the other. Pulled off a California version of jitterbug probably not seen in this gymnasium since the 50's. We'd gained an appreciative audience- most of them standing aside and clapping in time.

Lil wouldn't allow Rick to play wallflower and I had to hand it to him, he was really trying- not as adept as at basketball but there was a hint of promise. I say hint.

The jitterbug contest was announced. The song, one of my favorites- Johnny Be Good. A fast tune.

"You ready, Kitten?" We'd soaked up water, chips and sloppy jos with cole-slaw on a break. Bonnie was more than ready, she pulled me out to the dance floor.

Bonnie put her eyes into mine and I showed her some new steps. Needless to say, no one else had a snow ball's chance. We won a hundred dollars and a cd collection of great 50's recording artists.

We sat out the twist contest. To Rick's surprise, he and Lil won the best dressed event. Lil bounced like a rubber ball next to her geeky basketball player boyfriend in his flood pants and penny loafers.

While Bonnie attended the ladies room, I asked the band leader for a favor. I twirled the mike and as Bonnie reentered the gym a spotlight found her and I sang YOU'RE 16 to her- a perfect song for my peaches and cream, soon-to-be lioness girl. The wonder on her face as I bopped to her belting my heart out was priceless. I only hoped Lil had snapped pictures.

"That was so much fun," Bonnie went on and on and on and on.

"Sure was," I agreed completely.

"I don't think I've ever had this much fun getting so tired before."

"Kitten, good dancing takes effort. I have the best time with you. The concept of fun. . .you are fun. The most fun I've ever had in my life."

"Riordan. . ." I couldn't resist those exquisite lips another second. My mouth watered. I covered hers tenderly, tasting, daring to explore. Her arms slid up my t-shirt clad chest and as far around my neck as she could reach.

Her sweet response thrilled me and I let myself get a little more intense. Ah, too much. Bonnie's breathing changed and she pulled away, eyes wide and a question in them.

The smoldering coals inside my chest refused to be banked and I leaned in. Bonnie's hand on my chest raised a barrier against my advance.

"Riordan," she squeaked, her chest heaving.

"Hmmm. . ." I tried again, but her hand remained adamant. I delved into her questioning eyes.

"You're looking at me different tonight," she whispered, unsure of herself.

I straightened a bit, "I've made you uncomfortable?"

"N...not exactly," she stammered. "Am I easy to read?"

"You've been open to me mostly, not always. Most people are easy to read, interpret, by facial expressions, a shift of eyes or body position. Psychics know this- the cons anyway. I want you to tell me what it is you're feeling right now."

"I," she looked away. I gave her a minute to regroup. "At what point did you stop aging? Was it after you could shape shift and travel?"

I tried to remember; it was never important to me, but for some reason it was important to her.

"I guess, Kitten. I don't know. What's bothering you?" I inquired.

"If I stopped aging now, would I be enough for you?"

It took a second to glean her meaning. I smiled at her, delicately lifted her sweet chin. "Yes, Kitten. You'd be plenty. I'm looking at you tonight and imagining how it will be when the only home I take you to is ours. When I can hold you in my arms all night."

"I...I'm no...not ready to sleep with you," Bonnie stuttered in an inadvertent, but awfully beguiling manner. Not that there would be a whole lot of sleeping, but I knew what she was intimating.

"Bonnie, I know that. Please forgive me if I got a little carried away. You are utterly delicious. Hold on, I'm putting my 'patient man' hat back on."

"But Riordan, you are a man, a gorgeous man. . .maybe you should go out with other girls, older girls," her eyes began to water at the prospect.

My fingers caressed her temple to her cheekbones to her lips, then her chin. My eyes never left hers. I couldn't make my love for her any more apparent. I wanted, needed her to understand her worth.

"You're being silly- my hormones do not control me. My love for you has precedence now over every aspect of my life. If you need me and I'm not there, just thinking my name will have me with you in an instant. I do not want and certainly will not spend time with any woman but you. Do you understand me?"

"You don't have to commit. . ." she faltered. We'd just got into the jeep. I shut it down and turned to her.

"Now you're being exasperating. I love you. Let's step outside and I'll shout it for the world to hear," I made for the door handle, but she tugged at my arm.

"Will you know when I'm ready to. . .?" I felt the heat of her blush and envied her teeth their grasp on her lower lip.

"To make love?" She nodded, eyes averted. I chuckled softly, "Oh yes, Kitten, I'll know, believe me, and you will, too. Right now your hormones are experimenting. You're unsure of yourself. That's all right. I'll know the difference between your feelings of teen-age ups and downs and the reality of our love coming to fruition- about the time you are of marriageable age."

"When will that be?" Bonnie whispered, fascinated.

"I don't think I'll ruin the surprise. Time for you to go in." The look of shock stayed on her face as I led her to her door, leaned over and gave her a chaste kiss and hastened away. I'd need to mind my p's and q's very carefully.

Chapter 44

The night of the dance had made up my mind.
I recalled my covert confab with Bonnie's father.

"Mr. Lance, I'd like to talk with you," I
cast my gaze about searching for Bonnie and
blocking my thoughts.

"What is it, Riordan?" He noticed my
search. "Bonnie's still in the bathroom. You're
kind of early. Come to think of it, don't you
think it's time you called me Jim? Mr. Lance is
getting to make me feel an outsider. I appreciate
your respect, but I hope we're friends by now."

"Thank you, sir. I better wait 'til I ask
my question. After that you might rescind your
offer."

He was now alert and on guard. I could
fathom the myriad scenarios running through his
mind as the father of the girl I'd been spending
all my free time with.

"Sir, I'd like to give Bonnie a gift- a very
special gift," I began slowly.

"Well heck, son, you had me worried," he
noticeably breathed a sigh of relief.

"I'd like to give Bonnie a ring," I added a bit more stress.

"A ring," he repeated, puzzled.

"Yes sir. You could call it a promise ring or an engagement ring," I laid my cards fully on the table.

Mr. Lance folded his arms across his chest- eyed me speculatively. "Is she pregnant?" He asked, knife-like point blank.

"No sir," I straightened. "I'd never dishonor Bonnie that way. I assure you she is untouched."

"You plan on eloping with my daughter?"

"No sir." I would not have wanted to be him. But I was being totally honest, as he deserved.

He nodded thoughtfully, contemplating how to defuse this situation.

"Riordan, don't you think she's a little young at 16 to be engaged? How can she know you're the one? She's never been out with anyone but you." He tried logic; but there was no logic involved in what was between Bonnie and me.

"I understand your concern, sir. I'm not pressuring Bonnie- as if that were possible."

Mr. Lance grunted affirmatively on that point. "I don't want my daughter to make the same mistake her parents did, rushing into a marriage we weren't suited to." He grimaced, and I realized he still loved his wife even though she'd moved on.

"I've no intention of addressing marriage until Bonnie is at least 18. I just want her to feel confident in the way I feel about her. I think she has a hard time believing someone would want her." Did I explain sufficiently?

Mr. Lance pinched the bridge of his nose. This revelation hurt him and I certainly didn't intend that.

"I can see that. Abandoned by her mother, an absentee father. . ."

"Sir," I broke in. I liked and respected this man; I didn't want him to suffer.

"You mean her for a potential bride, right?" He'd regained his composure and was now the father, the one with the ultimate responsibility for Bonnie.

"In the future, sir. At any point, I'll step down and away if she says so."

"And if I say so?" He qualified.

"I think Bonnie should be the one to accept or decline," I patiently stood my ground.

"Then why even bring this up to me?" His tone belied his mounting aggravation.

"I respect you, sir. I'm totally in love with your daughter. I've never met anyone like her." Oh too true.

"You're not the typical high school senior, are you Riordan? Red Hawk says you've been around the world- sort of self-taught."

I stood resolute as he continued. "I can't deny you've brought out wonders in my little girl. Have you been in love before?"

"Unequivocally, no."

"I'm not ready to lose her. . ."

"Sir, if it's up to me, you'll never lose her. I've no intention of taking her away. My future home is here in this area- helping my grandfather and establishing myself. Trips away will always be necessary, but this will be my home base. You may have concerns about my financial prospects. If you call this number, my banker, Quince Sheldon, has been notified to answer any and all questions you may have," I placed a card in Mr. Lance's palm.

"You've thought a lot about all of this?" His mien portrayed that of the truly impressed.

"Yes sir." We eyed each other, gauging until Bonnie appeared on the cabin porch.

"I expect I'll have to leave the decision to my daughter. If you hurt her. . ."

I nodded. That went without saying. "Thank you, Mr. Lance."

"The name's Jim," he proffered his hand.

Saturday, Valentine's day. We didn't have a date, but I planned on a bit of sky watching after helping Bonnie with night chores.

"What were you and my dad so secretive about?" Bonnie, after unsuccessfully attempting to read my mind, broached the mystery.

"I don't know what you're talking about," I shrugged, my lips yearning to twitch.

"Oh yeah? Maybe I'll tickle it out of you," she tried a different tack.

"Please try, Kitten. 'Cuz I know where your ticklish spots are." We lay upon the roof, supervised by the stars- who winked appreciatively at us as they arabesqued in the sky.

"You're not going to tell me?" She couldn't believe it.

"I enjoy watching you work with that stallion- he really cottons to you," I tried a Bonnie tactic.

"Riordan?"

"I wonder if he'll let me ride him?" This was fun.

"Riordan?"

"We could go out riding together." That did it.

She rolled atop me and began tickling my waist- not happening. I rolled her over and tickled her speechless- no more questions. When I was satisfied I had the upper hand, I kissed the tip of her nose.

"I've a present for you; it's up to you to accept or decline, either way the present is yours whenever you like. When you're 18 I'll have an important question to ask, but for now. . ." Her kitten curiosity peeked.

I recalled the event that brought the stone in the ring to me. I'd recently arrived in India, land of maharajas and way too many extremely poor. It was one of those dire, destitute individuals, or so I thought, that I'd rescued from a stoning.

The old man was considered an outcast in those days when the caste system dictated one's life. Some of that still exists. He berated me for saving him. When I simply smiled and accepted his ingratitude, his tone took on a different relevancy.

"Ah, I know who you are." I was sopping up knowledge like a dried sponge in those days, so I kept quiet.

"Yes, I know why you're here. They told me you would come."

"They?" I'd not been long enough in the country for anyone to know me. I'd simply been passing through when the first stones let fly.

"I've stayed alive as long as I could. Thank you for finally arriving-" as if I were late for a dinner invitation. His gnarled fingers reached into a fold of his dusty loin cloth and he placed an object in my hand.

"This stone came from the stars. One day it will be important to you, as a gift for a gift. It will save the life of what you hold dear. Never lose it. You must vow."

He was serious- as serious as imminent death makes a body.

"Very well, sir. I shall keep it safe. I thank you. . ." Before I could finish thanking him, he died. The spirits conjoined me to adhere to my vow.

The stone had never seemed to have any special appeal-around four carats of a moonstone-like, opaque something or other. Not until Bonnie, did I remember it, pay extra attention to it and intend the stone for her.

I discovered a special attribute. What I presumed was a diamond was not. I now believed the old man's riddle was nearer an answer. Instead of a dead rock that needed light to enliven it as a diamond does, this stone was a light- a star unto itself. Its dull façade was a ruse.

I'd had it set in a silver band constructed of Celtic style woven circles. Not trusting it to a jeweler unsupervised, I'd waited until the band was finished and watched as the man set the stone. His many questions went unanswered.

My guardian spirit stretched and purred as I placed the ring on Bonnie's left hand ring finger. I didn't allow her a moment to respond, but went on.

"Whenever you doubt my feelings for you I want you to study this ring. It doesn't matter if you're in the dark or in daylight. I love you." As I said the words, the stone flashed.

"Riordan, did you see that?" Bonnie murmured, enthralled. I laughed, delighted. "The ring responded! It sent a current through me- like it's alive!"

I told the story of how I'd come by the stone. "It was meant for you, Bonnie. I know it. Do you like it? I could get you something different," I equivocated, knowing the answer.

"No. Tell me again," engrossed in watching her ring, she lent me her hearing, telepathic and aural.

"Greedy, aren't you? I love you, Bonnie." This time, I examined the stone and its wondrous flashes of color. This time, an echoing light flashed in the sky.

"Bonnie?" Her eyes flew to mine.

"Riordan CatSkill, I love you," misty, green eyes met mine. With this declaration a revolution of colors lit the stone and continued unabated for several moments. "Riordan, look," her chin lifted from my mouth, to the stars.

Apparently our shared spirit guide was not the only approving audience. The stars applauded our future, too. The Pink Lady looped the loop and the others made geometric figures, based on straight lines, of course. A veritable fireworks display ensued for our eyes only.

"If the stars are souls gone ahead of us, passed shamans and holy men and other spiritual souls, it would seem we have many, many friends."

Chapter 45

It took a lot of coaxing to get Bonnie to turn in.

"I'm too excited. . ."

"Kitten, you've got school tomorrow, remember?" My final warning to her. The ring a complete success.

Somewhere amidst a peaceful rest, dreaming of the day I'd make Bonnie my wife, a scream ransacked me. The first syllable of my name had me pulling on jeans, the second syllable- I was with Bonnie.

'Riordan,' subconsciously she'd kept the scream telepathic otherwise I'd have run into her father in her bedroom.

Huddled, shocked, in the middle of her bed, Bonnie clutched blankets around her like fortress walls. I scooped her up, soothingly intoning her name and held her on my lap. She collapsed into me, tears trickled down my bare chest.

I rocked her for a few minutes allowing her to achieve a fairly normal breathing pattern, then, urged her chin up.

Brushing her hair back, "Tell me, Kitten."

"Riordan, it's horrible. Something black and evil is c...coming to. . ." and she broke into sobs again.

'Grandfather, where's Chac?' I silently sent out an urgent communiqué.

In a moment he replied, 'Grandson, he's in his jungle lair, but he's quite perturbed- I can hear his roaring. What have you done?'

'I gave Bonnie a ring,' we continued, silently.

'A ring?' I sensed grandfather's concern on several fronts.

'Grandfather, tomorrow, please. Bonnie's had a most disturbing nightmare,' I telepathically begged off.

"Bonnie," I lifted her chin again and kissed away her tears. Her coherency returned, albeit with heartbreaking inconsistency.

"I'm here, everything is safe." For now. "Tell me what you saw." She hiccupped while I stroked her back.

"A black mass bearing down on us. We became separated and i...it shifted shape. I saw it focus on you- all the evil possible bearing down on you and you fought it and. . ." she choked. Her hands wrapped about my neck, over my shoulders- assuring herself I was really with her, unharmed.

"Bonnie, it was just a nightmare. You have them once in a while. Was this one any different than normal?"

"Y…yes. We're not swimming tomorrow and my dad's home." That's right; the previous nightmares were held at bay by the presence of her father and brought on by the advent of swim class.

"Tell me the other bad dream." I was interested to see if she'd remember any more about the usual nightmare while in the throes of tonight's terror.

"Only blackness, then nothing, but this dream was not like those. This time a black beast was after you. A fight until death. When I saw you overwhelmed, I began to scream. Riordan, what is it? Why is something after you?"

Her innate senses had made her aware of part of the impending arrival of Chac. Prophetic dream, spirit sent. Would the rest of the explanation wait 'til class with grandfather? Knowing my Bonnie, the answer was no.

"Bonnie, you have nothing to fear. . ." I began.

"Riordan, the only fear that would destroy me is the loss of you." Her teary, strained face, looking up at me, made me yearn for immediate battle and for a resolution to this mess.

"Kitten, that's not going to happen- I promise." I would keep that promise.

"Granddaughter, do you understand what my grandson has told you about Chac?" Class had begun.

"No, Grandfather. Not really. I can't believe a, a shaman, like an evil witch doctor, wants me." Bonnie was holding her own this morning, thank you, Spirits.

"Although your powers are not fully realized, the jaguar man has sensed your existence since Riordan's arrival has induced your true nature to hasten to the forefront; he believes you can be of great use to him. His purpose is to consolidate power as an avenger. He wasn't always like that, but today his only interest is himself—gaining strength and wreaking havoc on all who've despoiled his jungle and taken away his perceived dominant role. If the picture in the cave tells the story, you've called forces into play here. Not all of the participants have yet arrived, but I know we're meant to be your teachers and protectors."

Grandfather paused, seeking Bonnie's affirmation of digesting what he was saying. Nodding slightly, she confirmed he should go on.

"I believe, Riordan. . .the way the two of you face each other in the drawing, are meant as a couple, even though you're still not at your promised level of power. The Great Spirit has a special purpose for you. A young white woman shaman must be extremely rare- this endows you with a particular appeal Chac seeks to extort. He's definitely coming for you."

Bonnie swallowed hard and curled into my chest. I held her as protectively as I could against this terrible revelation.

"What you saw in your dream last night is not necessarily fatal. As the most powerful shaman in the northern hemisphere, Riordan has been delegated not only your mate, but the only potential adversary that could face Chac. The others of the circle, including myself, are obviously protectors, but must bear something more in the way of, as yet undesignated roles. After all, half of the circle is missing. We must wait for the spirits to divulge their full purpose while we prepare you for what is coming. I expect they sent the dream to hurry our program of preparation."

Bonnie looked up at me, fearfully concerned, "Are you really as formidable as grandfather says? Are you that powerful?"

"Know this, Kitten. No one, nothing breeches my territory, and you are my territory." The grim resolve on my face, I hoped reassured her. Instead, she shuddered at the implications. I began to stroke her back once more, adding a calming energy.

"Can't we call the police when he shows up?" my Kitten asked.

My brow quirked and I stifled a great burst of laughter, "Bonnie, do you really think police could stop ME?"

Chagrinned, she huddled in my lap as grandfather continued.

"Your progress has been most remarkable, but we must proceed at a more rapid pace," Grandfather solemnly instructed.

"Why does he think I'll go with him?"

Grandfather and I exchanged looks. "He'll not deign to give you a choice. And he'll bide his time, until it's warm, content in his perceived, omnipotent strength."

"Because I walk this world with stealth, Chac doesn't know what form his true adversary will take," I mused.

"Yes, Grandson, and he doesn't know of your human visage- we still have that advantage. He must think a lowly, male class mate dares to think he's in love with Bonnie- not worth his time as of yet. The daring to put a mark on my Granddaughter is what upset him last night- somehow he sensed an assumed boy staking Bonnie as his. Only the lovely Wyoming cold and his supreme arrogance keep him at bay for now. The spirits want you healthy, Granddaughter, and will most likely aid by keeping your future dreams more benign- now that you've been apprised of Chac's potential."

"Healthy? Now I'll worry myself to death," Bonnie shuddered, her face drawn from her prophetic nightmare and its surreal interpretation.

"No you won't, Kitten," I fixed a look of absolute determination on her. "You will not worry. I will take care of you."

"How can I help it?" She cried.

"I suppose I'll have to find ways to distract you," I bent to her mouth and kissed her- our first public kiss which caused her to blush furiously.

"He came last night because of the ring? Can I prevent him. . .?"

"Try not to worry, Granddaughter; I see that he senses some boy paying close attention to you. I doubt he knows of the stone's propensity to use light. . .I can't read that part clearly. My guess is he's more perturbed that a boy continues to hang around you, but the ring and the boy he considers as irritating inconsequentials."

Grandfather continued after a moment's break. "Although Chac considers a human boy easily disposed of, we must now show you how to block your mind- keeping it only to yourself. You must begin to walk with the stealth of your spirit guide."

"Bonnie, there are many ways Chac will attempt to induce you to go with him. Drugs, frequencies, hypnosis. . ." I stopped, as grandfather had a task for me.

"Grandson, leave us. Gather ten plants. Give us an hour and then try to communicate with my granddaughter."

I nodded, kissed Bonnie's hand and left, intent on locating benign and poisonous plants. For a time I watched through Bonnie's eyes.

"Grandfather, do you think my ring has power?"

Silently, grandfather observed her. She wasn't used to coyote teaching, I cautioned him.

"I…I see that's for me to discover," she looked crestfallen.

I sent her a mental pat on the back and a silent last few words before minding my task. 'Shamans have tests, Kitten.'

'Bonnie,' I used my easy going call- no response. I waited to be sure, then, hammered a more insistent 'Kitten' at her. I felt her will power waiver- it's hard to resist the one you love. But in this case it would serve to meet the requirements of a necessary test.

She started to answer, 'Rior. . .' I heard grandfather cautioning her to focus. She walled herself off to my repeated entreaties. I gave her a break for half a minute.

'Bonnie,' I felt my call tentacle to make inroads, but she held out. This time there was no intimation of a response. Bonnie had erected a bastion of self-defense. She was unable to hear my 'good girl.'

I spread a bundle of desiccated foliage in front of Bonnie, willy nilly- nothing to give away a particular plant's attributes.

"Granddaughter, use whatever sense you feel is up to this task. Pick out the harmful ones."

Bonnie's face took on a frown of concentration as she checked each of her senses in turn for the answers to grandfather's test. Her right hand slowly waved over the array. She picked out four plants and gave them to grandfather.

"Wait," she said. Two more herbs were set aside. "Those can be beneficial or not depending on how they are used." She looked up- the straight A student seeking approbation.

Grandfather smiled one of his infrequent smiles, "Excellent, Granddaughter. Excellent. Sensing when the wrong energies are present is vital."

I had an idea. I rearranged all of the plants. "Bonnie, try something for me- use your left hand, now."

Grandfather's eyes widened imperceptibly. I'd told him how the stone responded to our declarations of love- how it had a light all its own.

I sensed Bonnie question the stone. It flashed an angry red over the harmful plants, a pulsing pale lavender over the beneficial ones and alternating white and red atop those with dual purposes. We were all suitably impressed- this was a power to not take lightly and to explore further.

"Granddaughter, it is imperative you keep yourself blocked from everyone except Riordan and myself- you must be sure no stranger has access to your thoughts. If Chac, and he most likely will disguise himself so as to appear non-threatening, gains entry to your mind, he will suck your will. . ."

"And our job will become much more difficult," I cautioned.

"Practice, continually. Be alert always. Let the spirits and your ring guide you."

Chapter 46

The kids at school had oohed and aahed over Bonnie's ring after they'd seen it flash. Without the firelight inside the stone bringing it to life, it was rather ho-hum.

"Catskill, you're going to give the rest of us an inferiority complex," one of Rick's friends quibbled.

"Not me," Rick vouchsafed. "I'm ready to take you on-basketball's calling!"

"Great! Let's do it this afternoon. Bonnie's got driver's ed." I'd at least have something to do while waiting for her and Rick made for good company. The rest of the gang rolled their eyes at Bonnie.

"I forgot, you're still a kid," Lil taunted, harmlessly.

"Lil, we're all kids," Bonnie retorted.

'Not me, Kitten,' I silently quipped to my girl.

Lil's nose rose, "But some of us are nearer grown up than others." Bonnie groaned and I pulled her into my arms.

"Don't worry, Kitten, I don't mind robbing the cradle," I chuckled into her hair, tipped her chin to receive my mouth and sent her off to class.

'Bonnie,' I felt her mouth twitching as she decided whether or not to accept my telepathic call. She was stuck in driver's ed class after school.

Rick and I were kicking around, or should I say dribbling around the basketball court. He was giving me a decent workout, but I remained impatient for Bonnie's company.

My girl was a conscientious driver, no surprise there. I'd allowed her to take the wheel of the jeep on the drive home; more like implored her, as she had no inclination to drive.

The driver's ed class was required to gain a certificate acknowledging the student had passed a test on rules and regulations etc.

'I love you, Bonnie.' Through her eyes I saw the ring light up. The classroom was dark; the students subjected to a video of crashes involving DUI drivers and other 'inattentives'. Mr. Floyd, the instructor, glanced around.

'Kitten, I love you.' The light flashed again.

"Where's that light coming from?" Mr. Floyd demanded. "Who's got a flashlight?" The students twittered, looked around. All 15 and 16-year olds.

"Maybe there's a poltergeist," a smart aleck proposed.

"May I remind you, each one of you needs a certificate from this class to get your driver's license." Quiet ensued.

'Bonnie, I love you.' What fun watching the mayhem through her eyes! Something I'd not done with anyone else. I heartily approved the spirits steering me to Bonnie and love.

'Riordan, stop it,' she silently chided.

'Stop loving you?' I enjoyed being a stinker.

'No, never that! I don't know if I could live without you,' upset reigned in her craw.

'Better plan on living forever then, Kitten, because I love you, guaranteed, forever,' I soothed her.

'You're going to get me in. . .'

"Miss Lance, you seem to have something on your mind other than class. Why don't you answer the question?"

"Mr. Floyd, the answer is blood alcohol level. Do you want the parameters?" Bonnie, my multi-tasker was quick on the draw.

"Hmph," the instructor grunted.

'Riordan, I'm blocking you now,' she silently advised me.

'Go ahead, Kitten. I want to see if the stone blocks me.'

The stone did not and Mr. Floyd went on a tirade. Bonnie's lips curled up in a sweet smile as she put her right hand atop her ring.

I laughed, 'See you after class, Kitten.' But she didn't hear- the barrier was in place.

"Granddaughter, it's important for us to address your fears. Everything, no matter how trivial that gives you cause for concern."

She wriggled in her seat and crinkled her nose. How cute and oh so desirable; my mouth watered.

"Anything that gives me the creeps?" She qualified.

"Er, yes, the creeps," Grandfather replied, unexpectedly flummoxed.

"Spiders in the bathtub," Bonnie grimaced.

"D...did you say spiders in the bath...bathtub?" I asked, completely floored.

"Y...yes," she tentatively answered.

A monumental guffaw volcanically erupted from my gut. Unbelievable that the same girl who was going to take a broom handle to the football team in my defense, the girl who would sit opposite a wild mountain lion and converse, the girl who did not squeal when I pounced on her as my other self, the girl who tackled a recalcitrant black stallion- this girl now cast aspersions on innocent spiders because they happened to end up crawling in her bathtub! Oh, I was down. I was out for the count. I was rolling. I couldn't catch my breath, I was laughing so hard.

Grandfather tried to remain stoic, depict the proper aplomb for an instructor. But even he couldn't resist. His head turned and his face reddened trying to conceal his amusement. Wasn't happening- his shoulders began to shake. The tears rolled down his cheeks.

"Bonnie, Bonnie, Bonnie," I was reeling and she sat there dumbfounded. Her big, strong protectors all cracked up.

"Bonnie, woman you are a trip," I hiccupped.

"Well, I never. . .'

"Either did the spiders," and I went into another windfall of belly-wracking laughter. As did grandfather.

Bonnie harrumphed and then she, too, disintegrated. We blew off the gathered tension of the last months in fits or rather gales of hilarity.

"Riordan," question time.

"Yes, Bonnie."

"Can you block Red Hawk, I mean Grandfather?"

"Never had reason to try." What was she getting to?

"Grandfather can read Chac?"

"Yes. Chac thinks he's invincible, there's no reason for him to care one way or the other. I must give grandfather credit; I believe his mind reading powers are beyond extraordinary."

"Why doesn't Chac see you as a shaman?" This would puzzle her.

"For one thing, his self-esteem can't be bothered that he might actually have a true rival. That's impossible for him to contemplate. For another, I've shielded my shamanic identity. As grandfather said, he also can't see what I look like in this form. He only sees a hovering boy as the equivalent of a fly-easily disposed of."

"But you won't be, Riordan?" The worry haunted her eyes.

"No, Kitten. Chac's in for a surprise," and I secretly relished the thought of bringing him down.

"I think you should practice blocking grandfather."

"Is that an intuition?" I mulled over the idea. One should never write-off intuition.

"I think so," Bonnie hedged.

"Very well. I can see that might be beneficial; I've never had reason to, but I don't expect it to be a problem."

"Would Chac sense I'm blocking him?" She kept up the line of inquiry.

"I don't believe he will. He knows you have potential. You're blocking him will most likely lead him to think you've got a lot to learn- that you're stumbling about. He's sure he's the only one worthy of being your teacher."

"But it's possible?" Her face begged a placating touch.

"Anything is possible, just don't worry, Kitten, I'm here."

"I hope I can transform before he comes."

I tried to reassure her. We were getting closer to warm weather, the final countdown. Grandfather and I expected the jaguar man sometime in June. Thank the spirits for Wyoming's long winter.

"Bonnie, when the Wakanda- the power, as the Lakota call it- the power in all objects is ready to fully wake within you, then it will happen. You must embrace change. Transformation is all about embracing the change, no fear- see the world as yourself, but also as another, your guardian spirit, sees it. I, too, am looking forward to your wild self, to racing you as my mountain lion mate. Know, Kitten, that it is going to happen."

Chapter 47

Looking forward to prom time is more of a girl's ambition than most guys. I was one of the male exceptions. Anticipating the sight of Bonnie regally clad in chiffon and high heels had me salivating.

Modeling off a custom fitted tux- well I could do that- to maximum advantage. Now, talking Bonnie into all this. . .

"You'll teach me ballroom dancing? Isn't there anything you can't do?" She looked at me in wonder. I ate it up.

"You think I've been sitting on my thumbs for 150 years?" I gave her a puppy dog grin. "I'll teach you to dance with the greatest of pleasure. Let's go find you a dress."

Most of our classes were finished except for finals. Unlike our class mates, the imminent exams did not give Bonnie or me, cause for concern. Besides being A-students, there were bigger fish to fry. Chac put penny ante to the idea of tests. Everything in proper perspective.

Bonnie was staying pretty cool. Whether it was because she believed whole heartedly in me, or that the cave art prediction cast members were not yet all gathered- she didn't allow fear to override her life. I kept her mind on more appealing topics.

In fact, the list of her fears consisted entirely of spiders in the bathtub, deep water and the loss of my love. Of these, I'd still not relieved her of the deep water 'nemesis', though I felt we had made progress with spiders. Finally she'd accepted the future belonged to the two of us together. I wasn't going anywhere without her.

The gym took on a Roaring Twenties, speakeasy décor for prom. Prohibition-minded moms provided a genuine claw foot tub and kept it stocked with artificial gin- some kind of punch concoction sans alcohol. Horrible tasting stuff.

Zoot suits vied with fringed Roaring Twenties dresses for attention. Feathered, sequined headbands swayed and sent out swirls of color as the light struck them. Long strands of beads twirled and caught in fringe as the dancers attempted cha-cha's, the Charleston and the Lindy hop.

Those not in the full spirit of the mix, donned respectable, modern tuxedos and formal gowns. As for myself, I'd headed for the south of the border look- a custom fit waist jacket, red cummerbund, tuxedo pants and Latin-American formal dancing shoes.

I'm not being totally impartial, Bonnie was exquisite in a white off-the-shoulder Latin dancing dress of graduated length. The crystal dotted bows at the tiny, capped sleeves and the crystal-decorated skirt which cavorted around her marvelous legs, twinkled forth miniscule rainbows with every step she took. Her little feet encased in satin, ankle strap, dancing heels had me raring to go- on the dance floor.

Her father placed one of her graduation presents in her hands early. A strand of pink pearls graced her neck, intimately. Perfect for Bonnie. I showed her how to release the lion pendant from the gold chain and it now hung on the pearl necklace with admirable contrast.

I decorated her wrist with a corsage of fragrant, pale pink rosebuds. Grandfather and Jim made over us, posing Bonnie and me and snapping pictures for all they were worth- took turns doing it. We left the two of them watching baseball games.

The DJ had his work cut out for him, mixing up the song list to keep everyone happy and yet still maintain the gist of the Roaring Twenties theme.

"You up for a tango?" I invited my girl.

An interesting smile lit her face, "Lions tango?"

"This lion does, Kitten," I held out my hand. I'd learned from a Brazilian artiste and I taught the dance to Bonnie using every possible physical and extra-sensory nuance.

The tango is the most romantic dance of all and we were in the spotlight as the other dance floor occupants vacated to give us plenty of room.

With Bonnie's eyes into mine, we used every square foot of space. Twirls, dips, lifts- pulling Bonnie to me and then gently thrusting her away. Attraction and resistance, long glissading steps- romance in every breath, in every movement.

"Riordan?" Bonnie softly sighed into my neck as I pulled her up into my chest from a final dip.

"Hmmm. . .Kitten?" Spirits help me, I prayed. She was delectable and I ached as one starving. How long would I have to wait? I kissed her glistening temple before slaking my thirst with her sweet sweat drops.

"I don't know if I can wait until I'm 18," sweet, pink lips admitted in a breathless whisper as her eyes glowed.

My heart flip-flopped. I groaned into her hair, held her away from me.

"I guess we'll not tango again for a year and a half." Our eyes locked for an eternity long after the music stopped.

Coming to my gentlemanly senses, I led her to our table. All of our new friends waited, spellbound.

"Riordan, did you know you're up for prom king?"

"I don't think so, Rick," I certainly hoped not.

Lil and Vera chimed in, "All of the girls were divided. It was between you and Rick. Matt didn't stand a chance after his behavior last fall." Huge grins and conspiratorial looks all around.

Bonnie excused herself and I went in search of ice cold water- for both of us.

Rick and Lil sported the crowns for prom king and queen. But later that night when I sang Michael Jackson's THE WAY YOU MAKE ME FEEL, complete with moonwalking (but no crotch grabbing), to my girl, Rick tossed me the crown and I set it on Bonnie's head.

Chapter 48

'I think he's here,' Bonnie telepathically sent a tremulous alert. Sticker and even Stalker were barking menacingly. Handsome paced, reared and sitting back on his haunches was prepared to jump the fence if Bonnie needed him.

'Bonnie, remember the last thing in the world he wants is to harm you. I'm watching everything through your eyes. Do just as you would if a stranger showed up and you were alone. I'm with you. I love you.' The most serious event of my life to date. Bring it on to ME, jaguar.

Bonnie swallowed hard, pulled out a drawer, reached for her hand gun, put it close by. Her Celtic forbearers would have been proud. She had more guts than any 16-year old had a right to.

The cabin door opened; she stood in the doorway- called the dogs to her. With their lips revealing ready-for-battle fangs, Sticker and Stalker backed toward Bonnie- keeping the stranger in view.

"Who are you and what are you doing here?" Bonnie demanded, no trace of fear. Bravo, Kitten!

"Hi, my name's Chuck Jaeger. Your dogs don't seem to like me." Cunning Chac had chosen a most 'charming' disguise- a self-effacing young man with a movie star face and the kind of body any teenage girl couldn't help but be interested in. Except for my Bonnie.

"My dogs don't cotton to uninvited callers," she inscrutably informed the faker.

"Sorry about that. I was in the area and heard you were standing an exceptional, black stallion at stud. I've started a small breeding operation and I hoped to find out about him- his breeding and such. You're Bonnie Lance, right? My friends told me your name."

Bonnie looked around, no vehicle. "How did you get here?"

"Some friends dropped me off. I told them I'd meet them in a half hour at the end of your driveway." Bonnie knew this for the lie it was. She hesitated as a smart, alone girl would.

The clean-cut guy stood there, hands at his side- totally benign. Only the animals and Bonnie knew better. Grandfather also kept an eye on Bonnie from a high distance. We didn't want to give anything away, but we were prepared.

"Yes," she said.

"Could you tell me about the stallion, I mean while I'm here. . .? Or I could come another time if that would be better?"

"Just a minute. Stay," she told the dogs.
They vigilantly guarded the cabin entrance.
Bonnie thrust the hand gun in the waist band of
her jeans and donned an oversize long sleeve
shirt.

Sticker and Stalker flanked her as she
walked toward Handsome. The closer Chac got to
the corral, the more riled the stallion became.

"Is he always so wild?" The jaguar mused on
how easy he'd make cat food out of the beast in
front of him; I saw it in Chac's demeanor.

"No. He doesn't like men, in general. He's
registered Thoroughbred, never raced. Five years
old, perfect legs. . ." Bonnie rested an arm on
the top fence rail; her other stayed close to her
pistol, although it would not aid her.

Chac kept two dogs distant from her. He
made pretense of watching the stud, but his real
focus was on Bonnie.

I sensed his inquiring tentacles attempting
to read her. Bonnie appeared oblivious, but her
barriers remained firmly in place. Chac smiled a
movie star smile- completely lost on my girl; his
eyes betrayed his true feelings at her
disinterest. And after all the trouble he'd gone
to.

"You're going to tell me you handle this horse?" This quipped in mock disbelief as Handsome stationed his body at Bonnie's side, ears laid flat back and teeth-bared muzzle venomously thrust out at Chac.

The geldings and the broodmares exhibited their awareness of the conflicting vibrations in the atmosphere. The geldings snorted in their stalls; the mares called their foals to their sides in the corral beyond the barn. Hector and his harem of chicks had abandoned pecking for bugs and as if it were nightfall, had rounded themselves up and high-tailed it for the coop, and safety.

"Yes, I have a rapport with him." No brag just fact.

"Show me," he challenged, tongue-in-cheek.

Bonnie slid between the rails, gently pushed Handsome over. He bowed his head to her, but his alert eyes and teeth kept Chac at bay. I had to hand it to him, what courage! The dear fellow had no idea, which for once completely endeared him to me.

Chac played along. In not wanting to harm the one he'd come to acquire, he'd not upset her at this time by destroying her would-be-bodyguards. But they were no match for Chac. He knew this even if they didn't have a clue.

With a hand under Handsome's jaw, she guided him away from Chac to the far fence, climbed the rails and slid across the quivering stallion's back.

Bonnie put the stud through his paces, giving Chac a wide berth. She played her part- Oscar worthy. Where did she find the strength? So young, so untried, so mine.

The jaguar man was impressed. He had to be wondering about her current powers- if they had manifested yet. Her blocking him did not faze him. As I expected, he assumed she was innocently blank.

Bonnie slipped off Handsome, patted his neck. "You'll need to speak to my father if you're interested in bringing mares."

"And when will he be available?" Chac continued to play-act the mare owner.

"I expect him anytime." Bonnie was reluctant to inform Chac her father wouldn't be home for two days.

"All right then," Chac tapped the top rail and made as if to leave. But stopped and turned to her.

"Tell me about yourself, Miss Lance?" He sought to gain her eyes. Immediately, I sent a silent warning. Bonnie gazed at everything except the jaguar man- to his frustration.

"Nothing to tell. I work here with my dad. I'll tell him you called." She didn't want to appear anxious to get away, though she certainly was.

Bonnie went through the fence, much to Handsome's dismay. He preferred her close. Sticker and Stalker stationed about her, resuming guard duty. Wonderful animals.

"Come on, I'm harmless. I'm not that much older than you. We could be friends." He smiled a semi-convincing, cajoling smile that did not quite reach his eyes.

"I think you should go. We can talk further when my dad's home." Bonnie kicked the dirt, but her wide-angle vision kept her mindful of Chac's least movement.

Now Chac grew more perturbed, though he hid it fairly well. He began to pelt Bonnie with a frequency which would bring her under his thumb.

'Bonnie,' I warned her. 'Keep your guard up, but pretend you're beginning to feel ill. Slowly feel worse. Pretend NOW!' I thundered, prepared to go to her assistance if necessary. I felt all through her body as Chac's power assailed her, attempting to subdue her- make her malleable.

"I...I'm not feeling so good r...right now," she placed a hand on her stomach, kept her eyes from his.

"I'm sorry, Miss. Sorry if I've upset you.
Maybe you should go lie down, take a nap," his
tone force-faked concern, but was actually quite
gleeful. Chac believed success was at hand.

'Say yes, Bonnie,' I instructed.

"I…I think you're right." A sweat had begun
to break across her forehead. Chac pelted her
relentlessly- there was no harm in his attack, at
least physically. It was the acquisition of her
will he was after. Once he'd subdued her in that
manner, carting her back to his lair was simple.
Bonnie resisted with just as much endurance as she
could muster. Every cell of my being ached to go
to her, end the charade, and send that vile
miscreant straight to hell.

"I'll be back later, Miss Lance." A promise
and a threat, I knew. Bonnie, hand at her
stomach, ran for the cabin, the dogs protecting
her flanks, Handsome screaming his outrage. Chac
smirked at the protectors and disappeared.

'Bonnie?' I beckoned. No answer. 'Bonnie!'

Chapter 49

"Chac," Grandfather addressed his unwelcome visitor.

"Red Hawk," the jaguar man nodded.

"You're a long way from home," Grandfather inclined his head.

"Only temporarily. I was in the area and thought I'd stop and see an 'old friend'," Chac qualified.

Grandfather wasn't fooled. Chac had returned to his aboriginal mien. 'Old friend', indeed. Tall, heavy, dark skin, long black hair, piercings in his ears, nose and lips- a most unprepossessing sight. Tattoos of ancient origin writhed from his shoulders to his hands. It was no wonder he'd disguised himself in a harmless mien for his first visit to his mark.

My attention flagged between Grandfather and Bonnie. If she ignored my third call, I'd be with her in an instant. But she called me.

'Riordan,' her voice was shaky.

'Are you all right, Kitten?" I battled to keep my place.

'Yes, I'm getting myself together. I'm sorry. I blocked you so you wouldn't see me throw up. Whatever he did to me- awful,' she coughed, shuddered.

With a sigh of relief, 'You did great, Bonnie. Chac tried casting a spell on you. He intended to take you without any resistance after visiting grandfather. In your fight against his pummeling you with a frequency you're not used to, your system rebelled. You however did not surrender- you're an absolute wonder! I love you. Remember our plan. Get into position now. And never block your being sick from me again.'

Our telepathic communication ended, I attended to Grandfather's conversation with Chac.

"I've traveled north for an acquisition." Grandfather remained closed, uninterested at this admission.

"I've come for a white girl." Entirely too much pride in his boasting.

"You think to take a white girl from Wyoming to the deepest South American jungle? You expect her to survive? I wouldn't have believed such of you," grandfather expressed shock.

Chac barked a laugh, "Not an ordinary girl- a future shaman."

"A white girl shaman, hmmm. . ." Grandfather feigned disbelief.

"Play coy all you want, old man. Perhaps you know this young girl. She doesn't live far from here," in his arrogance, Chac didn't even deign to look around- bad sign for a cat.

"Do you think you can take a young girl from her home without a backlash of people up in arms?" Grandfather added dismay to his disbelief. "Have you lost your senses?"

"I know I can take her," Chac retorted with the over- confidence of one who's never been personally challenged.

"You can't stop me Red Hawk. You know I can clip your wings. I wouldn't want to 'old friend', but I will," Chac warned cheekily.

"I was just about to go fishing," Grandfather gathered several bamboo poles. "You used to have an appetite for fresh fish, as I recall. Care to join me? If your acquisition can wait?"

"Oh, she'll wait. Fresh fish sounds very, mmm, appetizing. Let's go," Chac accepted the poles and followed Grandfather.

We'd reconnoitered the stage for our play act with great consideration. Chac, as a jaguar, loved water. If it came to a fight, he'd most likely have poisoned his claws- the cheater, and a battle in a lake (there was an exceedingly deep body of water on Grandfather's property) would help protect my hide. The poison didn't faze me, but it entailed redirecting the use of healing energies; I'd been cautioned to keep all my powers focused on defeating Chac. Plus, I was as adept in water as on land- a hoped for advantage.

"Ah, young Riordan, any luck?" Grandfather hailed me as he and Chac came into view. I held up a stringer sporting three sizeable fish.

"Chac, a young friend of mine- Riordan. An 'old friend',-Chac." I nodded without making eye contact, concentrating on my line.

"Perhaps this young man knows of Bonnie Lance?" Chac jumped right in- no nice guy small talk as with Bonnie.

I glanced over at my adversary. His height just shy of mine, Chac carried an additional forty pounds. Sometimes weight interferes with stamina. We would see. . .

"Bonnie, yes I know her." And I drew the proverbial line with, "She's my fiancée."

Chac hissed, "That's too bad."

"Too bad?" I queried, set down my fishing pole and gave him my full attention with a block still in place on just who I really was.

"Yes, too bad, boy. The girl is mine." Way too much conceit, that's for sure, I thought.

I stepped forward as any human would upon having a gauntlet thrown at him by one suggesting harm to a loved one.

Grandfather spoke up, "Now Chac, if this young woman belongs to Riordan, why would you want to take her?"

"Belongs? Huh, she belongs to no one yet. She's still an innocent, but she will be mine. She's waiting for me as we speak." An evil grin of complaisance spread across his leathery dark face. His black eyes gleamed with anticipation.

"You, boy, can live or die, I could not care less. It's up to you- stay out of my way and live. Be foolish enough to get between me and the girl and you will suffer the consequences," he threatened, maliciously.

"What if she doesn't want to go with you?" Grandfather asked. I remained impassive, prepared.

Chac roared a conceited laugh. I couldn't wait to shove that down his throat.

"I can give her the world. Together we'll have power beyond imagining. What girl would turn that down?" He was blind sure of himself.

"And when she does turn you down?" I tossed the proverbial wrench across the proverbial line.

Chac cackled, "She's in my power as we speak- waiting for me. You can't stop me, foolish boy." His long, sleeveless shirt, open in front, fluttered as his chest swelled. He was the definition of hell and damnation- evil personified.

"Chac," Grandfather soothed- the mediator stepping in.

The jaguar man looked at Grandfather. I was beneath his contempt. A bug to be crushed.

"Why not give her a choice? You say she can't resist you-why not give her a chance to choose her own future?" The mediator put forth his suggestion.

"Bah! A waste of my time," Chac sneered, contemptuously.

"Or maybe you're afraid? What if she's beyond your power?" I tossed out.

"Boy, you make me laugh," except he wasn't laughing.

"A bet, then," I offered.

"A bet?" Chac's eyes lit up- gambling was ever a favorite native pastime.

"You call Bonnie to you. If she comes at your call, we'll stand down," Grandfather stated.

"As if I care if either of you stand in my way. Boy, you know nothing of me. Red Hawk, you should caution this ignorant boy," he practically spit 'boy'.

Grandfather finished the terms of the bet, "If the girl refuses your summons, and instead comes to the call of her fiancé, will you go home and leave us all in peace?'

Chac was quiet for a moment. Perhaps his self-confidence gained a sense that everything was not as it appeared.

"Are you afraid, great Chac?" I taunted.

His self-obsession cornered him- no backing out. "Bah, very well."

"We have your word?" Grandfather asked.

"I agree," Chac solemnly nodded.

"After you," I conceded.

Chapter 50

Chac stood omnipotent. I knew he was lifting his spell, the magic that never took, preparatory to summoning Bonnie.

Without the least concern, he beckoned my fiancée. No response. His expression did not betray his feelings at the lack of Bonnie's presence, not at first, but a slight frown of concentration formed on his ugly countenance.

Noticeably he now put the full force of his will into a command for her appearance. The sole answer- a stir of leaves rustling in a light, cool breeze. Unlike Wyoming's ubiquitous winds.

He couldn't fathom the mystery of non-compliance. It had probably not happened to him before. Waves of anger began to roll off the old shaman.

"Give up?" I respectfully asked.

"Very well, boy. Show me." The dawn of my true identity had begun to color the self-indulgent horizon in his brain.

I took a deep breath, 'Bonnie.' Within seconds the rustle of footsteps brought Bonnie into my arms.

I held her to me. "Perhaps a little quicker next time?" I said for all to hear.

"I'll work on it," she smiled, her eyes solely for me. I kissed her upturned face. Her arms wrapped me tight.

And then she looked to the jaguar man sans movie star disguise. I warned her not to show fear. Not soon enough, but she regrouped admirably. Only I could feel her heart's slight pounding, as if it were my own and it was, after all.

Chac smoldered at my 'insouciance'. He now recognized the proverbial tossing of the wrench and he was deadly angry as he regrouped.

"Chac, you cannot deny they belong to each other," grandfather advised, hopefully.

"Come here, girl." He may as well have commanded the wind. Bonnie straightened, her arms loosened from my waist. She would defy him on her own two feet, but she swallowed hard at the living nightmare standing in front of her.

"Girl, you are much too young to saddle yourself with this 'boy'. Don't be stupid. With me you can have everything you've ever dreamed of," Chac tried enticement, almost a plea- something totally outside his range.

"All of my dreams have ever been of Riordan," I felt Bonnie's eyes light with the fire of her honest admission.

"You dream of a 'boy' when you can have a man?" He pulled himself up into his most imposing, gruesome stature.

I, for one, was more than ready to knock 'boy' down his throat with whatever teeth cared to join. But I stayed cool. I'd spent 150 odd years studying and engaging in battle.

"Chac, you've given your word. Have a quiet journey home," Grandfather tried to end the impending confrontation with a simple reminder to the beastly shaman. However, the concept of honor was unknown to Chac.

"I'll go and the girl will accompany me," Chac would not go quietly.

"I'm staying here," Bonnie did not flinch- stood resolute. I would let her have her say. It didn't matter. I'd have to fight.

"Then this 'boy' will suffer the consequences," he sneered.

"You gave your word to leave in peace if I did not respond to you. Now you renege." Chac simply smirked at her.

Bonnie's hackles rose. If she'd been a shaman now, she most likely would have erupted into my lion mate. Instead, she rounded on him.

"What kind of a man are you? You've no integrity. Your word is worthless. How dare you!" Bonnie fired at him.

"Watch it, girl," he sneered malevolently, but kept his position. Wary of me, finally.

"You think to drag me away against my will?" She challenged.

"Either come now or he will die," Chac threw in his final trump card.

Bonnie played poker- refused to surrender. "The moment Riordan ceases to exist, half of my heart and my soul are no more. I live and die as I see fit. My life is tied to his. All you will own of me is an empty shell, a corpse. Is that what you came for, my dead body?"

"Pretty words, girl," he snapped.

"Look at me, liar and thief. Know that I speak the truth," she held her head high, uncompromising.

For a moment silence held sway. Chac perused Bonnie thoughtfully, weighing her words. The words of a young girl, an ignorant girl, he scowled. Surely no one this young would die for a teenage obsession?

The shaman roared. The jaguar is the only feline in the western hemisphere to roar. Its sound is enough to send most everything, everyone, scurrying for cover. Even the betrayers of his homeland grabbed rifles in response.

"Bonnie, go to Grandfather," I disentangled her, pushed her behind me and into Grandfather's hands.

Chac metamorphosed into his black jaguar other. The answering snarl of my mountain lion guide responded to his challenge as I shifted to meet him on equal turf.

He remained still, momentarily non-plussed. Then burst into action, flying at me, claws extended, jaws wide, fangs intent.

I bounded away from his attack- let him exhaust himself. I'm remarkably large for a mountain lion, but the jaguar's body exceeded mine. Using my agility, I sidestepped his initial charges- Ali would have been proud. The lake, I intended as my last resort.

We circled each other. He'd not expected his adversary to be such a powerful shaman in his own right. We gauged each other's potential, anticipating the strikes, prepared the correct defenses and responding retribution.

Chac thundered at me, claws swiping- I danced away. This dance of onslaught and agile sidestep continued until my superior stamina weighed in as an advantage.

With a final roar, Chac used every last bit of strength to bowl me over. I allowed him to commit himself, bounded away and Chac struck the water some ten feet inside the edge of the lake.

I rushed and flew atop him, my claws raking his shoulders as my jaws sought the life pulse in his neck. He bucked and together we rolled in the water, sending out violent waves.

Chac's heavier body gained the upper hand. My hind claws raked his underbelly continually, seeking to rend his hide into submission while avoiding his fangs and suffering his raking talons.

The poison in his obsidian claws was washed from the wounds he inflicted on me by the chill, cleansing waters. He attempted to hold me under, initiating my first strategy of using all available strength to bowl him back under me once more and refill my lungs with oxygen. As I surged up, I lifted him.

'Grandfather, now!' The red hawk dove and dug his talons into the scruff of the jaguar's neck and began to peck at Chac's hell's night, glassy eyes.

The jaguar released me, reared out of the water. I vaulted up only to see the beast work at dislodging the red hawk with a swat of his huge, wet paw and angry shake of his head.

Cascades of water shot in all directions. Chac's left eye had irrevocably suffered. Pus like liquid boiled from the remains. Bits of black fur clung to the talons of the hawk.

Buffeted by the jaguar's defensive maneuver, the predatory avian flew without power of wings, landed crumpled at Bonnie's feet. Grandfather transformed back into human form, bruised body, broken collar bone, crushed shoulder. . .

Chac and I resumed our tango.

Chapter 51

As if a second language, strange yet intimately familiar vocalizations- snarls, growls, hisses, were welling up from deep inside me, vying for release from my core.

Something completely thrilling and unknown was coursing through me, fueling every cell.

My protective instincts were roused, urged into action. My territory was invaded by a malevolent beast and my mate locked in lethal combat.

Without conscious intent, I paced the edge of the lake.

Chac's jaws closed over Riordan's muzzle, biting, seeking to drown.

"Rrrr. . .," I felt my teeth gnash. Embrace the change, Riordan had advised, and now he desperately needed me. Grandfather lay working his magic to heal himself, but I feared it would be too late.

I gave the right of way to my spirit guide and prayed- help me to help him.

One last deep "Rrrowl" burst from me and I was racing- the supreme speed I'd previously denied, I poured on. My body bounded, no longer as a simple girl, but now coupled with my destiny, my spirit guide.

From the depths of my brain, I heard a challenge issue forth. I'd kept my focus on the jaguar, needed it for this hardy antagonist. He thought he had me pinned, but I gained the upper hand, my claws raked his underbelly unmercifully and my front legs pushed him down further into the water. Chac's muzzle closed over mine. . .

I was sure to Bonnie it looked like I was in trouble, though I bided my time. Chac would tire or bleed out his guts before I ran out of breath.

That growl, again. NO! 'BONNIE, NO!'

Faintly, I heard Grandfather begging, "Granddaughter, no, no. . ."

My haunches powered my spring, following the demand of my intent, green-gold cat eyes. I landed atop the jaguar.

My fingers- no, claws- lethal, long, lion claws skewered into Chac's shoulders. I'd overshot slightly and could not direct my fangs into his neck.

But, with the instinct of a top predator, I bit onto a black felt, perked ear- gloried in the blood swathing my lion tongue. I tore the ear from the jaguar's head.

My claws now sought a different purchase and the jaguar's left eye, the remains of it, evacuated his skull. He would see no more with it.

The beast roared and released CatSkill, my mate. A furious toss of his head, swipe with huge paw, and I could grasp no more. I was flung backward, my head hit a solid, unforgiving wall and. . .

It was my dream, my nemesis. The dream of. . .flashes of color exploded through my brain. Then black. . .nothing. . .

Unexpectedly, suddenly, Chac relinquished his devastating clamp on my muzzle. I took full advantage of his divided attention. My mouth wide open, I fastened my fangs on his exposed jugular area. I bit deep and tore for all I was worth and spit out the offending mouthful.

The jaguar disappeared, submerged. I thrust out of the water, sucked my fill of oxygen. But there was no time to revel in my conquest.

"Grandson- Bonnie- drowning!"

I shifted to my human form and dove deeper and deeper into the churned, watery battleground, every cell focused on its other half- the whereabouts of my Bonnie.

Her body slumped down through the cold, flotsam flecked depths- eyes and mouth closed. My soul screamed for her as I caught and cradled her. I catapulted from the lake and rushed to lay her in grandfather's hands.

"Bonnie," I whispered and bent to resuscitate her. Grandfather lifted a hand covered in Bonnie's blood.

"Grandson, listen to me. You must take her to the hospital. NOW. Use the jeep. I've stopped the bleeding. It's imperative you take her there now. GO! GO!"

I'd never heard such urgency or volume in Grandfather's voice. Her wet body melded to mine as I flitted through time and distance to the jeep, held her in my lap and forced the old vehicle to speeds it had never known before.

Chapter 52

"I need a doctor," I yelled to the shocked
mannequins that parted before me. The emergency
room nurses, unused to seeing war refugees in this
relatively small town, were slow to move out of
stock-still mode.

I strode through carrying a small
unconscious bundle, dripping water and my blood in
my train.

"Here, sir. In here." A white-coated,
stethoscope bearing man ushered me into a room. I
heard him bellow for nurses and other
accoutrements that weren't registering- my brain
locked in limbo over Bonnie's non-responsive body.
I gently laid her on the bed.

"Sir, you'll have to leave," a pushy nurse
broke in.

"He stays," the doctor ordered to the
shocked nurse.

"Bag this, please." He'd pried open
Bonnie's mouth and retrieved- I nearly crumpled-
Great Spirit, give me strength! She'd taken off
Chac's ear and held it!

The doctor issued orders. I heard a request for a name.

"Bonnie Lance," I managed from limbo.

"We'll need to get in touch with her parents." I gave her Mr. Lance's cell number. My hand rested on Bonnie's foot.

"We're going to take pictures of her skull," the doctor instructed me. "We'll need to control any swelling- the bleeding's stopped, that's a good sign. Her pulse sounds strong."

He sensed he'd not be able to recommend a nurse to tend to the multiple bleeding wounds on my face, chest and arms yet, so he allowed me to follow Bonnie to radiology. The results confirmed the doctor's suspicions of fractured skull.

She was placed in ICU. The nurses set off to fulfill their orders. They'd dressed Bonnie in a hospital gown, washing her body beforehand. The requests for me to leave the room were countermanded by my intransigence and the doctor's orders.

Soon after, the doctor and I were alone.

"I know who you are, CatSkill. I also know that you could not have prevented any of this. Right now she rests in a coma. There is no pain."

Pain. I remonstrated with myself. How could he know? But I did. I finally understood the significance of Bonnie's nightmare, her fear of water. Wasn't a coma a black sleep? Nothingness?

He misconstrued my deadly visage. "You must not fret. She will return. We just have to wait." His words continued to come out of a fog. I turned my attention on him.

He held out a hand, "Doctor Gunne."

"Dragon," I murmured. He nodded.

Mr. Lance bolted into the room; saw my forehead resting on Bonnie's small, listless hand. Took in my tattered clothes, wounds and the still, ghost-white face of his daughter.

"Bonnie," he choked. "Riordan?"

"Mr. Lance," the doctor introduced himself. And in enough detail as if he'd been part of the audience, he told Bonnie's father what had happened.

"A jaguar- there are no jaguars in this part of the country," Jim shakily eyed Bonnie.

"It could have been a private pet turned loose or one that escaped, sir," Gunne attempted a plausible excuse. Mr. Lance slumped into a chair opposite me and held Bonnie's other hand.

'Bonnie,' I telepathed my love- the stone, alone, rewarded me with a flash.

Meanwhile, some busybody had contacted the police and Dr. Gunne tried to waylay the interrogator. He could have insisted, as only a shaman is able to, but I faced the officer.

The uniformed public servant's eyes bulged and he whispered a contrite prayer or curse or whatever. My appearance said it all.

"Son, I hate to bother you, but I'd like to confirm that the creature is dead," his fingers nervously plied his note pad and pen.

"The body sank," I stated without any inflection. "I slit its throat."

Dr. Gunne handed over the bagged ear. To his credit, the officer controlled the quiver in his hand and passed the bag to a younger assistant who was half a second from releasing his shock-stricken guts. The senior officer pushed him out of the room.

"Must have been like a Tarzan re-run out there. You've got to be the toughest young man I've ever met. Good luck to you, son." He turned to the doctor, "Somebody needs to tend to this young man."

"CatSkill," Gunne was careful not to touch me. "Your grandfather has brought you some fresh clothes." Then, for my ears only: 'It is important for you to begin your healing. When Bonnie wakes, if she sees you like this, she may well suffer a relapse.'

"Come, Grandson," my Grandfather beckoned.

In a daze I changed my clothes and let the healing energies flow through me. I'd slow their aftermath so as not to startle the hospital staff with miracles. They'd got a good enough look at my wounds to know they were not superficial.

I returned to Bonnie's side. The attending nurse, a new one, issued an ultimatum.

"You must leave- family only." Mr. Lance sat shell- shocked, unreachable.

"I'm her fiancé," I explained, peaceably.

"Doesn't count. Now please go or I'll have to call security," she added to my blank resistance. Her hand touched my forearm and I nearly erupted.

"You and whose army," I growled at her, literally. She was momentarily dumbstruck; coming to her senses, she moved around me to call for reinforcements.

Dr. Gunne, gleaning the discord, hastened back to give a reprimand and ordered her to post on the chart- Riordan CatSkill to have complete access to the patient, 24/7.

Near midnight, as Mr. Lance folded asleep in his chair, I asked my peer. "Why isn't she responding to my healing?"

"I can't tell for sure. Maybe you're too close to her. Even your Grandfather hasn't had an effect, except to staunch the bleeding. She's in the hands of the Divine for now. Please don't think she's suffering. It's as if she's sleeping without dreams. We must wait."

Without dreams, without me. If I hadn't been sunk in such despair, I might have questioned Gunne's words right then. . . I lifted Bonnie's be-ringed hand, turned it, kissed her palm and with her hand resting in mine, I hid my face and for the first time in my life felt tears maneuver unchecked.

Chapter 53

"Riordan," Mr. Lance attempted to broach the subject in stilted, choked-off words. "I want you to know, I don't hold you responsible."

This added to my remorse because she had come to my defense and her father knew it.

"Bonnie would wade into hell to save. . ." he broke and turned to hide his feelings, his shoulders trembling.

Day 5. Still no response.

With orders to be called at the slightest change in Bonnie's condition, Mr. Lance had gone back to work. He worried about the escalating hospital bills. He needn't. Though he'd not accepted my offer, I'd already directed the statements to my banker's attention. Dr. Gunne had written off his portion.

Bonnie slept hooked up to the necessary fluids. Her vital signs remained strong. We had managed to control the swelling of her brain.

Rick and Lil stopped by with flowers, wishes and prayers. I felt and allowed Rick to put a hand on my shoulder in commiseration. I was grateful for his presence. Lil brushed Bonnie's hair back, kissed her fingers and placed the kiss on Bonnie's forehead.

"Riordan, why don't you come with us? Let us buy you lunch. If Bonnie see's you pining away like this, losing weight, when she wakes up, you'll be in trouble."

"Thanks, I won't leave her. I'll welcome her scolding."

"You've been here constantly?" Rick frowned. I nodded.

"Where do you sleep?" Lil asked.

"Usually on the floor, more comfortable than those chairs."

Rick and Lil exchanged sympathetic looks. "All right, then. If you won't come with us, we'll bring something back for you, OK?"

"Thanks, Rick, Lil. You're good friends."

"There are others who'd like to visit, too," Lil added.

"Sure," I absent-mindedly replied.

"Everyone we know is praying for her," and the unsaid, and for you.

Day 17. Midafternoon.

The tiniest flicker of a tendon in Bonnie's hand, as ever, resting in mine. 'Dr. Gunne,' I sent a silent communication and in an instant he appeared by her bed.

Her eyelids fluttered and as a baby newly born, opened, felt the shock of the bright light, closed and slowly squinted open again. Dr. Gunne dimmed the light's intensity.

Looking around in wonder, but not in recognition.

"Get Mr. Lance on the phone," Gunne whispered to an attending nurse.

"W...where?" She croaked with nearly impotent vocal chords. I presented her with a cup of water, cautioned her to sip when she tried to gulp.

"You're in the hospital, Bonnie," I soothed.

Dr. Gunne unnecessarily held her wrist to check her pulse. "Do you remember anything?" He queried.

"N...no," she wore the blank look of a storied Rip Van Winkle invalid.

"Wh...who are you?" She studied me. "Wh...who am I?" Her face crumpled.

The fissures in my heart fractured anew and more fully.

Chapter 54

There's nothing left for me to do. At night I guard the shell that harbors my love. As I have the entire summer.

In answering a call from my reservation group, I left Bonnie for several nights in the hands of her father. As it turned out, she cried, tossed and whimpered for the entire time. Neither the doctor, Grandfather, nor her father could stem her innately-inspired disquietude in my absence.

When I slept on the floor by her bed, she rested in serene peace. On some level, metaphysical? cellular? she recognized and required my presence.

Awake, she was a body going through the motions- without an inner light- seemingly on hold, without memory. Even the animals, heads low, basked in depression, silently waiting.

Dr. Gunne's admonitions to "just wait" were too frequent to offer any kind of reassurance.

As long as the shell of Bonnie drew breath, I would too. But only for that, however unspecified, time.

Chapter 55

A slim woman with short, dark hair exited an economy version of a SUV at the Lance homestead.

"Can I help you?" Mr. Lance asked.

"Hello, I'm a friend of your daughter. Would it be possible to see her?"

Bonnie's father swiped at his jeans and gestured helplessly to the cabin.

"Thank you."

The girl who answered the door had prominent cheek bones and was clad in baggy attire; she bore slight resemblance to the curvy teenager of three plus months ago.

"It's time, dear," the woman said.

The young girl gazed at the visitor with polite interest as a frown began to crease her forehead.

"Block yourself and return," the woman laid a hand on the girl's forehead and then placed the same hand, now glowing, on the patient's heart. "Riordan CatSkill needs you."

The frown receded to serenity and recognition. "I know who you are," the young face brightened.

"Of course you do, dear."

"Riordan?" I started, but the woman caught me by the forearm.

"Not in view of your father, dear," the woman smiled in thankful gratification.

I raced out the door. "Dad! Dad!" Sticker and Stalker, alert in an instant, ran to greet me, bowl me over is more like it. Apparently they'd given up on hearing my voice again.

Handsome picked up his head and pirouetted and piaffed. My dad broke the door of the chicken coop in surprise and Hector and his harem flapped, clucked and hastened everywhere.

"Bonnie!" He scooped me up and swung me about just as he used to when I was a kid.

"Dad, I'm all right. I…I know, I know who I am. . . I have to find Riordan."

My dad gave me a last heartfelt hug, used his sleeve to dry his tear-streaked face. "Go get him, honey! Hurry back!"

Inside the SUV, the woman cautioned me to wait until I was out of my dad's line of sight.

"You know where he is- surprise him. Keep your block in place." I didn't question her; I was too excited.

I let the Wyoming wind I loved rush over my face. It was getting cold. What was the date? How long was I. . .? How was Riordan?

I did know where Riordan was and that wasn't all I knew. Around the last bend from my home, I thanked her and flitted through time and space to the entrance of the cave. How had I acquired this knowledge?

My heart thundered, fit to burst, as if an addict confronted with an over-supply of his favorite source of well-being. I gloried as the energy poured through me and I embraced my other identity.

My kittenish body slipped its shoulders between the narrow rock walls of the entrance. As only a cat can negotiate such tight places. My block still remained in place even if I wasn't sure why. But I heeded her advice.

There he lay at the base of the ancient cave art- a male sleeping beauty. One hand thrown over his head and the other rested on his stomach. He was gaunt, but so was I. The dark could not hide a single detail from my cat's eyes.

I salivated in anticipation and with the utmost stealth, I padded to his side- my block in place. And woke my dream cougar with a sloppy, rough, lioness French kiss.

His eyes flew open- shock, disbelief, gratitude- all played across the stage of his human face.

"Bonnie! Kitten!"

I purred and he shape-shifted. Lion and
lioness rolled gleefully together.

Thousands of miles to the south, in a
secluded, untrammeled remnant of thick jungle
foliage, a roar resounded. It vibrated out with
intense rage and a malevolent promise of
vengeance.

ACKNOWLEDGEMENTS

To Hillary, my literary guinea pig friend for inadvertently putting me on this path

To my cheering section: Celeste, Rebecca, Renae

To my sister, Desiree, for her tireless endeavors to acquire my materials and for introducing me to computers- what a chore!

To Bob and Brian- computer gurus extraordinaire!!!

To Carol for inspiring me

To all the wondrous muses that fascinate my life

THANK YOU! THANK YOU! THANK YOU! THANK YOU! You're AWESOME!!

Please look for part 2 of the CATSKILL trilogy-CATSKILL'S LIONESS in 2015. Learn more about the protective circle and of Bonnie's special talent as well as a new rival for her affections and the coming. . .

If you would like to correspond with me, please address: **lisaannettepowell@gmail.com**

Available at Amazon.com or contact me for personally signed copy.

And many thanks for sharing your time with me!!!